HE LOVES ME NOT

C.M. NASCOSTA

MEDUAS
EDITORIALE

Contents

Author Note

You've Got Mail is elite, and I won't hear a single word to the contrary.

If you've never seen it, you should put this book down and go watch the movie immediately.

(And then come back and read your book.)

I already know I didn't make our Joe Fox character even half as charming as Tom Hanks,

but I think our Kathleen Kelly was a more than makes up for any shortcomings.

My eternal gratitude to Nora Ephron for creating one facet of my personality with her love stories.

It's Giving Manifestation

PART ONE

The SS Sunk Cost

SUMI

PinksPosies&Pearls: *I have a confession to make.*

This is going to sound bananas, so don't judge me. I'm giving you fair warning.

I haven't told anyone I'm moving.

I haven't said a peep to anyone yet. Not my family, not my boyfriend.

I haven't told anyone but you. It's like you're the only one who knows me. The real me, at least.

I haven't even quit my job yet

Isn't that ridiculous? What is wrong with me?!

PinksPosies&Pearls: *the school year is finally, FINALLY over.*

Pretty soon we'll be in that home stretch of spirit days and graduation rehearsal.

*Which means, at the very least, I'll **have** to tell my principal and union contact.*

*And if I'm telling my job, I can't **not** tell everyone else in my life.*

Again - what is wrong with me?!

I don't even understand what my thought process was on this.

I guess I just wanted to keep it for myself for a little bit.

Is that selfish?

"Do it for the plot or take the L, Chapin."

"Too late, I'm already bored. L rizz."

A swell of voices cascaded over each other in a waterfall of incomprehensible insults and jeers as Sumi tipped her head back, staring up at the ceiling, phone securely concealed beneath a book. Her students were speaking their native tongue, of which she had only the most rudimentary grasp, and as long as they weren't doing each other any bodily harm, she couldn't be moved enough to translate. Not when she was so close to the finish line.

The house had a sunroom. It was the thought she kept coming back to, over and over again, a giddy bubble of excitement crowding her lungs as she envisioned nights spent there, stretched out on the long, low sofa. She would be able to see the moon from the walls of windows, would be able to see the night sky all around her. The windows in her condo were undersized and high on the walls, often leaving her feeling as if she were in a cave.

Even though the possibility that she would wind up stumbling down the two shallow steps into the sunroom and go sprawling on the floor was, dare one say it, an inevitability, for now, Sumi was enamored with the sunken space.

She was going to fill it with plants. Hanging baskets of trailing greens, her cebu blue and manjula pothos, training her golden to climb over the curtain rod, her pink lady callisia and strings of rubies and pearls cascading down in delicate ropes. Succulents on the low coffee table, with her prized pink princess philodendron and albo monstera providing pops of unexpected color amongst the greenery in places of honor near the sun-filled windows.

Of course, the house boasted other things — wonderful, sumptuous things — that her current condo was lacking. A walk-in closet. A deep soaking tub in the attached en suite bathroom, wide and long enough for her, she'd confirmed the day she'd clambered into it, fully clothed. There was a kitchen fit for someone possessing far greater culinary ability than she possessed, and for the first time in her life, a formal dining room. Sumi had a feeling none of these things were actually extraordinary, but when compared with the decade spent in her current condo, her twenties in even smaller apartments and student housing, and the open-concept house of her childhood, the kitchen island and dining room made her feel as if she were moving into a palace.

Most importantly, the house was in Cambric Creek, a thriving multi-species community an hour away, with an excellent school district and not a single job opening to which she might be able to apply. New town, new house, new job, a whole new life, just waiting for her to roll up to the curb with the moving van.

Sumi listened idly to the pockets of chattering students around her, their nonsensical conversations blurring together into a slurry of unconnected thoughts and slang.

"Deadass, did you see his drip?"

"I know, but he's so baby girl."

"It's giving sigma."

At the start of the year, the principal had pulled together a staff meeting, sitting them all down to review an endless list of new slang they had to learn in order to communicate with their middle school charges.

She had glared down in disdain at the time as they reviewed the packet, a glossary of nonsensical terms she was certain would wind up displacing something far more important and valuable in her brain storage. The script to some obscure 90s horror movie, or the meticulously rehearsed dance steps to a pop song routine she'd performed with her two best friends in the school talent show when she was fourteen — all more important than committing the new meaning of *Ohio* to memory.

It hadn't mattered. She had always been adept at acclimating herself to her surroundings, code switching on a dime and mirroring the behavior and speech patterns of those around her. Her students' slang had crept into her vernacular without her full conscious approval, but no matter how many times she had looked over the list since the fall, Sumi wasn't any more confident she knew what *skibidi* meant that afternoon with just two weeks of the school year left than she had been at the start.

She wondered what would happen if she began using her newly acquired slang on the street, outside of the controlled chaos environment of the school. If she appropriated bites of strangers' food and explained she was simply collecting a fanum tax, or if she told the handsome, unsmiling barista she saw every morning that she was earning a degree in Advanced Rizzenomics, would her friends and neighbors laugh, or would they think she was having a psychotic break?

Sliding her phone out ever so slightly from beneath the book, she continued to type.

PinksPosies&Pearls: *I'm going to plant lilacs at the new house, I think. I love the smell of lilacs in spring.*

They're all bloomed out at this point in the year, but that's something to look forward to

Think of it — no more classes, closing my eyes in my own house,

and smelling the lilacs right outside the window.

Like I said, don't judge me too harshly. And wish me luck!

The cat's gonna be out of the bag after this week.

"What about you, Ms. Trent?"

Her eyes snapped up at the sound of her name, realizing the group of girls at the front table had been talking to her. Sumi smiled brightly, not letting them see her mild panic at having lost herself in one of her daydreams in the middle class.

"What about me? Repeat the question, please."

The girls giggled, rolling their eyes before the ringleader piped up once more. "MacKenzie and I are both going to camp this summer."

"And I'm going to Europe to visit my grandparents," one of the other girls quickly interrupted.

Sumi smiled, nodding. She'd already heard the details of the girl's impending trip, as had the rest of the class, the rest of the school, probably the pigeons outside. Her mind quickly filled in the blanks, catching up with the question she's likely been asked.

"I'm going to be doing some redecorating this summer," she told them, not mentioning that the redecorating would be taking place in a new home and that she would not be returning to the school in the fall. "My plants are all getting pot upgrades."

Fortunately, the answer was suitably uninteresting to them and they did not press.

If this opportunity had presented itself the year before, she would have spent this week breaking the news to her students, preparing them for a new homeroom teacher and team leader the following year, making introductions and easing their impressionable minds through the change as easily as she could. Fortunately, it wasn't going to matter to this group. Her two years with this crop of kids was up, and they would be moving on to the junior high the following year, leaving her behind and likely never thinking about her again.

That suited Sumi just fine. This was the easiest break of her plan, the most painless, the most seamless. Everything else was a bit stickier, but this, at least, she could walk away from with a clear conscience.

You said you wanted a do-over, right? No time like the present, Pinky.

It wasn't that she disliked teaching.

She hated everything about it, had done so right from the beginning, knowing she had made a terrible, terrible mistake two weeks into her master's practicum, before she had even completed the degree. By then, though, it was too late. Too many years in school, too much money, too much of an investment to walk away from. The sunk cost fallacy of her life.

She liked kids, or at least, she'd thought she did. She liked imparting wisdom and shaping young minds, at least in theory. But the reality of being surrounded by other people's tweens all day long — stinky and vicious to each other with no boundaries to speak of, distracted by screens, never actually reading the books they were assigned and turning in essays that had been fed to them by an AI program — was mostly terrible. She had been kicked in the face the previous year trying to break up a fight, sent home carrying her tooth in a paper cup, only to discover her union-provided dental coverage would still require several thousand dollars from her out-of-pocket.

Since then, Sumi had mentally checked out. There were teachers who felt called to the profession, who called themselves educators, who *loved* it . . . she simply wasn't one of them.

It was *embarrassing* being in a relationship with Jordan at this point. He was the loudest voice on the front for public education in the state, with his name in the paper and his photo on industry websites, visiting rural species-specific schools and large public schools like the one in which Sumi taught alike. **Visiting** *schools. I've visited the space museum; that doesn't make me a fucking astronaut.*

It wasn't that Jordan was a *bad* boyfriend. On paper, they were perfect — the middle school teacher and the educational activist. They'd been together for three years, three years in which he had gone from the local school board to the state board, and as he inched closer to his own lofty political aspirations, Sumi had begun to consider if she was, for the first time in her life, nothing more than a bit of arm candy. After all, she ticked an awful lot of boxes that played well with his constituency of middle-aged teachers. She was plus-sized, both mixed race and mixed species, even if she was human-presenting, and she just happened to be toiling away in the very profession he championed. *You're the diversity hire girlfriend. That's it.*

Perhaps that was why this windfall seemed like such a life-changing opportunity. *Life-changing. A life-changing opportunity. No time like the present, Pinky.*

When the door between the joint classrooms swung open, Sumi nearly fell off her chair in her haste to conceal her phone entirely, breathing a sigh of relief when it was only her co-teacher.

Meredith taught math, reporting that the kids were just as over-reliant on their phones to feed them answers in her class as they were in Sumi's. Sarcastic, with a caustic tongue and a very low threshold of patience for the *this is the noblest profession!* teachers' union and school board, she and Sumi had become fast friends the instant their classrooms were paired.

"You know, if *I* inherited a million dollars from a strange relative, the very first thing I would do, without reservation, would be to buy my coworker a new car. Like, the *first* thing I would do. Before I even paid my own bills. I think that says a lot about my character, don't you?"

Meredith had perched on the edge of her desk, blocking out the trio of girls sitting in the front row, keeping their conversation as private as it could be amidst the cacophony of her chattering students. Sumi snorted in response.

"Wow, you've really been giving that a lot of thought. It's giving sainthood, no question."

"I know, so sigma of me. The second thing I would do is turn in my resignation and walk backward out of Mark's office, slapping my ass.

All the way down the steps, out the front doors. They'd be able to hear me slapping on the other side of town."

Sumi buried her laughter in her palms, squeezing her eyes shut. *This is your chance. This is your chance to tell someone for real.* "Does that mean you're not going to hold it against me if I'm not back next year?"

It was the best she could do. She couldn't bring herself to actually say the words out loud before she had officially resigned. She knew the way teachers in this district gossiped, knew how fast the ignition turned on the gossip machine. If she told Meredith, their room para would know before Sumi even cleared the doorway to leave for the day, half the building knowing before she hit the parking lot. Even though she wasn't coming back, she valued her professionalism enough to want the principal to hear it directly from her, and she didn't want Jordan finding out through the whisper network.

At least . . . she didn't think she did.

"Girl, I'll hold it against you if I *do* see you in three months. Slap. That. Ass. All the way out the door." Meredith scoffed, helping herself to one of the mini chocolates Sumi kept in a bowl at the edge of her desk. "Maybe you should take a year off and travel, see the world. Wait, will Jordan go with you?" Reading Sumi's expression of uncertainty at the thought, she unwrapped another candy. "Good, that's the right answer. You should buy one of those huge sunhats and sleep with a bunch of hot twenty-five-year olds. If you're not being railed on your private sundeck by some unnamed stranger with a six-pack, what's the point of anything."

"I didn't realize hot twenty-five-year olds were interested in middle-aged fat women."

"They are when she's loaded!" Meredith exclaimed from around her mouthful of chocolate. They both quickly turned, checking to see if any students were listening in, but it didn't matter. Too engrossed in their phones, too deep in their own shrieking conversations to notice or care. Meredith turned back, rolling her eyes. "Don't forget the luncheon today. Is Jordan going to be there?"

When she groaned at the reminder, one of the front row girls finally lifted her head, eyebrows raised in interest for a moment before turning back to her conversation. "I forgot all about it," Sumi admitted. *Mother fucker. So much for taking another load of boxes to the house.* "I'm sure he will be," she went on despondently. "Are you kidding? He could never resist a captive audience hanging on his every word about his favorite topic."

"His favorite topic being himself," Meredith put in helpfully.

"I could never bring Jordan on a trip like that." Sumi felt her cheeks heat, emboldened by the conversation. "Leaving work? With no one to impress? Who would he perform for? He'd wither like an orchid."

The other woman snorted, taking another candy. "Maybe there's somebody else who ought to see you slapping your ass on the way out. Just sayin'."

"Maybe I just want to do some quiet, off the grid dream job," Sumi blurted. "Make jelly and bake pies. I don't know, maybe I'll open a flower shop. I love flowers."

"I told my husband I wanted to open a bookshop after the kids are in high school. I just want to sit and read, enjoy the peace and quiet, maybe have a little coffee bar. He said I was describing a living room and those don't make money. Turned the den into a library for me; said it was cheaper. He even put in a little coffee station. Seriously though, if I was in your position . . . I wouldn't need to think twice about coming back. But really, a new car. The *first* thing I'd do. And make sure your replacement understands the way this works. They *supply* the candy, I *eat* the candy."

She would stay friends with Meredith, Sumi vowed as the other teacher crossed the room, popping her last chocolate in her mouth before pulling the door shut behind her. *That's what social media is for. And you're good at talking to people on that, at least.*

She hadn't told many people about the inheritance.

It had hurt, knowing there had been someone from her mother's side of the family *right fucking there* all along, but there was no one to blame. Her father hadn't known. The great aunt in question had never known how to find her. When the probate paperwork had caught up with her, the documents originating from an office less than two hours from the house she'd lived in for more than twenty years, she had cried bitter, heartbroken tears, but now she was wrung dry. No point in regret. Nothing left but the life savings of a frugal couple who'd owned their own successful business and a house in an affluent neighborhood of a town in the midst of a real estate explosion.

They all thought she was going to sell it. Her boyfriend, her father ... everyone thought she would sell the house, put the money in the bank, and keep on living the status quo.

Everyone but ChaoticConcertina, who was enthusiastically supportive in her plan to run away and start her life over again.

After all, how could she not?

She was forty years old and felt as if she were being given a do-over of the last twenty years. A docking of the *SS Sunk Cost*, a chance to do the job she'd always dreamed of doing, a chance to own a house, own a business, a completely fresh start. A mulligan on her life, an opportunity to be *happy* rather than simply exist. *No time like the present, Pinky.*

He was right, and so was Meredith. *Slap your ass all the way out the door. It's a big, bouncy ass, so they'll be able to hear you coming all the way in Cambric Creek.*

Pushing to her feet before the bell rang, Sumi idly wondered if she was going to regret it. The clock was running down, and maybe she'd look back at this week wistfully once it was done. *Who knows?* she thought, bending to retrieve a pen that had been pushed off the desk when Meredith rose. *Maybe once you're out of here, it won't seem that terrible. Maybe you actually love these kids and you're too close to realize it.*

"Gyat!"

Her face flushed and her eyes narrowed as she snatched up the pen and straightened, whipping around to face the 12-year-old at the far corner table, smug in his exclamation over the bouncy ass in question.

She wouldn't need a slang cheat sheet in her new life, she reminded herself. *Nope. You're not going to miss them at all. Fuck these kids.*

When the dismissal bell rang only a moment later, it was all she could do to call out to their backs, reminding them of the following day's spirit week theme, sighing in relief when she was left alone in the classroom once more. She only had to get through the rest of the week, and then she'd never have to think about any of them again either. *No cap indeed.*

ChaoticConcertina: Today I was at the coffee shop the same time as a bunch of kids

Too young to drive, but apparently old enough to come to the coffee shop unsupervised.

Since when do kids drink coffee? Did YOU drink coffee when you were 14?

Am I the only one who missed out on a caffeine addiction in middle school?

Do we really want them MORE hyper?

Anyway

I moved to the end of the counter as the group of kids was leaving

And promptly put my hand in a puddle of something they left behind.

It was too thick to be water.

Was it coffee? Was it vomit? Snot? Some kind of dark matter secretion?

Did I put my hand in a puddle of puberty?

I don't know, but I wanted to cry.

Is this what I have to look forward to in a few years with my daughter?

Mystery puddles?

Why aren't these kids in school?

ChaoticConcertina: You'll get absolutely no judgment from me.

This is a judgment-free zone.

Would it have made a difference if you would have told the school 2 months ago?

You're still leaving and they have all summer to fill the job.

*Are **you** dodging mystery puddles all day?*

If you are, I'd just walk out right now. Fuck that place.

Your family and friends will understand.

This is a huge opportunity for you! Why wouldn't they understand?

Remember, it's a gift from your mom. Don't let it go to waste.

No judgment at all. How many of us wouldn't love an opportunity to hit reset?

ChaoticConcertina: *Hey wait, do I get to help you spend the inheritance?*

Because your collection **desperately** *needs a red mambo*

Oh, and some of those ridiculously expensive anthuriums.

I'd like to amend my answer.

If you don't get some insanely rare, incredibly delicate specimen for your collection,

then ALL the judgment. And yes to the lilacs.

Good luck letting the cat out! Can't wait to hear how it goes.

It had become a part of their daily routine.

She would close the door behind the last student and flip off the lights, luxuriating in the silence and avoiding the congestion of the parking lot for a little while, settling back in her chair and reading his midday message. Swinging the door shut after the last student went scrambling out of the room after the dismissal announcement, Sumi dropped into her chair with a grin. Sure as clockwork, his response to her early morning whinging was there, causing a bubble of warmth to move through her as she grinned.

He was funny. He was more than just a little dramatic. He made her smile and laugh every single day, as she did then, the sound of it echoing in the empty classroom. *And he's a stranger. When was the last time Jordan made you laugh? Why haven't you put this much effort into your actual relationship?* Sumi pushed away the little voice, unwilling to entertain its treachery.

PinksPosies&Pearls: Yeah, it was definitely a puddle of puberty

You're probably going to go through it again now

Get ready for your voice to move through three octaves in every conversation

Are you sweaty yet? Don't worry, you will be soon!

Sorry, I don't make the puddle rules.

Her grin faded slowly, remembering that she needed to put in an appearance in the teachers' lounge, and that Jordan would be there. Her stomach flip-flopped as she gathered her things, a quiver of guilt moving through her. *It's not like you're doing anything wrong. You have a boyfriend. He has a girlfriend. You literally don't talk about anything that could get you in trouble. It's not like you're exchanging nudes and getting off together.*

She knew her inner voice was right, but that didn't prevent a tiny bit of guilt from gnawing at her conscience. *You're guilty over everything else. Guilty because you haven't told Jordan the truth, that you're selling this place and leaving town. You need to rip off the bandage and get it over with.*

That part was true, she was forced to concede. She was tired of tip-toeing around the truth. But. The undeniable truth, Sumi was forced to admit, was that if ChaoticConcertina was someone in her actual daily in-the-flesh life, she couldn't promise even to herself that they wouldn't have already hooked up.

She was just a few feet away from the door to the lounge when her phone buzzed.

ChaoticConcertina: *It's a good thing I stand behind a tall counter most of the day.*

The seconds seemed to audibly tick by as her eyes read his words, lips moving slightly as she repeated them in a murmur to herself before her brain latched onto the implication. She honked like a goose, earning strange looks from her coworker exiting the lounge. It was the very first time either of them had ever alluded to anything even remotely sexual, and *she* had inadvertently opened the door.

Sumi dropped against the wall, hand over her mouth as her shoulders shook in renewed laughter, warmth moving up her neck. *Not here. Not now! Jordan's here. You have to wait until you get to your car.*

The lounge was crowded with bodies, every teacher in the building seemingly packed into the tight space, along with the school board, pumping hands and tacitly reminding everyone that they existed. If Jordan was there, Sumi knew she would not need to look hard to find him. He would be where he was most comfortable — holding court in the center of the room, speaking on the subject over which he was most passionate — himself. *Sure enough.*

"Did you happen to read the story they did about me in the Ledger? I wouldn't say it was a hit piece, but it certainly wasn't flattering, nor truthful. They did mention that I went to Spencer, however. So at least I got the impressive part in there, am I right?"

The collection of people standing before her boyfriend all laughed, right on cue. Sumi hoped her smile did not resemble a grimace of pain.

That they were all human went without saying. The entire teaching staff was. There was one girl in particular, a petite blonde, staring up at Jordan completely besotted. She was from the board, Sumi thought, recognizing the woman from a few of the meetings she'd attended.

"At least they managed to get your good side, Jordan," another board member piped up. "The photo is of your head and not your ass, even though that's what you were talking out of the whole interview."

Another volley of laughter amongst the group, as she slowly edged away, making her way to the food. *He won't even notice if you're here.* After all, he noticed so little. Anyone with eyes could see the missing knickknacks and pots and pans in her kitchen, the pared down living room. *Are you really hiding anything if it's happening out in the open?*

Her thoughts turned almost involuntarily back to her phone as she picked up a square of cheese. How she responded to his message could change the tenor of their conversations for good. *You might need someone to lend a hand. Wouldn't want you to get a cramp.*

"Are you counting the minutes yet?"

Sumi jumped, nearly dropping her phone. *That's what you get. You're in a public school, surrounded by co-workers and your boyfriend, and you're thinking about offering a virtual hand job to an online stranger.*

It was one of her coworkers, a teacher from the other team in her grade, piling tiny canapés on a paper plate. The union had been providing a party tray of snacks every day for the last week, of which she helped herself to each afternoon before heading to the house. A thank you for another great school year, they said. *Please be sure to cast your vote*, she knew was the hidden subtext of the miniature quiches and carrot sticks.

"You know I am," the other woman went on. "The parents this year, I thought they were going to be the death of me. One mother, she called every single week for a touch base. Lady, your kid is already getting straight A's. How much more do we have to talk about?"

Relaxing into the commiseration, Sumi laughed, still gripping her phone. She *needed* to put it away. *Jordan's going to see you, and you know how he feels about people and phones. And what if he says yes? Are you ready to follow through, trade nudes? What if it ruins everything?*

"I already told my husband I'm not sure how much longer I can do this."

Sumi raised her eyebrows at her coworker's disclosure, sliding her phone into her bag. *This can wait.* She needed to think through how she would respond, and didn't want to do anything hasty that would jeopardize a relationship she had come to depend on. *See? You're not the only one who wants to walk out!*

"What would you do? I mean, if you're not teaching, what would you do instead?"

"Oh, I didn't mean quitting," the other woman laughed. "Are you kidding? Between the two of us, we've got another decade on our student loans. But I don't think I can do middle school for another two years. Especially with kids at home. It's so much grading, constantly following up with assignments they never turn in. You know how it goes."

Sumi nodded, knowing all too well how it went.

"I used to do early education, and I would be happy to go back. When you go home for the day, you actually feel like you're off the clock. Second-grade is the sweet spot. You're past the crying stage but most of them are still sweet enough. These kids? With their hormones? I'm going to wind up in jail if I have to do this for another two years."

The other woman paused to stuff her mouth with caramelized onion and feta cheese in puff pastry as Sumi sympathetically laughed her agreement. *Damned middle schoolers and their puddles of puberty.*

"But if I weren't teaching," she continued around her mouthful, "I've always wanted to open a B&B. But that would require a bigger house and nicer furniture and the desire to get up and make strangers breakfast. But if we're talking second life dream jobs, that might be it."

"I've always wanted a flower shop," Sumi blurted, heat spreading over her cheeks. *Why don't you put it on a sign and start wearing it around, that might be less obvious.* "Just a little place, nothing too fancy or big, where you can stop in and get a bouquet to brighten your day."

"That sounds so nice. It can be on the same block as the big house for the fancy furniture I don't have."

"That speech was just *riveting*, wasn't it? We're so lucky to have someone like that on the state board. There's just so much riding on what happens next, don't you think? Have you voted yet?"

The bespectacled older woman had come out of nowhere, appearing at their elbow. Jordan must have given a speech, Sumi realized. One that she had missed, dillydallying in her classroom, catching up on her messages from ChaoticConcertina. Another tiny pang of guilt shivered through her as the older woman stuffed a miniature quiche into her mouth, waiting for someone to answer. *It's giving emotional affair.* Sumi said nothing, knowing her grimace-like smile probably made her look feral, annoyed at that treacherous little voice. *You wouldn't need to have an emotional affair if your emotional needs were being met. They're barely being acknowledged.*

She would tell her principal at the end of the week, she vowed. The final week of school was a short one, then teachers had another few days cleaning out their classrooms. Hers was already nearly empty. She had already begun the act of permanently moving out, and was confident she'd have the entirety of her classroom in a box by the last day of school. She could avoid the banquet dinner, the speeches, the union vote altogether. *After all, what does it matter?*

She hadn't cast a ballot the last time the union had called for a vote on some contract issue either. Instead, she had gone to a free floral arranging class being sponsored by the botanical gardens. Sumi knew other teachers bolstered their degrees with drop-ins and lectures and workshops every few years, but she had never felt moved to do so. Flowers and plants were what she loved, and if she had to spend her days breaking up fights and constantly asking her middle school charges to put away their phones at the school Monday through Friday, shouldn't that mean the rest of the time belonged to her? To do what *she* wanted?

The class had focused on vase designs, something she could do in her sleep, and she had left in such a good mood that she'd decided to stop off and treat herself to a fresh manicure, not remembering that she had been meant to vote that day until the following evening.

Jordan had been incandescent. He didn't do *anger*. Anger was 'for people of a small intellect.' He had never blown up at her, never raised his voice. He didn't need to. The palette of his emotions were hued with sanctimony and disappointment, his metaphorical paintbrush dipping into indignation and self-righteousness like a seasoned master. He'd made her feel terrible without raising his voice at all, which was somehow worse than if he had simply argued with her.

When her team peer began to speak, Sumi made good her escape. This room, she thought, making her way to the door, was full of teachers just like her on the surface — barely making ends meet as they bought supplies for their classrooms every year out of their own pockets, contemplating that they would likely be paying back student loans until retirement. They were career educators, they gave everything they had to their students and schools, uncaring if they had sufficient retirement accounts or if they found themselves playing bouncer in the hallways more often than they actually taught anything. She didn't share their passion, had already mentally checked out of this job, and was ready to close this chapter of her life. *Close the whole damned book and pick a new one.*

It wouldn't do to go changing the type of relationship she had with ChaoticConcertina. Not right now. Not when she had come to rely on him so much to be her voice of reason, her therapist, the keeper of her innermost thoughts and dreams. After she was gone, after she had settled into her new home and her new life . . . maybe things could change. Their energies matched, at least, they did online. *Compatible rizz for sure.*

It was a bad idea to change anything now, but after she'd started over again . . . she wouldn't rule it out, Sumi thought, pulling away from the school, feeling the possibility of what the future held thrumming within her.

After you're someone new, maybe he can be part of the new vibe. Deadass.

The Flashback You Should Have Been Anticipating

SUMI

I
t all started when she joined the houseplant server earlier in the year, seeking advice on her ailing Swiss cheese philodendron.

DiscHorse felt oddly comfortable — more private than most of the other popular social media platforms, completely absent of the typical audience one found on CrowdJournal, which mostly appealed to her parents' demographic. One could find a community for almost every interest, reminding her of the message boards and blogging communities of her teenage years.

The evening she had typed out her initial message to the group, it had been quiet, with only a small handful of respondents, none of their advice particularly good. It wasn't until she'd gone to bed that a response had come, the notification pinging on her phone screen.

ChaoticConcertina: _Sounds like an issue with soil content?_

Have you repotted lately?

She'd straightened in bed, light from her phone illuminating her face as she read the response, quickly tapping out a more detailed summary of the plant's progress.

ChaoticConcertina. Their profile was empty beyond username and pronouns. He/Him.

Instantly, Sumi was on her guard. She was no stranger to men online, who often left her asking the age old question: why are men? He'd asked a few more questions, had given her the best advice, asking for photos.

When he sent her a DM after she had posted the photo of the pathetically sagging plant, she prepared herself for the inevitable dick pic. *Block him and forget about it.* To her light shock, all he'd done was let her know that he was going to ask a friend of his who owned a shop specializing in rare houseplants.

Sumi assumed he was lying. Surely a place like that didn't exist in the real world, where jobs were something one primarily looked forward to leaving each day and where consumers couldn't be bothered to support an entire business specializing in monsteras and hanging jades.

There were flower shops that sold the odd planter, home improvement superstores with seasonal greenhouses, and if one was lucky enough, a year-round garden center, but even those tended to place their emphasis on outdoor growing. A houseplant store. It was such a silly, stupid thing to lie about. She'd huffed, rolling her eyes at the mere thought. *Does he think you were born yesterday?!* Perhaps it was because she spent her days with middle-schoolers who lied as often and easily as the most hardened criminals, but Sumi considered herself a good judge of truthfulness, and this seemed as probable as all of her students showing up on time on standardized testing day.

> **_ChaoticConcertina:_** _I'm going to save your photo, if you don't mind._
> _I'll pop in tomorrow on my way to work and show her._
> _I'll let you know what she says!_

He'd done exactly that. She'd not actually expected a response from ChaoticConcertina, outside the lingering threat of an unexpected dick pic. When the top left corner of her phone screen displayed a notification from the chat server app two days later, Sumi expected another unhelpful response from another member of the server, swiping open her phone with only half-interest.

> **_ChaoticConcertina:_** _The most likely culprit is a bit of rot at the root_
> _beneath the point you can feel with a finger._
> _Probably started when you repotted last month._
> _If you're using vermiculite, swap it for perlite and an equal part orchid bark._
> _If you have access to fresh bone meal, a little bit works wonders._

She'd stared at her phone on her lunch break that day, eyes widened, shocked that he responded at all and flabbergasted by the photo he had sent. It was an example of each of the items he'd mentioned, assuming she was a novice. She was familiar with perlite and bone meal, but she had _never_ in her life seen anything like the shop in the background, looking like something from a dream.

Antique cabinets and mismatched marble-topped tables stood behind him, topped with ceramic pots and glass Mason jars, beakers and bud vases, all bearing clippings from various plants. From the ceiling, the trailing vines of pothos and jades, strings of hearts and strings of turtles, zebrinas and ivies. On top of the closest table was a sawhorse draped in a scarf of rich emerald, and on top of that was an old-fashioned librarians card catalog cabinet, the drawers pulled out, with vibrant green strings of pearls cascading to the surface below.

The hand that held the container of orchid bark was large and well-formed, tawny with an olive undertone, with long fingers and raised veins, the kind of hand one envisioned if one were fantasizing about being held down and fucked within an inch of one's life—

"Whatcha lookin' at?"

Her room para had startled her from the inappropriate thought that day, nearly causing the phone to escape her grasp. Sumi had squeaked in shock and fumbled the phone, hand moving over hand as if it were a slippery fish intent on evading capture.

ChaoticConcertina: If you don't have access to it, you can buy it online.

The bone meal, I mean

Like, that wasn't advice to go commit murder just for fresh bone meal

You definitely shouldn't steal someone's bones

*Unless it's a **really** nice philo*

Then it's your call

He was real. If his hand was anything to go on, and it was all she had, he was gorgeous. *You can't tell that from a hand, what's wrong with you?* The shop was real as well, like something out of one of her most fevered dreams. Someone out there, wherever it was that ChaoticConcertina called home, had a plant shop, living their best life, she had no doubt. It was everything *she* wanted.

It was the very first time Sumi admitted it to herself — *she* wanted her own little shop, airy and bright and full of flowers, a place that was hers, where she would never be in charge of standardized testing preparations and would never again have to break up a fight between twelve-year-old girls. *It's giving aspirational. It's giving dream life. It's giving manifesting.*

She'd wandered into the pretty little flower shop in her neighborhood later that same day, feeling an itch beneath her skin, her feet propelling her to the shop almost without her full conscious consent. *The Lucky Lily by Bloomerang.* There was a tree growing right through the center of the sales floor and a wall of refrigerated cases containing buckets and buckets of flowers. She could choose a premade arrangement from the case or select her own individual stems à la carte, which was her preference.

"Bloomerang is your parent company?" she asked the friendly woman who checked her out, whom she knew to be the owner. Sumi had been in the smaller shop at least a dozen times before, but never before had she felt compelled to ask questions. She'd never had a reason to. Now, though . . . the thought of that plant shop whispered at the back of her mind. She loved all of her plant babies but knew she was nowhere near knowledgeable enough to run a store like that.

Flowers, on the other hand, *that* was a language she spoke. The way other women joined book clubs or took voice lessons or horse riding lessons or playing intramural sports, she had done workshops at the Arboretum, volunteered at the garden, taken several different courses on advanced floral arrangement, offered through various community centers and enrichment programs. As a young teen, she had completed several summers' worth of certification at summer camp, and developed what was probably a not completely healthy obsession with the Victorian's secret language of flowers. Sumi heated, remembering her "vicious Victorian" phase, when she carried a tussie mussie around the halls of her school and gifted friends and enemies alike carnations in symbolic colors.

A flower shop had been something she'd long dreamed of, although it was never something that she considered realistic. She was captain of the *SS Sunk Cost*, and there was no port in sight.

"Yup, we're technically a part of their franchise. It's nice though, because they really let each shop operate independently."

Her lungs had felt overinflated, pressing on the walls of her chest as if they might buckle outward, turning her into a balloon. *A franchise!* She had never seriously considered this latent little fantasy of hers, always reminding herself that she had spent too many years on teaching to throw it away. *And you don't know the first thing about starting up a flower shop.* But then again, she had never asked.

"So like, do they just slap their name on your shop and take some of your profits? You had to do everything else?"

The woman behind the counter grinned broadly. "*They* actually do everything, if you can believe it. I own the shop with my mom. This was always her dream, and once I looked into it, it seemed like a pretty profitable system in place here. So, you have to find your own industrial space and secure the building. But if you're accepted as a franchisee, they come in and do everything else. They cover the cost of construction and they supply you with everything you need to open. All the equipment, all of the distribution contacts and contracts."

"So . . . is it not really your shop then?" Sumi asked, already resigned to disappointment. *If it seems too good to be true, it probably is.* "I mean," she added quickly, realizing how her words sounded. *Way to be an asshole.* "Like, no offense. I didn't mean that to sound rude. But if they're paying for everything, aren't you just an employee?"

At that, the blonde woman barked out a laugh. "Technically yes, but you start paying it back immediately. It's kind of like financing a house. Everyone always says 'they bought a house', but isn't the bank the one who bought the house? You have to use Bloomerang's contractor, but you hire your own shop designer and it can look however you want. The only thing all the shops have in common is the tree. So we pay a fixed amount every month back to the parent company to pay back the cost of the initial build and set up, plus a percentage of business for the licensing. And our rent," she added with another laugh.

Sumi slumped, her stomach sinking. *There's no way you would ever be able to afford all that.*

"And it's a fixed term, so you're not paying back your startup loan indefinitely. If you don't pay back within that fixed time, I believe they have the right to come in and take over. But," she added quickly, seeing Sumi's expression, "it's honestly *so* easy to keep up. Basically all the franchises fulfill their online orders, so business is never, ever slow. That's where their real money is, the brick and mortar end of it is a drop in the bucket for them. So all of those online flower orders get pushed directly to the franchise stores first, before independent stores get anything. Obviously they keep a percentage of it, but *you* make the money on every order. It would be a racket if it weren't always busy," she laughed again. "Mom and I only have sixteen months of payback on our startup loan and I've been doubling the payments for the past year. It's that busy."

"What happens when you pay it back?"

"Then it's yours. You still pay the franchise royalty every month to have the name over the door, but that's worth it for the business you get from the website. I did this for my mom, but now it's going to be a profitable business I can leave to my daughter."

Sumi swiped her card as the woman wrapped her small bouquet. *That's all you want. An opportunity to do something you actually enjoy.*

"Are you thinking about it? I can put you in contact with my franchise manager if you are, she's super easy to work with. At the very least take her card. You can do your own investigation online."

"Thank you," she called back over her shoulder, leaving the shop a moment later with the franchise manager's card taped to the front of her paper-wrapped bouquet. Every nerve in body seemed to be vibrating as she walked home with a bounce in her step, thrumming with *possibility.*

She never would have ventured into the shop that day if she hadn't been feeling good about herself, and she couldn't deny *why* she was feeling on cloud nine. She never would have had that first conversation if she hadn't been buoyed by her interactions with ChaoticConcertina.

PinksPosies&Pearls: *I did something wild today. Crazy for me.*

I had a conversation with someone about franchising a business.

Opening my own shop!

That's all it was, just a conversation.

It's not like I have the money to do anything right now.

Shockingly, teaching is not keeping me stocked in gold bars.

But just having the conversation felt good.

Like I might actually follow my dreams someday.

His response came only a few minutes later.

ChaoticConcertina: *Revolutions begin with a conversation.*

All of the inventions that have changed our lives probably started

with two people just having a conversation.

A conversation is a spark, Pinky.

I'm proud of you! It's the first step to anything you want to change in your life.

Keep feeding it and let it ignite.

That had been the beginning.

Completely innocent, she regularly reminded herself as the weeks went by. They talked about plants, and what could be more innocent than plants?!

He cultivated Hoyas. Dozens of different variegations, various sizes and styles and ages. Hoyas and ficus, sending her photo of a rubber tree that seemed to be as tall as the room itself. She showed off her collection of philodendrons and monsteras, sharing a photo of her prized pink princess, feeling oddly giddy to be doing so.

There was no one in her daily life who knew or cared about her actual passion, much less shared in it. Both her co-teacher and their team assistant claimed to have black thumbs, and while Jordan knew she had a condo full of houseplants, Sumi suspected he viewed them much in the way as he viewed the coat tree or the bathroom mirror — something that existed, that was a part of the house, unimportant and unworthy of attention or discussion.

To have someone who not only cared, who was not only interested, but someone who *shared* her hobby — who had wisdom to impart and exclaimed over how beautiful her collection was had been intoxicating. ChaoticConcertina's reaction to her pink princess had been appropriately enthusiastic and admiring. *He gets it! Someone actually understands!*

A few hours later, when he sent her a photo of a pink variegated hoya, telling her it was called krimson queen, one of the many in his collection, Sumi suspected she was toeing her way down a dangerous path.

ChaoticConcertina: *She looks like she would want to have tea with your Princess.*

PinksPosies&Pearls: *She does, I'm obsessed.*
I kinda want to start staging my plants to have tea parties now.

ChaoticConcertina: *And you should!*
You can probably monetize the views on DreameStream.

By the end of that month, Sumi had realized she'd spent more time talking to ChaoticConcertina online than she had talking to her boyfriend Jordan, who slept beside her two nights a week. He knew that she was a teacher, and she knew he ran his own business. They didn't know each other's names or locations; didn't know the specifics of each other's lives outside of the broad strokes and had never shared face-identifying photos. Those details seemed strangely unimportant. What he *did* know was far more personal.

Sumi had confessed to him that she didn't actually enjoy being a teacher, that she felt trapped in her own life, a trap of her own making, for which she alone held the key. She knew he was divorced and that his ex-wife had moved for work, drastically limiting the time he spent with his 9-year-old daughter.

Since then, they had settled into a schedule.

They were rarely online at the same time. She was an obligate early riser, her alarm having the temerity to go off each morning before the sun had even made an appearance, while he was a night owl, based on the timestamps of his messages. Sumi would send him embarrassingly long messages each morning, starting them before she left the house, finishing her thoughts sometime during homeroom.

By the time the 3 o'clock bell rang, there would be a response. His afternoon response would be brief compared to the book she had written, but Sumi no longer felt self-conscious over that. They would trade messages back and forth sporadically over the course of the late afternoon and evening, and then after she went to bed at night, Chaotic-Concertina spilled his guts.

ChaoticConcertina: Have you ever considered how much of our identity is sewn up in the brands we use?
The products we consume?
Loyalty to a particular brand of toothpaste.
A preference for one giant tech company-created cell phone
...over the other giant tech company's cell phone.
The visible logo on the clothes we wear.
ChaoticConcertina: Whether or not you buy your dish soap from the supermarket
...or the superstore
or even worse!
from a giant online retailer who delivers it to your doorstep,
no interaction with your fellow citizens required.
I had a realization this afternoon, as I was placing an inventory order.
I used to get almost all of this stuff from independent vendors.
I had a basket guy, a box guy. The woman who did our packaging.
ChaoticConcertina: One by one, they all went out of business slowly.

I guess that's the nature of the beast, right? Nothing stops the engines of commerce.

And now I'm ordering all of these individual things from one catalog, one charge.

It's so much easier. The prices aren't much different. It's improved MY workflow.

And I can rationalize that this choice was made for me, but I've still participated in it.

The people who make the money off our choices have no idea who we are.

Most of them don't care to learn. They don't care about the communities they destroy.

But still we make their products who we are, how we judge each other.

But I DID know these people, their faces and their names.

And I don't know how we excuse not judging ourselves for being complicit.

PinksPosies&Pearls: Ugh, How dare you.

How dare you make me contemplate capitalism and my part in it this early in the day

I am the "even worse" no talking required

You know what half of my identity is?

The size of clothing I buy. The logo doesn't make a difference.

That little number is all that matters, because it determines everything else.

Whether or not I even bother stopping into a shop, the styles I'll be stuck with.

Whether or not I want a quarter of my wardrobe to consist of shirts with no shoulders.

Because of the size on my tag, the fashion powers that be have determined who I am.

I have to dress a certain way because of my size AND profession. No deviation!

PinksPosies&Pearls: *And the same is true on the other end of the spectrum!*

My tiny-boned sisters are locked into dressing like teenagers indefinitely.

And I'm stuck dressing like their mother. It's maddening.

Maybe I should just embrace that I like talking to my plants more than people

What's the dress code for a bog witch? That's what I want to be.

But like, a sexy bog witch. That'll attract the right sort, right?

ChaoticConcertina: *Absolutely. I sense sexy bog creatures in your imminent future.*

It was a relief. If she were the only one using their friendship as an invisible therapist, she likely would have stopped after the first week or two, messages tapering off until she was back into her routine of drudgery. He matched her early morning vent posts and ruminations at night, balancing the scales of their friendship, giving her something to look forward to each morning – a prize that had been long absent from her life.

And if she occasionally closed her eyes and tried to envision that strong, well-defined hand holding hers, well . . . Sumi decided that was *her* business.

Then her great-aunt died.

An aunt whose existence had been completely unknown to her, her maternal grandmother's sister, a family she'd never met. Sumi and a second cousin on the other side of the Unification were contacted as the closest next-of-kin, named beneficiaries to an estate they'd done nothing to earn.

PinksPosies&Pearls: *I know it doesn't make sense to be upset.*

Or at least, to be as upset as I am.

But I'm heartbroken that I didn't know her.

My mom died when I was little. Sometimes I can't even picture her face without a photo.

I've had my entire life to get over it, but I feel like a part of me died with her.

I don't know anything about Japanese culture. I don't know anything about Sylvan culture.

My dad did his best and my stepmother was always good to me

But I was still cut off from half of everything I AM.

I've never known anything about her family.

I've never known grandparents or aunts and uncles.

PinksPosies&Pearls: *So to find out that I had a relative so close . . .*

We could have met for lunch, we could have had tea.

She could have been in my life when I was growing up.

I could have been in hers so that she wasn't alone at the end.

I have this money now and everyone is telling me how happy I should be but I'm heartbroken.

Trigger warning for a MASSIVE overshare, sorry []

She was mortified with herself for sending something so personal to the stranger on the other side of the screen, but she couldn't deny that it felt good to get it out.

Her father was human, white, and from the unification. He'd met her mother when he'd been an architecture student, studying on the other side of the world, and her mother had left Japan with him to start a new life as a professor's wife and give birth to a half-sylvan baby girl.

Sumi had not been born with the shimmering markings around her eyes and on her face that other sylvans possessed. They tracked down her back, visible only in the most daring outfits, but absent as far as the outward world was concerned. She did not have the elongated fingers, but *did* have their slightly tapered ears. At least, Sumi told herself she did, obsessively comparing the shape of her friends' ears her entire life.

She didn't have any *noticeable* outward markings that distinguished her as anything other than human, feeling cut off from the photo on her dresser of her beautiful Sylvan mother every time she looked in the mirror. She didn't know anything about her mother's Japanese heritage and culture, didn't speak the language, didn't know any family.

But now she was a beneficiary to this stranger, a stranger who shared her blood, her mother's blood, and she couldn't help feeling cut off from all of it all over again.

When she went to bed that night, her head ached from all the tears she had cried. She was embarrassed for the over-the-top overshare, but there wasn't anyone in her daily life to whom she could vent in such a way. She didn't want to make her father and stepmother feel poorly, and her much younger step-sisters — both human, both white, both the majority race and the majority species — couldn't possibly understand. She didn't have close girlfriends, not close enough for something like this, and Jordan viewed every topic in which he was not the center as a problem to solve. Rather than a supportive shoulder for her to cry on, he'd told her it was an opportunity for investment. ChaoticConcertina, as pathetic as it was, was the only judgment-free source of solace she had.

__ChaoticConcertina:__ Please don't apologize.
I totally get it, you've got a lot more to unpack just cashing a check.
I don't understand what you're going through specifically, but I get it.
I'm a pro at "there's more to it."
My grandfather started his business when he came to the unification.
My dad was already a teenager, grew up working in the shop until he took it over.
A few years ago he was diagnosed with a progressive disease.
The dementia is slow, but it's steady.
It doesn't matter that I have a degree in something else.
I'm the eldest, I'm the only son. I was the first one born here. This is our family's business.
But there's not a week that goes by that I don't think about selling it.
The industry we're in has changed tremendously in the past two decades
It's almost all online now, so brick & mortar is a liability.

ChaoticConcertina: *Everyone tells me to sell, get the money for the land and the building.*

I'm in an area that is rapidly developing, so I know I would make a mint.

But it's not just a shop. It's not just a business.

It was my grandfather's dream. It's been my dad's whole life.

And I can't just sell that off like a used car.

ChaoticConcertina: *Think of this as a gift from your mom, Pinky.*

Everyone you know will tell you how to invest it, what you should do with it.

And I guess I am too — Spend like it's a gift from your mom.

Take a course or two and learn about her culture. Join a mixed-species group.

Do something that makes **you** *happy, and then remember that it's from your mom.*

And think about how happy **she** *would be to see you so happy.*

And don't ever apologize for venting here.

When she'd read his message the following morning, Sumi sat before her laptop, shoulders shaking as she sobbed, beyond grateful to this empathetic stranger who understood her so well.

PinksPosies&Pearls: *Thank you for understanding.*

And yeah, that's exactly it. There's more to it than people see on the surface.

I'm so sorry to hear about your father's diagnosis. I can't imagine how hard that is.

I know my mom was sick for a long time, but I was too young to remember her decline.

If you ever need to just scream into the void, the over-sharing void is here to listen.

I guess talking to each other is a hell of a lot cheaper than therapy, right?

Thinking of this as a gift from my mom is honestly probably the very best advice

so thank you for that as well.

If her inheritance had only been money, she likely would have done exactly as he'd suggested. Inquired into whether or not there was a multi-species support group in the area. Taken a class on Japanese Art, on kimono, a beginner's language class. After all, the handful of classes she'd had time for back in undergrad seemed very far away.

If it had been just money, she would've done exactly that.

But it hadn't been just money, even though the money was substantial, a life-changing amount for her. The little nest egg she'd accumulated in fifteen years of teaching would have been at home in a pigeon's nest's, a tiny crumb compared to what she had gained from this unknown relative. Along with their savings and assets, her mother's aunt had also left her home, the home she and her husband had lived in for more than thirty years, in a town called Cambric Creek.

She went to see it alone.

Sumi couldn't articulate why she didn't mention it to Jordan, why she didn't want anyone else there. *No, that's not true.* She would have been happy to have *one* person there with her . . . but he was an anonymous screen name.

The house itself was an L-shaped single-story brick beauty. It had a slightly retro feel in its design, but it was bright and airy, with a long backyard and the sunken sunroom she loved at first sight. The kitchen amenities far outran her ability, but there was a cozy breakfast nook beside a wall of windows, and on the other side of the paned glass, an empty bird feeder. The agent had laughed when Sumi had clamored into the tub in the master bedroom's ensuite, squealing in delight to find it fit her ample frame.

The north-facing bedroom was heavily shadowed at that midafternoon hour, but the walk-in closet had track lighting, allowing her a good look at every inch. *You're actually going to be able to start dressing like **you** again!*

She had always loved frilly dresses and sweeping, dramatic silhouettes. The problem with dramatic silhouettes when one was a size 20, however, was that even the most modest neckline was too bodacious for teaching middle school. She had been taken to task several times early in her career for her wardrobe choices, even though there had been nothing wrong with any of the outfits, she had wanted to scream at the time — feeling as though she were being held accountable for having large breasts and a big ass in the first place, as though she could eliminate them if her clothes were frumpy enough — it hadn't been worth the battle. Turtlenecks and A-line skirts had been her near daily wardrobe for fifteen years, the turtleneck swapped out for a clavicle-hugging shell in the warmer months.

She could fill this closet with the clothes she actually liked to wear, diaphanous dresses of lavender and creampuff confections with pink ruffles and slits up to her thigh. Her favorite article of clothing was a dusty pink Grecian-style dress with gathered shoulders and a deep V neckline, slit up several inches above her knee. She would wear it every week in this place, would buy it in every color in which it was made, and if hormone-addled 12-year-olds wanted to stare slack-jawed, it wouldn't be her problem. Her cleavage was going to be allowed to breathe for the first time in more than a decade.

That was, if she decided to keep the house.

There's no question. This is it. This is home. The instant the thought invaded her mind, Sumi knew in her bones it was true, tears burning at the corners of her eyes. *A gift from your mom.*

After she'd left the house, she had driven to Cambric Creek's little downtown afterward, parking her car in the public lot and walking around the horseshoe of businesses that ringed a long oval-shaped park in the center of town. There was a charming little gazebo, and a bandstand at the far corner that one could access by any of the meandering pathways cut through the greenery. Around the park were more than a dozen different businesses in Victorian-style buildings. A hardware store, an old fashioned-looking ice cream parlour. A coffee shop that had a steady stream of traffic, and all around her, bustling about despite the fact that it was late afternoon on a weekday, were residents and shoppers of every conceivable species.

She'd dropped to one of the many stone benches enhancing the space, overcome with emotion at the sight of her soon-to-be new neighbors, bustling about this ridiculously charming little town. The agent handling the house, Elspeth, was a tiefling, and once Sumi got over her initial shock, she was able to pay attention to the woman's recitation about the house and the neighborhood. She had mentioned it was multi-species, but Sumi couldn't have envisioned *this* in her dizziest daydreams.

A chattering mothwoman shopped with a tall, tusked troll, a trio of fox-tailed young women in identical school uniforms, a goblin with several children on cell phones, instructing them to *pick up your heads and stay out of the way!* She watched a tall, broad-shouldered ogre with burnished gold horns shoulder his way out of the coffee shop, passing before her bench before he disappeared into the building on her left, his thick black glasses sliding down his brick-red nose as he did so. There were humans here and there as well — at least, people who looked human from a distance. They could have been elves or werewolves, Sumi reminded herself. *Or Sylvan, like you.*

She could find herself here in this place. She could find the piece of herself that it felt as if it had always been missing.

Sumi decided there was nothing compelling her to rush back home, and took her time strolling around after getting her own coffee from the busy cafe. After looping Main Street, she cut down a little side street close to the bench where she'd sat, just around the corner from the center of town. There was a stationary shop, a little sandwich bar, and a clothing boutique that seemed to be exclusively for goblins and gnomes. The last four or five spaces were empty, likely all part of some larger business that had closed.

FOR RENT

Her lungs over-inflated once again, leaving her feeling as though her toes might leave the ground, floating away like a turtlenecked balloon. *This is a gift from your mom. Think about how happy **she** would be to see you so happy.*

This was her opportunity, Sumi realized. This was her chance to dock the *SS Sunk Cost* for good. *You can sell your condo, use that money to pay the rental lease on this place, at least for the first year.* She owned a house free and clear; it would be silly not to live in it. Especially in a place like this, where you can finally figure out how to feel whole. If the florist at the *Lucky Lily* was to be believed, her Bloomerang business would thrive here. *They provide all the equipment, the distribution contracts, and the customers. All you have to do is live your dream life.*

It was with that energy that Sumi set off in search of a flower shop, a plant store, even a supermarket that sold premade bouquets. She wanted to bring something home from this place to put in her condo, to remind her why she was packing up, why she was walking away from her life into the unknown. *The Perfect Petal. Viol, Violet & Vine.* She frowned down at her phone, knowing she needed to make a decision quickly. The red light wasn't going to last forever and she didn't know her way around. Both sounded promising . . . But *Viol, Violet & Vine* would've required turning and looping all the way back around the town square, back in the direction from which she had just come. The light turned green. *The Perfect Petal* it is, she thought, following the sign that advertised *business district.*

Maybe you wouldn't be able to rent that space at all. Maybe the business district is the only option. The thought made her frown, but she quickly saw that Cambric Creek was packed with businesses. Little storefronts, long restaurants, sidewalk cafés and quick service counters, a veterinarian next to an eyeglass shop beside a small pharmacy. There wasn't any indication that business was restricted to the business district.

Don't get ahead of yourself. You are going to call the number from the building today.

She noticed, as she drove, that the sidewalks were tiered in this place — standard concrete, a shallow trench that rippled with moving water, and a section of neatly trimmed grass, just as wide as the concrete. Some stretches of road even had a lane of sand. It wasn't until she took a closer look that Sumi realized the different sidewalk materials were specific to accommodate the different species of residents. A slender cervitaur walked on the grass, laughing with her companion, a goblin wearing chunky soled shoes, clicking along on the concrete.

On the other side of the street, a blue skinned little girl with webbed fingers hopped along the water trench, splashing until her mother turned swiftly, the little girl instantly ceasing her splashing. Accommodations for more than just the human majority. It was a revelation. In that instant, Sumi nearly regretted her vow to leave education, thinking of how much good accommodative policies like this would have in classrooms. The moment was fleeting. That would be a noble cause to take up . . . For someone else.

The instant she stepped over the threshold of *The Perfect Petal*, Sumi closed her eyes, head dropping back slightly. Vegetal and green, the crisp herbaceous smell of freshly clipped rose stems invaded her senses, the cotton candy sweet smell of the blossoms and pungent note of eucalyptus following after a few more steps. There was a long wall of refrigerated cases that she could come to expect, although it seemed as if several of the shelves had been taken out, the premade arrangements spread out on the shelves that remained. The last case held the buckets of individual flower stems, although Sumi noticed there were half as many there as had been in the *Lucky Lily*.

The space was well-organized, with high shelves of baskets and empty vases, a counter where one could peruse half a dozen photo books, and a single table through the center of the space, containing dish gardens of ferns and spathiphyllum. The shop was compact and utilitarian, but it didn't possess the fanciful Parisienne flower boutique she envisioned in her head for her own shop. *Well, that's fine. You don't want to look the same as everyone else anyway.*

At the POS counter stood a pear-shaped woman with a waterfall of blonde curls spilling over her shoulders. Sumi felt her own smile raise as the woman turned, giving her beaming grin.

"Hi there! He'll be right out."

"Oh! Oh, that's fine. I was just going to pick up a little —"

"Okay, this is all I have. Do you solemnly swear you're not going to use it for something stupid? If I come by and find this on a jar of pickles, you are never getting anything from me again."

"It's going on the fruit baskets! How dare you!"

The woman threw up her hands defensively, her shoulders shaking in laughter, but all Sumi could do was stare. The man who had come out from the back room was striking. His features were sharp and angular, with an aquiline nose and strong jaw. His mouth was wide, his eyes so dark they seemed to glitter like obsidian. Something moved behind him, something brilliantly colored, still moving behind him as he dropped a hand to the counter. It was his tail, Sumi realized after what felt like a small eternity, watching the sinuous way it moved, swaying in an undulation so subtle, she might not have noticed it if she hadn't been paying such close attention to him. *If he wasn't so fucking gorgeous.*

He was a naga, she realized.

His tail was *beautiful.* Vivid violet scales, banded in irregular splotch-es of inky blue, and as he turned to hand a spool of gold twined ribbon to the woman at the counter, Sumi could see a brilliant iridescence, prismatic like a rainbow. His light brown skin seemed to glow against the pale colored button-down he wore, and when his gaze traveled past the blonde woman to land on Sumi, eyes widening slightly in surprise, she could see that he had lashes so thick and black that it almost appeared as if he were wearing eyeliner. He was stunning.

"I'm so sorry! I didn't even hear the bell. What can I help you with today?"

She was underwater, unable to decipher anything other than the deep thrum of his voice, the individual words lost in the vibration. As she watched, his dark eyebrows rose slightly, his head inclining minutely, appearing as if he were waiting for something. Somewhere in her brain, an alarm bell began to ring, a clanging clamor that seemed to rattle her teeth, that treacherous little voice screaming, just barely able to penetrate the fog she seemed to be trapped in by this man's almost inhuman loveliness. *He's talking to you! You're staring, your mouth is hanging open. Fucking hells, he's talking to **you**!*

"Oh!" she exclaimed, jumping in surprise, her inner voice finally penetrating to the worthless bowl of pudding in her skull. Heat burned up her neck, and Sumi knew he would be able to see it splotching her cheeks. "Oh, of course! You're talking to me! Of course you are!" *What an amazing first impression in your new home. The first person you meet is a gorgeous man and you go slack-jawed for five minutes.* She laughed in mortification, her tongue off and running without any input from her brain. *What the fuck is wrong with you?! This could be your new husband!* "Um, I'm so sorry to have interrupted. I-I was just going to pick out a few stems, if that's okay?"

He seemed amused by her outburst, a wry smile curving his wide mouth, showing her a glimmer of glinting white fangs. When he raised his arm to extend a hand out to the case containing the buckets of loose flowers, Sumi thought her knees were going to buckle. She was a sucker for a good forearm, and she always would be. He had his shirt sleeves rolled back to the elbow, showing off his sinewy forearm, long fingers directing her attention to the side wall. "Loose flowers are in the last case here, closest to the register. Price list is on the door. I'm happy to help you pick something out if you're not sure . . ." He let the question trail off as she dipped her head, moving to stand before the case, her eyes closed tight.

"I-I'm going to take a look at what you have, first. But thank you. So much. I'll let you know if I need you. *Help.* I'll let you know if I need help." *I'll let you know if I need impregnating. Like, right now. Maybe here on this table.* She was childless by choice and had no desire to change that, but if this beautiful snake man suggested he would be interested in breeding her right then and there as the smiling blonde woman watched, Sumi knew that she would be able to make room in her heart for his child.

His smile stretched a teensy bit further as she turned to the case in mortification, reaching out to the cool glass for support as he turned back to the other woman.

"Anything else, Grace? Or are you done pilfering my shelves for the day?"

"You should get the little purple asters," the cheerful woman said to Sumi's back, ignoring the handsome man entirely. *How is she able to do that? Maybe she's a witch, immune to his charm and eyelashes.* "And that deep red ranunculus, I just love how full they are right now."

Breathe. This is the language you speak. She turned with a grin, still feeling hot, but the cool glass had calmed her galloping heart a few degrees. "Ranunculus is actually one of my favorites. I think I'll do exactly that." She added a bit of lemon leaf and ruscus, a bit of dark purple statice, and two stems of cheerful yellow alstroemeria. Just enough for the small vase currently on her windowsill, as yet unpacked. *Attraction, admiration, optimism.* The meaning of her bouquet was almost prophetically on the nose.

The blonde woman's smile was cherry-red and beaming when Sumi carried her selections back to the register. She had a creamy complexion and a spray of freckles over her nose, and as Sumi forced herself to breathe, the other woman's sapphire eyes moved from her to the handsome naga so quickly she might have missed it if she had been looking at her phone, as she likely would have been doing anywhere else.

"Um, I'm processing roses right now—"

Her thighs clenched at the baritone of his voice. *When was the last time you were instantly attracted to someone this way?* She couldn't remember, it had been so long. *ChaoticConcertina, but that's different.*

"—If you wanted to see them. They're lipstick roses, pink and yellow? Or . . ." he hesitated, looking over her meager selection with an appraising eye. "Hold on."

That overfilled balloon sensation against her ribs again as he turned, his snake lower half moving him with a surprising amount of speed. Her teeth sunk into her full lower lip when he disappeared, a section of his long tail staying behind, keeping the door propped open. *That's strangely adorable?* When he returned, he carried wispy plumosus and two bright-colored stems of birds of paradise. The tropical flower was normally outside her bouquet budget, but Sumi supposed she could splurge today. *Because you're about to start a new life. Because you deserve it. Because he's gorgeous.*

"These are left over from a wedding I had this past weekend. They're almost bloomed out, so no charge. But they work nicely with your colors and it'll give it a bit of height."

She could have swooned.

"That's lovely!" the blonde woman hummed once he'd wrapped the flowers in a fluid, practiced movement. *You're going to learn to do that. Maybe he can teach you.* "You seem to know what you're doing, sometimes I'm hopeless with pulling things together. Bringing flowers to anyone special?"

Sumi hoped her laugh didn't sound as awkward to them as it did to her own years, trying to tear her eyes away from the throat his open collar revealed. "Oh, no. Just for me. I-I'm going to be relocating to the area soon, and just wanted to pick up something for my condo to remind myself why I'm packing."

The blonde woman's face lit up. "How wonderful! I'm Grace, by the way. New to the area! Ranar, did you hear that? She's going to be *new* to the *area*." Her voice was pointed, although her brilliant smile never cracked.

Ranar.

"Did you want your receipt printed?" It was his turn to completely ignore the blonde woman, smiling at Sumi warmly.

Breathe. You can do this. You are going to be professional peers hopefully someday soon. Maybe he'll give you his phone number for flower business emergencies and blow jobs. "Not necessary," she returned his smile. "I love the functionality of your shop. Have you been in business long?"

"It's a family business, so yes. I've worked here since I was too young to legally be working anywhere, but that's what happens when your parents run a business. Child labor laws cease to exist."

She wondered if her laugh was as tinkling as she tried to make it. "Well, it shows." She twirled a strand of her long dark hair around a finger, gazing up. *Advanced rizzonomics.* "Everything is so well organized." *Here goes.* "I've been thinking of opening my own," she admitted with a sheepish laugh, biting her lip in a way she hoped appeared coquettish and not confused. "Do you have any tips?"

His dark eyebrows rose once more, snorting. "Tips? For a flower shop? Yeah, don't do it. Save your money."

"Ranar!"

Sumi could barely hear the sound of the woman named Grace's exclamation over the sudden timpani of her own heartbeat.

"I'm serious!" he chuckled. "If you want to throw money away, just put it out with recycling. But call and let me know what night you do it."

Grace slapped the counter. Sumi felt frozen, her heart crashing.

"Look, don't let anyone else deceive you into thinking this is a dream job cakewalk," he said, waving Grace's sputtering away. "This industry is dying a protracted death. Everything is online now, and the online retailers have become greedier and greedier. Gracie, you *know* I'm right!"

The blonde woman, Grace, crossed her arms, glaring. Sumi felt kinship, like she wanted to line up beside the woman and join her in scowling.

"A few years ago, the big companies used to wire out all of their orders to shops across the country so that everyone got a piece of the business," he went on. "Now they're opening their own shops, these soul-sucking flower factories everywhere you turn around. It's getting harder and harder for small independent shops to turn a profit on anything other than weddings and funerals. That's great in the spring and summer, but you need to work yourself to death every single week from March until September just to pay back all your accounts and keep the lights on through the winter."

Sumi wondered how they weren't able to hear the sound of her heartbeat as it crashed against her chest, seeming to smash against the very walls of this shop. "Oh," she practically whispered. "The shop that's close to my condo, where I live right now, it's um, a Bloomerang franchise?" She didn't even have a chance to continue before he was pulling a face, and somehow even *that* was attractive.

"Greedy vipers who are killing this industry. And I know a thing or two about vipers. I'm sorry to be the bearer of bad news, but there's no way to compete with them."

She wasn't sure how her legs managed to carry her out the door, barely remembered getting into her car. Her hands trembled. She felt ready to shake apart. *No! This is your dream! He's wrong. Just because his business isn't good, doesn't mean you'll have the same problem. You will be a **part** of the industry, not the thing that's killing it. He's probably just stubborn and doesn't want to adapt to the new ways things are done.*

She was halfway home when she decided to pull off the highway, directing her car into the drive through line of a chain coffee shop and treating herself to an iced latte. *What an obnoxious man. What a handsome, obnoxious man.* Pulling out her phone, she quickly tapped open the DiscHorse icon.

PinksPosies&Pearls: *This has been the weirdest day.*

It's been amazing. It's been the happiest day of my life, thus far, I think.

*The house is **so** great. I went to see it for the first time, and it's beautiful.*

It already feels like home, and I'm so, so happy.

I am definitely selling my condo! Like you said, no time like the present.

PinksPosies&Pearls: *But then, before I drove home, I stopped into this little specialty store.*

And the guy who ran the place was such a jerk!

He basically shat all over my dreams

I only hope the rest of my new neighbors are going to be nicer than him.

She squirmed once she was home and tucked beneath the covers. *He was so handsome. Ridiculously handsome and he knows flowers. How is that not a match made in heaven? Ranar.* Stupid handsome, but also kind of a jerk. Sumi wasn't sure if she was giving the handsome naga a completely fair characterization, for nothing he'd told her had been delivered in a *rude* way, but still. *Tactless. Just his opinion, and I'm pretty sure it's a bad one. The Lucky Lily cancels him out.*

She avoided telling ChaoticConcertina anything more than that. *He doesn't need to hear that you were about to present yourself on all fours like a bitch in heat.* After all, she had determined that changing the kind of relationship they had would be a bad idea. *He's your friend and you can talk to him with no judgment. And you kind of need that right now.*

Sumi was gratified when her phone pinged a short while later.

ChaoticConcertina: *First of all, I am so thrilled for you.*
Congratulations!
I'm so glad the house is something you can see yourself in.
That's so exciting! It's time to start packing, huh?
Okay, secondly, fuck that guy.
Like, seriously. Fuck that guy.
There are always going to be jealous people who try to bring down others'
happiness.
Don't let them get to you. Don't give them the space in your life to affect you
at all.
I'm so happy for you, Pinky. Everything's coming up roses.

Suggestible (Still a Flashback)

RANAR

"**R**anar, what is *wrong* with you?!"

Grace wasted no time rounding on him; the pretty, dark-haired woman barely clearing the sidewalk with her wrap of loose stems before Grace was slapping her hand down on the counter once more.

"What? She was nice! Did you want me to lie to her? Doom her to heartache and probably bankruptcy? And you call yourself a people person?"

They both turned as the woman backed out of a parking space in front of the shop, pulling out of the shared lot a moment later, brake light flaring. He followed the shape of her car as it disappeared into the world beyond his windows, gone forever.

"Ranar, she was *flirting* with you. At least, she was trying to. She probably would've had more luck with this spool of ribbon."

Ranar rolled his eyes, snorting. Grace was a dreamy romantic who spent too much time with equally optimistic newlyweds, their rose-colored glasses too secure for them to see the sharp edges of the world beyond the fifteen-minute ceremony of their nuptials. *And this is why the divorce rate is so high.*

"Seriously, are your eyes okay?" She glared. "Did you not notice the way she was looking at you? The way she was laughing? Fucking stars, she was *twirling her hair*. I don't think she could have been any more obvious without lifting her shirt and asking if you liked her boobies and maybe wanted to take a squeeze."

"Gracie, you are out of your mind. That mothman has broken you. The buzzing of his wings is probably a decibel that's dangerous for humans. I hope the sex is good, because it's scrambled your frontal cortex."

"How?" Grace turned away in disgust, moaning out the question to the empty shop. "How can you be *this* stupid? How can I be friends with such a stupid snake? Have you ever even been on a date, be honest with me. How is it that you have a child?"

"Because that was an arranged marriage," he added helpfully, ducking easily when she flung the spool of ribbon at his head, catching it as it rolled across the counter.

"Yeah, and now I understand why it didn't work out."

Ranar nearly choked on his laughter as he turned away from the counter, critically eyeing the coolers where the woman had stood just a few minutes earlier. It was a wonder she was able to put anything together at all. Pickings were slim, and the meager order arriving that afternoon likely wouldn't bolster the display much.

"She was pretty." The words were out before he was able to control his tongue, not especially wanting to engage in this particular conversation with Grace, not wanting to have this conversation at all. His friend was well-meaning, but she was a little *too* keen to see him coupled, desperate to force him into meeting her and her mothman scientist boyfriend for an evening of couples drudgery, he assumed. There was no need to give her any encouragement, but Grace had already turned at his words, flinging her arms open. "I mean, if she *had* lifted her shirt, I absolutely would have taken the offered squeeze."

"She was! And she's brand-new in town. At least, she will be soon. You can get to her first!"

"I'm pretty sure she'd find that offensive, boobie squeeze or not. She's a person, Grace. Not a collectible. Besides, I don't have time for a relationship right now. As it is, I have like twelve orders in the queue for this afternoon."

Grace rolled her eyes. "Don't even pretend you won't have them all done within the hour," she snapped before closing her eyes, sucking in a deep breath, steadying herself as if this was the most aggravating conversation she'd ever had in her life. "Look."

Her voice was gentler, her tone a bit closer to her normal sunny disposition, and Ranar almost laughed out loud at the notion that he and his inability to spot the subtle flirtations of strangers were the cause of her near apoplexy.

"All I'm saying is you are selling yourself short. And yes, I think you need a head start because you're not nearly half as smooth as the majority of the men in this town. *And* don't get me wrong," she added quickly, already knowing the way he would turn the conversation. "I know you have a lot on your plate. I *know* you're dealing with so much right now and I don't envy you any of it. And I'm here whenever you need a shoulder to cry on. But you're one of the nicest guys I know. You're genuinely a good guy, and that's more than I can say for some of my other friends."

"If you compare me to Tris, I am never speaking to you again."

"And I just think," she went on a bit louder, ignoring him, "that all of this with your dad wouldn't feel like such a heavy burden if you had someone to share it with."

"I thought you were here whenever I needed a shoulder to cry on?" he challenged, fighting his grin as she stamped her foot. "I have you, Gracie. I have my friend online. I don't have the mental bandwidth to start dating someone new *and* keep this place going by myself *and* be the only responsible adult in my family. That's just a fact."

"Yeah, but you lied and told *that* woman that you have a girlfriend!"

"Because she said she had a boyfriend!" He turned to her, incredulous. "Now who's being obtuse? She's someone from my plant server, I didn't want her to think I was only talking to her because I'm on the prowl."

"Literally, *how* are you so bad at this? If it weren't for Ruma, I would be convinced you've never had sex before. That you've never even talked to a woman!"

Ranar rolled his eyes. It was his turn to ignore her, he decided. And he really did have orders to get to. "Grace, I appreciate you, and I hear what you're saying. It's just not a good time."

She sighed heavily, re-accepting the spool of gold ribbon before trudging to the doorway. She stopped just before pulling it open, turning back to him.

"Thanks for this. Just let me know if any orders come in, I'm pretty sure we have everything in stock for the standard and the extra-large basket. And it's never a good time, babe. Learn from my mistakes. This is one of those things you *make* time for."

Ranar rolled his eyes one last time as Grace made her exit. It wasn't a conversation he wanted to have, not even with himself. *How are you supposed to make time for a girlfriend when you barely have time for anything as it is.* Bending to the printer below the work desk opposite the POS station, he pulled out the afternoon's orders, glaring at the logo in the corner of each. *Bloomerang.*

It was galling, being dependent on the floral industry giant.

Perhaps, he allowed, Grace was right. He shouldn't have been as blunt as he was with the pretty stranger, but he was steadfast in what he had told her. Unless she wanted to be a wedding florist, which was a thankless job with endless hours and no shortage of stress during bridal season, there was no way to compete with the flower giant's latest scheme to cut out the middleman.

Once upon a time ago, people came into the shop directly for all their flower-sending needs. He had been a child — *big enough to help, old enough for some responsibility* — tasked with unwrapping boxes of vases and baskets, placing them carefully on the shelf and breaking down the packaging. They came in for roses before dinner dates, cheery baskets of daisies and sunflowers to send to a sick friend, stood in line to place orders for school dances and graduations, table arrangements for holidays and bouquets for the school play. He was old enough to remember the phone in the shop ringing throughout the day, customers who called the flower behemoth's 1-800 number to place an order, patched through to local little stores like his family's, all across the unification.

Then had come the fax machine. The whirring, buzzing click of an incoming fax was one of his keystone memories. The fax machine gave way to the wire service with the advent of the Internet, requiring a dedicated line and a modem, the unending noise from the dot matrix printer in the office like a song he'd been forced to hear for hours on end.

Now the entire industry was almost exclusively online, excluding weddings.

He understood the why behind it. The Bloomerang website was easy to shop, searchable by both price point and occasion, pre-made vase designs and twee containers for everything from birthdays to a sick co-worker. They had a bottomless national advertising budget to ensure they were the biggest name in the industry, owned multiple web addresses and toll-free numbers, ensuring that if one were attempting to order flowers, they would be on the receiving end of the request. *The Perfect Petal* had been a Bloomerang partner for as long as he could remember, buying into the wire service as soon as it became available, although the cost of membership to the service was ever-rising.

Orders from the service were sent directly to the shop and printed automatically throughout the afternoon, although there were fewer since the industry behemoth had begun opening its own stores.

The Bloomerang-branded flower shops were a blight on more than just the floral industry. They were a clarion call, a warning to every small business of the fate that awaited them once whoever *their* corporate overlord was decided that they, too, would cut out the middleman. Most people didn't see the invisible labor that went into every item they purchased in the course of their everyday, but he did. Ranar knew how many people were put of work when small businesses fell like dominoes, entire industries left in the hands of the corporate giants who'd bulldozed their way to be at the top.

He might have been tactless in his words to the attractive stranger, but better for her to hear honesty than be snookered in by aesthetic-driven social media, believing that this business was sustainable in the current climate. As it was, it was only Jack Hemming's disdain for human-run businesses and chain stores that was keeping his family's shop afloat.

He disliked being reliant on the Bloomerang wire orders, but at least he still had them coming in daily. It was more than some of his former peers could say.

On the days his father insisted on coming into the shop, as he had for more than forty years, Ranar had made it a habit to make a sweep of both the front of house and back several times a day. His father had a habit of taking the orders from the printed queue and misplacing them. Ranar would find them on the front counter, on the back cutting table, on the shelves in between boxes of floral foam. Once, he'd found a request for a casket spray inside the cooler next to a birthday arrangement, a juxtaposition that nearly sent into an existential spiral until he remembered that his grandfather had not shared the same illness as his son, remaining quick of mind and sharp of tongue until his final breaths.

It was easy for Grace to give relationship advice now that she was coupled. He appreciated his friend and knew that she was only looking out for his best interests, but if she pushed the issue, he would remind her that she herself had been a workaholic with no social life not that long ago, with*out* the responsibility of caring for aging parents and a limping business.

Besides, it wasn't as if he had *no one* to talk to.

Pinky had become a fast friend. It was nice, having someone else confide their troubles in him for a change, and really, all she needed was for someone to believe in her very attainable dreams. She was knowledgeable about plants, spoke the same language of humidity and south facing windows, possessing an adorable collection of strings of pearls and pink accented philodendrons.

Ranar had not been at all surprised when she had disclosed that she had a boyfriend, because of course she would. She was vivacious and funny, and he was positive he could tell just by the way she typed and the things she said that she would be beautiful. But the more he had learned about her partner, piecing together offhand remarks she would make, likely thinking he wasn't paying that much attention, the more annoyed over the situation he grew.

It was silly to be jealous of a stranger.

Even more preposterous to be jealous of that stranger's relationship with another stranger. It was a fact he reminded himself of often, not that it should have made any bit of difference. She didn't exist here in the real world, in his world. Now she was moving to someplace new and embarking on a new chapter in her life, freeing herself of everything that weighted her down. Ranar couldn't relate.

He was happy for his friend, hoped that she would be successful in her new adventure, and even if he occasionally wished the possibility of that meeting and seeing if they were just as compatible on the upright side of the screen as they were behind it become a reality, keeping their relationship as it was didn't detract for his happiness for her windfall. Didn't detract, but it did solidify the fact that she would never be more than his Internet friend.

And she'll be happy once she moves, when she starts over again. She's going to meet someone, and probably won't spend as much time chatting with the random plant guy. The thought had occurred to him shortly after she had confessed that she would be selling her condo and moving to this house she'd inherited, that soon her life would be too full for chatting with him.

It made him sad, but Ranar had reminded himself that there was beauty in ephemera. Some things weren't designed to last forever. They were lovely for a minute, provided happiness for a brief window, and then they were gone — like the flowers he sold.

He sucked a breath in through his teeth the thought, his mind flickering back to the woman who'd been in his store that day. He hadn't lied to Grace. She was pretty, beautiful, in fact. Long dark hair to the middle of her back, full and lush like a peony at the height of its bloom. *Was she really flirting with you? She couldn't have been.*

He wondered where she would be living once she moved to Cambric Creek, what her actual job was, outside of her ill-fated desire to join his ranks.

If she were single, Grace was right — she wouldn't be for long. Not around here. Some of his neighbors were the horniest folks in existence, and her full breasts and round hips would make a fast impression the first time she went grocery shopping. Once they found out she was new to the neighborhood, that would be the end. It would be a race to see who could be the first to stick their dick into her, and she would have her pick of the neighborhood.

She'll probably wind up with some big, muscular orc. That cyclops landscaper who never wears a shirt. Maybe a werewolf. Even if Grace was right and she *had* been flirting with him, which he thought was unlikely, once she saw her other options, she would be sure to lose Ranar's number. *No thanks. Been there, done that, have the postcard.* Everyone ought to visit the Heartache Hills once, but there was never a need to go back for a second stay.

He wondered if Pinky would encounter the same mentality when she moved to her new town — that she was fresh meat, a prize to be claimed first. He hoped she would find someone better than her current boyfriend. *Too bad it won't be you.*

At that thought, Ranar turned, slouching against the coils of his tail as he tapped the computed monitor to life, quickly clicking on the

DiscHorse icon. His palms itched, a desperate need to push Grace's voice out of his head, and besides —he always sent her a little mid-day missive.

> *ChaoticConcertina:* *Do you know what I really hate?*
> *Well-meaning friends.*
> *They're well-meaning, so no matter what they say and regardless of how much you*
> *don't want to hear it, you can't ever really be mad at them*
> *Because they're well-meaning!*
> *And if you ever tell them to stuff it, now* ***you're*** *the bad guy.*
> *"But I only meant well!"*
> *Add that to my petty list of grievances.*

Pinky had been halfheartedly venting about something her boyfriend hadn't paid attention to, asking Ranar if he were similarly coupled.

Obviously he'd had to say yes. What was wrong with Grace?

He had quickly answered the question in the affirmative, not offering any more details, secure in the knowledge Pinky wouldn't ask. He wasn't turning up in her inbox in an effort to solicit her nudes, and had no intention of ambushing *her* with an image of his frilled erections, and didn't want her to worry that it was a latent threat. Ranar rationalized that if she thought he had a girlfriend as well, they would be able to continue conversing as they had, with no undue pressure.

And in the event that she ever asked, it wasn't as there was no one in his life from whom he could draw details. He had dinner with one of his aforementioned horny neighbors once or twice a month, "dinner" that consisted of a bottle of wine he would bring and an entrée on the stove that she had made, a thin pretext for the sex they had in place of eating.

She's an insurance adjuster, he would say. *She has a blue kitchen and a fondness for copper tea kettles. A perplexing number of stuffed animals on the bed.*

The kitsune had no deep feelings for him and he had none for her, outside of mutual friendliness, but they were both single, both horny, and she enjoyed his cocks. He would go home sated, leaving her well-fucked, and they wouldn't do more than wave from their respective driveways when taking out the trash until the itch to do it again struck.

Pinky certainly didn't need to know about *that.*

PinksPosies&Pearls: *Oh yeah, that's a good one.*

Those people are the worst

Don't you have anything better to do with time other than be considerate of me?!

You know what else is terrible?

When people expect you to have a reason for disliking someone

"Oh what happened? Did they do something?"

Yeah, their vibes are mid

*I don't need to wait until they **do** something to make them an enemy*

A+ observations, you're already a better student than my whole class

Ranar shifted in place, grinning once he turned back to his orders, undulating slowly as his thoughts turned once again to the woman from that afternoon. ***Very** pretty. Was she really flirting with you?* This was Grace's doing, he thought in annoyance. If she hadn't been there in the shop when the woman had come in, Ranar would have rung her out without incident, might not have even noticed how attractive she was, and he certainly wouldn't be swaying here with heat in his belly if Grace hadn't put the fantastical notion that the woman was flirting with him in his head, which in turn sent it straight to his groin.

It was Grace's fault, but also his fault for letting his imagination run away with his online friendship. Puddles of puberty be damned, he *wasn't* a teenager with no control over his body's responses. He was a grown-up and he had work to do.

And this afternoon when you leave, you're going to pick up a bottle of Shiraz.

It was the kitsune's favorite, and visiting her that evening would be a sure way to get rid of this inch beneath his skin.

The Unsung Virtue of Ghosting

SUMI

ChaoticConcertina: *PLEASE take a moment to be awestruck with me*
Look at the STATE of this wisteria. What were they feeding it?!
A steady diet of cocaine and whiskey? Straight steroids?
You could swing from this thing!
We need to reevaluate, Pinky.
All the plants need to start living dangerously if this is the result.

"Active harm in the form of covert threats sent across classrooms, bullying on an indetectable scale, leaving teachers and administrators helpless to intervene. Diminished academic achievement from even the best of students, and a no-contest tool of distraction for those already facing classroom challenges."

From the corner of the table, the subtle vibration of her cell phone made Sumi bite her lip, squirming in her seat. Her eyes darted to the edge of the tablecloth as surreptitiously as she could manage. It certainly would not be a good look to interrupt her boyfriend's oration on the detriment of cell phones in the classroom, nor did she want to prove his point about dwindling attention spans by checking the message notification. Particularly when she was sitting here at the table, squeezing her thighs together at the thought of another man's arm.

The vine in question had been impressive. Not nearly as impressive as the arm that gripped it, though. At least, not in her estimation. It was the same big, well formed hand, long fingers tightened around the thick, invasive wisteria. He had wrapped the vine several times around his forearm, almost as if he were giving her peep show to what was undoubtedly the sexiest part of a man's body. She was able to see popped tendons, the vine almost gray around the warm, nut brown of his skin, the photo cutting off right at the edge of his nicely defined bicep.

She had whimpered when the message came through, caught unawares, emptying take-out containers into serving bowls. She wasn't prepared for the sight of that sexy arm, nearly rocked off her feet by the bolt of heat that hit her like lightning, shivering down her back and igniting between her thighs. *What's he sending you now? The flowers laying over his thigh?* Sumi closed her eyes, imagining the cascade of fragrant purple flowers on their shared stem, a thick, curving raceme, fat with blooms.

"A district-wide banishment is the only thing that will halt the spiraling of our current educational crisis, yet our current powers-that-be won't entertain the suggestion! It's ludicrous. I'm begging someone, anyone to make it make sense."

It took a great deal of restraint to point out to Jordan that he didn't need to perform here, for there was no audience for his bluster, no enthralled teachers hanging on his every word. He technically wasn't wrong. Phones were an ever-present distraction for students. Even the most riveting lecture on a 60-year-old book couldn't hold a candle to the instant gratification of scrolling through an endless array of thirty second videos algorithmically chosen just for them. *That still doesn't mean I need to hear about it from someone who doesn't spend their day in the classroom.*

Instead, she focused on her plate, composing a message in her head, one she would send the moment she was able to be alone with her phone, provided there wasn't actually a cascade of wisteria-covered cock waiting for her. *My condo officially goes on the market this week. Like you said, no time like the present. I've applied to be a franchisee in my dream industry and for a business license in the new neighborhood. Every time my phone pings, I practically faint.* Her agent had called during her drive home, and Sumi had given her the official go-ahead. *What are you waiting for? The sooner it sells, the sooner you can close this chapter of your life for good.*

If there *was* a wisteria-covered cock in her messages, her message would be very different. *Interested in a gardening buddy? I'd love to lend a hand pruning that.*

That gods damned florist in Cambric Creek had broken something in her brain. She'd been horny since her ill-fated visit to his shop, a slick, ever-present pulse between her thighs, wondering how, exactly, his cock was concealed. Academically, she knew it was held in a genital pouch on the inside of his body, but she wanted information *beyond* the scientific mechanics. *Does he like his slit ticked? If he gets turned on in the middle of the day, does it just pop out?* She imagined being there, visiting his shop again in her favorite, low-cut dress, employing her every feminine wile to make his dick hard, to make it slither out. *And then what? Does it just retract on its own? Or does he need to come?* She would be willing to offer her support. It would be the neighborly thing to do, after all.

Since then, it was as if every innocuous thing ChaoticConcertina said had a double entendre, inflaming her further. It was an easy transference of her lust. After all, she already *liked* him. He was kind and funny and he understood her better than anyone in her actual daily life. He had sexy hands and now, she could see with painful clarity, a sexy arm attached to it. *Who knows? Maybe he's as handsome as the naga.* She didn't want to change their relationship, at least, not now, but if she were to open her phone one morning to find the long-expected dick pic, she wouldn't be upset.

"It's an addiction," Jordan went on, tapping his index finger against the table as if to emphasize his point. "We are witnessing the destruction of civilized society in real time! Entire generations are being brought up with screens as their primary caregivers. Is it any wonder they can't pass the timed state exams?"

"You know what else isn't good for civilized society?" she cut in, keeping her voice light as she forced herself back to reality, annoyed to be doing so. "Bringing your work home with you every single day. Don't you talk about this enough all week long?"

Jordan rolled his eyes. "That's the problem, we don't discuss it nearly enough! At least, not with any of the folks who can do something about it. But none of *them* are willing to try and—"

He cut off abruptly, raising his hands with a sheepish grin, as if she'd caught him sneaking treats from the cookie jar, his every word and gesture feeling condescending to her.

"But you're right, enough shop talk."

They were both quiet then, focused on their food, the subtle vibration from the edge of the table making her hands itch. When Jordan spoke again, she wished she'd never said anything at all.

"How did your meeting with the agent go?"

Sumi froze. *How does he know?! He has your car bugged. You accidentally patched him in during a call. He's known all along!* It took several excruciating seconds for her to realize he meant the face-to-face meeting she'd had with the agent the previous weekend, making her realize how little they'd spoken since then. *You've already started moving out right under his nose and now you've barely talked in a week. Would he even care if you're gone?*

The meeting with Elspeth had gone exceptionally well. It was an uphill battle to get through work every day because her mind was already far away, settling into her new life in Cambric Creek, meeting the neighbors, discovering all of the secret charms a small town promised to hold.

Not that she could tell him that.

"It went well," she said guardedly. "The other beneficiary isn't challenging anything."

"That's good, no family to squabble with over flipping it then. She thinks it'll sell fast?"

Jordan always spoke with the artless self-confidence of someone who'd never been incorrect about a single thing in his life, ever. Sumi avoided her boyfriend's eye as he tucked into his food, waiting for her response. She knew she ought to come clean . . . but she was tired. Tired and ready to just disappear.

"Mhm. She said selling won't be a problem."

What her tiefling real estate agent had actually said was selling her condo in the city wouldn't be a problem, as long as she didn't hold out on price.

"This *is* a very nice neighborhood, and the proximity to schools and shopping is always a plus," Elspeth had agreed with the bullet-pointed list Sumi rattled off as what she thought of as the condo's main selling points. "But the unit itself is small, so there's probably not going to be a lot of interest from young families. And the singles who are more the market demographic aren't going to care about things like proximity to schools."

Sumi was forced to concede the point. *You can't afford to carry both places.* Not if she wanted to quit her job, which she did without question. *You'll wind up spending the entire inheritance on this mortgage and the house's taxes.* There were two strategies they could work with, the tiefling went on to explain.

"We can either go in high with a bottom price in mind and see what you can get in the middle, or else you figure out what your asking price needs to be and you hold firm on that. It's totally up to you, but my suggestion is we go with plan A. Let's see how much you can get. I'm going to have our attorney lean on the court a bit, see where we are with probate and closing the lien . . . and then you'll have a bit of a remodeling budget once you move. That's the goal!"

Sumi chewed her spicy noodles thoughtfully, chopsticks ready with another bite immediately. Keeping her mouth full was a ready way to slow the conversation, she had discovered over the last three years with her boyfriend, and if he couldn't control the pace of things, the line of questioning would be abandoned. *The pace, the topic, the mood.* She was desperate to be fucked, but the notion of it coming from the man she'd spent the last three years with left her cold.

"That's fantastic, babe," he enthused, not seeming to notice her distinct lack of enthusiasm for the conversation. "What a great opportunity this is. I was looking up some of the properties for sale in that town and holy shit. They are in a real estate boom!"

"It's because it's multi-species," she agreed weakly, thinking of how *nice* it had been. "Towns like this are on the rise, but this one is old and affluent. They already know what they're doing." *What are you doing?! Why are you adding to it? Just let him change the conversation before you have to tell him everything right now!*

Jordan's brow furrowed as he chewed thoughtfully. "I suppose ... but do you really think those sorts of whole towns are necessary? Enough to justify the cost of living? I mean, don't get me wrong, I'm thrilled you're going to make a profit flipping this place. It just makes you wonder who it's serving and what the benefit really is."

Despite her desire to change the subject, his words brought her up short. Sumi turned, her mouth hanging open, not even remembering that she was meant to be filling it, her chopsticks hanging in space above her plate as she gaped in disbelief.

"I mean, don't you think it's better to just integrate everywhere?" he went on bullishly, seeing her expression. *Why did you say anything at all?* "We learned years ago that it doesn't serve children on IEPs to be removed from their home classroom; that's why we have integrated learning with classroom assistants."

Deep breaths. Of course he would use something from the schools as his example, too used to being called noble for doing so. *Just change the subject and eat your dinner. Let him keep talking about cell phones if it makes him happy.* Unfortunately, at that moment, there seemed to be a misfire in the communication from her brain to her mouth, as she drew breath for her rebuttal. *Fucking typical.*

"Jordan, that is not the same thing at all. The *point* is integration. It's not 'human by default but you're allowed to live here,' the way literally *every*where is, including our school district. Be so for real. The entire teaching staff in my building is human, and more than half of them are white. I only ever have one or two non-human kids in my class every year. You know who their friends are? The other one or two non-human kids. It doesn't matter if they're even the same species. And I went through the same thing! When I was little, all the Asian kids stuck together. It doesn't matter if there's a difference in language or culture, especially in early education. They stick with whoever feels safe, and 'safe' is usually *not* the majority."

She was breathing hard when she cut off.

Othering those who were different was something at which humans excelled. Growing up as sometimes the only Asian student in the classroom meant a childhood of duality, a daily game of "one of these things is not like the others," different facets of her personality she had learned to employ at different places and at different times. That was her experience, and *she* presented as the majority species.

She had lived in the city for more than a decade, shopped in the same neighborhood as her students' families. She knew how sparse the species-specific products were, had seen with her own two eyes how more often than not they were placed in the back of the store or else on a low, hard-to-reach shelf.

Sumi had no doubt that if multiple grades were given access to the cafeteria for one joint lunch period, she would find all of those nonhuman students sitting together, regardless of age. She knew the impetus behind those goblin and troll and mothfolk children banding together, for the same reason she had often found herself seeking out other Asian schoolmates — they were small fish in a pond of plentiful bigger fish, and there was safety and comfort in numbers.

"The benefit is accessibility," she went on in a quieter voice. "The houses, the roads, the buildings — they're all built to accommodate *more* than the majority. The schools are a mix of different species living together, not humans and one or two non-human kids. If you don't think that sort of representation matters, consider that you're a white human man and the whole world is built for you. I don't know, maybe you ought to get into the classroom for a while, try subbing. It's one of the many reasons why I'm not—"

She broke off again, her voice having risen without her notice. *There you go. May as well say it. Let that cat out for good.*

"That's why I'm considering not going back next year. Anyway, that's the reason for the housing prices. It's a very competitive market with no sign of cooling."

She backed out at the last moment, softening the sentiment, but at least she'd introduced the idea, Sumi told herself. *There. Let him be offended. By the way, I hate teaching. I've hated it for as long as you've known me, and if you ever noticed anything you'd know that. I'm going to quit my job and open a flower shop. But thanks for dinner.*

Jordan was quiet for a long moment.

"Well, good, that's what you need," he said at last.

Sumi blinked. *That's it? Just like that?*

"Just make sure she lists highs so that you don't wind up short changed. As far as the school . . . I don't think you should be making hasty decisions right now. You've got so much on your plate with everything . . . but maybe you're right. Maybe it's time for something new." He gave her what she knew was meant to be a supportive smile. "The high school always has openings. If you want to make the move, maybe now *is* the right time."

Fucking unreal. Negative rizz. If you stay in this relationship for another week, you're going to spend the summer having a nice menty b.

"Look, I know you're in a hurry to be finished with everything and probate is taking forever, but it's not worth cutting off your nose to spite your face, Sumi."

She kept her eyes on her noodles, murmuring her agreement. There was no point in doing anything else. And, it was true. Cambric Creek seemed to be suspended in an ever-increasing real estate bubble, and her listing agent did not think there was any danger of it popping.

"It's not the kind of community that's going to see a downturn anytime soon. You know, think of the big tech cities out on the West Coast. This is like a microcosm of that, only instead of developing software, they're building a self-sustaining ecosystem. This was just another suburb two decades ago. Housing prices weren't any higher than they were in the neighboring communities. Well, a little higher, because there have always been deeper pockets here, but this has all been in the last twenty years or so, ever since redeveloping the downtown became a focus. Excellent schools, very family oriented. You're just outside of the city, so there's never a want for anything that you can't get. I think you will be *very* happy with this investment."

A gift from your mom. No time like the present, Pinky. Sumi couldn't agree more.

"Once this sale is through, I think you should definitely look into some investments," Jordan went on, oblivious to her inner turmoil. "Did you talk to that financial planner I sent you?"

"I wound up setting up an appointment with the guy my dad suggested. He's from that firm that does all the big ads during the Ketterling finals." The look Jordan gave her was one of a disappointed parent. Her eyes narrowed, and Sumi forced herself to pick up another mouthful of noodles, jabbing her chopsticks at the plate. "I called the number you gave me, but it wasn't a financial firm. Why would I talk to some tech company for this? To invest it in some fake online money I wind up losing in three months?"

Across the table, the offense was instant. "Crypto is the future! Sumi, be serious. Do you think we're going to be reliant on something as outdated as the Federal Reserve forever?"

"I don't want to lose my real, spendable money on game tokens!"

Jordan rolled his eyes, shaking his head as if she had brought home a report card with low marks. "You would be foolish not to invest at least a chunk of this inheritance in a future currency. You should call my guy before the rates go up."

"Oh, so now it's an act fast offer? I thought I wasn't supposed to rush into anything and cut off my nose to spite my face, dad."

Reaching for the peppered beef, Jordan went on, ignoring her dig entirely.

"Did you see my video? 60,000 views already. Kelley from the board was sharing it over to the union's CrowdJounal page to give it an extra boost. Did you see it? I call out the governor, and I do *not* hold back. Recess. Is. Over."

And just like that, we're done talking about me. Not rolling her own eyes at that moment was an exercise in self-control. *Recess is over* had been the unofficial-official slogan of Jordan's campaign for the state board of education. Hearing him use the phrase on its own in conversation was, as her students would say, high-key cringe. *Kelley from the board. She's probably the blonde. Perfect, your replacement is all lined up.* She huffed at her internal monologue as the phone was pushed before her.

"*I, for one, don't like the Orwellian future our children are facing. It's high time we take time out to be present. It's time we take the phones out of our kids' hands and give them back books. It's time we took our message to the steps of the capitol. And if they don't want to hear it, the Governor's mansion is right around the corner. Recess is over!*"

Sumi squinted at the phone screen, internally cringing again. She wondered if Jordan had ever been asked who the *our* in question was, whenever he talked about *our kids*, seeing as he was unmarried with no children of his own and had barely ever been more than a substitute classroom teacher for a single semester before running for the school board. *Stop it, now you're just being mean. It's not his fault you've got a foot out the door. You've been here for three years, don't pretend that you didn't fall for his schtick at the beginning.*

It was a relief when he received a phone call a short while later from one of the interns in his office. Sumi watched as he frowned, casting his eyes about as if his laptop might appear in her small, eat-in kitchen, fully knowing he'd not carried it in.

"You should go home if you still have work to do," she told him as earnestly as she could. "I have a pounding headache. I'm taking a shower and going to bed. If you have to talk things over with the team, I don't want you to have to whisper because of me." It was a terrible excuse, but her words were pointed enough, and he nodded, taking his leave just a few minutes later.

She had once asked ChaoticConcertina if he thought she could simply ghost her life. She had asked the question in jest, clarifying that that wasn't actually her plan. But as the days went by and Sumi found that she still couldn't bring herself to have the conversations she knew needed to be had, ghosting seemed like a better and better idea.

She didn't want to be told that she was being impulsive, didn't want to hear that she was being irresponsible. She didn't want to be told by people who didn't understand how she felt that she was going to regret it.

She'd been making the hour-long commute to the house a few times a week, not coming home to her condo until it was dark. By the time she would need to hire actual movers, Sumi was determined that there would be nothing left but the furniture. *And he hasn't noticed a single thing.*

She was judicious in her purging. If it did not bring her joy, if it was not useful in her daily life, if it was not enormously sentimental — it was not coming. *This is a fresh start, right? You don't need to bring every bad decision with you.* If it didn't spark joy, she was leaving it behind, and that included this relationship. *Fax, no printer.*

Sumi tiptoed to the door once she heard his car start in the short driveway, creeping up to the sidelight as if he might still be lurking on the porch, waiting to catch her. It wasn't until his headlights turned out of her driveway that she relaxed, opening the door just enough to peek her head out, watching his taillights disappear around the corner. *Alone at last.*

To her slight disappointment, the messages she had received during dinner were not from ChaoticConcertina.

The first was from Elspeth. *You must be the luckiest teacher in the world. I think we might already have a buyer! I had dinner with some colleagues from my office and the one has a niece relocating to your city. She's not interested in anything big, doesn't want to have to worry about upkeep or yard, but she's not keen on renting. I think your condo would be perfect for her. Do you want to see if she's interested in making an offer?*

Sumi closed her eyes. She was ready to walk away from all of it.

If it would sweeten the pot, I'm willing to leave all major appliances behind, they're all new within the last five years. Furniture if she wants it. Let's go for it.

There was no sense in beating around the bush, no point to dragging her feet any longer. She had a new life waiting for her in Cambric Creek.

The second notification was an email. *We are thrilled to welcome you to the Bloomerang family, pending approval of your business license.*

Tears filled her eyes. She was going to be a business owner, was going to have her dream job. *You're going to make new friends. You're going to learn about Sylvan culture. You are going to find the pieces of yourself that have been missing all these years.*

And maybe she would meet someone new. After all, she'd visited one single establishment and had practically proposed to a stranger. *A rude, handsome jerk.* Maybe there would be someone there in Cambric Creek who caught her eye, who would be attracted to her curves, her long dark hair, her love of pop culture and flowers and aptitude with Gen Alpha slang. *Or maybe you and ChaoticConcertina can finally meet up.* The thought made her shiver. She thought about that hand, that perfect, long fingered hand. The strength in it was evident. And that arm!

Sumi bit her lip, rolling quickly to retrieve the toy from her bedside table. The lowest setting on the dual armed vibrator was a deep, rumbly buzz against her clit. Those fingers would work magic on her body, she knew it. And after all, he knew her so well. He knew her better than anyone, at this point. He shared her interests and supported her dreams. It went without saying that he would finger her like a pro. *He would pay attention to what you like and know just how to touch you.*

A tilt of the wand, increased pressure against the side of her swollen pearl, just the way he would know how to rub those long fingers. She envisioned that lithe arm, sinuous and strong, sliding the shaft of the vibrator into her slickness, her eyes instantly rolling back at the way it rumbled and thumped against her inner walls. His was the kind of arm that had the stamina to go to the finish line. He would be able to finger fuck her until she was screaming, rubbing her clit to completion, never even slowing down until she came on his hand, clenching around his fingers.

She clenched around the vibrator instead, wishing it were thicker, girthier, more like a real cock, more like whatever ChaoticConcertina was packing. The little vibrating mouth continued to work against her clit as she rode the orgasm, her back arching off the mattress as she shook.

Tomorrow, Sumi thought, once she was under the covers her eyes heavy and her body sated. She was going to ask him about his girlfriend tomorrow. *Maybe they're not even serious.*

Maybe, she thought with her last vestige of consciousness, it was time to *ask* him for a dick pic.

A Flattened Atlas

Part 2

MEDUAS EDITORIALE

The Rizzler

RANAR

PinksPosies&Pearls: *I broke up with my boyfriend*

I had NO intention of telling him I was leaving.

I was just going to ghost.

He found out from one of his toadies in the union after I resigned.

He had no idea I hated it.

And that's super sad. How could he not?!

How did he not know? Did he know me at all?!

PinksPosies&Pearls: *It's for the best though.*

I made a decision not to bring anything with me

that doesn't bring joy into my life

*I am leaving a **depressing** amount of stuff behind.*

That relationship was part of the pile. And that's sad too.

I'm so excited to have a fresh start

and to follow this ridiculous, irresponsible dream

PinksPosies&Pearls: *But I'm sad for myself.*

I'm sad for the person I've been.

She hasn't been very happy,

and I don't think I realized that until now.

The worst part is the little voice in my head. W

hat if I screw everything up?

What if I think I'm leaving all these unhappy things behind,

*but **I'm** the reason they're like that in the first place?*

I'm not going to get another do over.

Just feeling very sorry for myself today, for absolutely no reason.

Do you self-sabotage with a little voice

or are you like, emotionally well-regulated

If you tell me you can't relate

because you're well organized and never talk to yourself

and you're like, madly in love and deliriously happy & always take your vitamins

I'm probably just going to eat a wheel of cheese for dinner

__ChaoticConcertina:__ Hold on

I can't hear you over the sound of triumphantly cracking my knuckles

I'm going to relate to this so hard

you need to be prepared to be embarrassed for me.

I already told you I'm like my family's all-terrain vehicle.

My sister is the cute little coupe

they fawn over and lovingly wax twice a week,

I'm ol' reliable in the garage,

expected to keep everyone safe AND take them off-roading.

95

Well, that's just the tip of my dysfunction.

My ex-wife and I had an arranged marriage.

I know that seems archaic to some folks here,

but it's common in our species' culture.

It's basically an online dating service run by your relatives.

We spent months getting to know each other

ChaoticConcertina: *before she even moved here.*

I supported us while she went to school,

we made plans to have a baby when she finished.

Everything was running like a well-oiled machine.

We got along super well,

we lived together well, we co-parented well.

We genuinely thought we would fall in love

That the passion would just download eventually

like an automatic update.

But we were never more than friendly roommates

who sometimes had sex.

We tried to make it work,

but neither of us wanted a friendly, loveless marriage.

ChaoticConcertina: *And after nearly ten years,*

that's all we had.

It was an amicable divorce,

we even did that well together.

But that was almost five years ago.

I've been single for half the length of time we were together.

And I haven't been in a serious relationship since.

And even though I know we had good reasons,
I can't shake the little voice in my head.
What if it was you? Maybe you're just unloveable.
*Great, Pinky. Now **I'm** going to eat a wheel of cheese for dinner.*

If he were a betting snake, Ranar would have gone all in on the gamble of his location the next time he saw the beautiful stranger from that day in his shop. The odds that it would be at the Black Sheep Beanery couldn't have been any higher. Sure enough, as he quickly crossed the road on a brilliantly sunny morning, maybe two weeks after that first fateful meeting, there she was, standing just before the coffee shop's doors, tapping on her phone.

That morning she wore a cornflower blue dress with a deep-V neckline, the bottom point of it reaching the middle of her back. From his vantage behind her, he could just make out the shimmering, arrow-like marks on her skin, the dark waterfall of her hair concealing the rest. *Sylvan.*

Ranar wondered if she had already moved into the neighborhood, and where she had settled. Wondered if she'd already met some preening orc from the Ketterling Club. *Had she really been flirting with you? It doesn't seem likely.*

"Oh!" Her full lower lip caught between her teeth as his approach made her turn, eyes widening slightly at the sight of him there behind her. "Um, hi there! Nice to see you again."

This is your chance. Be charming, if you're capable. **Don't** *be an asshole, if you're capable.* He grinned down, hoping there wasn't an alarming amount of fang in his smile.

"Nice to see you as well. Have you made the move then? I hope it went smoothly for you."

She laughed lightly, her eyes darting behind him to watch his tail as he coiled off the direct path on the sidewalk. "Oh, um, I'm getting there. Moving truck comes at the end of this week. Are-are you going in?"

She nodded toward the Beanery's doors. He thought she seemed hopeful, quickly biting her lip again, her eyes once more to his tail.

"I am, but I'll be using the side counter. It's a bit more accessible for those of us with . . . well." He gestured to his thick length of scales. "This usually doesn't work out too well with the standard queue."

"Oh! I-I wondered how you . . ." Another high-pitched, slightly nervous laugh. "Although, from what I've seen, it seems like they do a pretty good job of accommodating . . ." She trailed off, sucking in a breath and closing her eyes. "Sorry, I-I've lived in human cities my entire life, so this has all been a *lot* to take in. They're good at accommodating more than the majority here. From what I've seen, almost every business does a great job with it. It's nice. *Really* nice. If my former place of work had been half as accommodating as even the little shops in town seem to be . . ." She trailed off again, hands closing into fists, furious with herself, he thought. *There's no need to be.*

"There are codes all the businesses have to follow," Ranar cut in, saving her from her stammering. "Home builds as well, unless you're grandfathered in, and all of those houses are in Oldetowne. Doorways have to be a certain width, a certain height. Can a minotaur walk into your business without ducking his horns? Can an ogre fit in your seats? Can an elf reach the sink? Counter clearance, depth . . . it's all considered. You won't find too much done with only humans in mind. And it *is* overwhelming, so don't beat yourself up."

Her little laugh was self-deprecating, but at least it brought her smile back, her dark eyes sparkling as she turned her face back up to him. *She really is beautiful.*

"Well, that's kind of you to say."

"No, really," Ranar insisted. "I avoid going to the city at all costs. Just the thought of spending a week surrounded by humans gives me a panic attack, so I get it. This isn't what you're used to and it's a lot to take in." She laughed again, like a tinkling little windchime. *Oh, do not try your hand at being poetic. You know that won't end well.* Ranar cleared his throat, forcing the little voice in his head to go away. "And it doesn't help that one of the first new neighbors you met was some tactless naga with no filter and a problem with projection."

At that, she burst out laughing, a genuine, full body laugh, dropping her hand to his forearm as she covered her mouth, shoulders shaking. "I mean, you were still *very* nice about it."

He waved her words away with a grin, feeling the heat of her hand sinking into him like a brand. *You're going to ask her out. Just do it, one little sentence. Would you like to go out sometime?* "Don't make excuses for me. I could have been much less of a jerk about it." *Would you like to get married sometime?*

"I'm sure you'll think of a way to make it up to me."

That sounded like flirting. Didn't it? "Can I buy you coffee? We need to get in line—"

"I use the mobile app," she blurted, a flush moving up her face. "At least, that's what I've done the two times I've been here. It's-it's a whole lot in there."

"It's always like this. The only other time you'll see this many people in one spot is at the Saturday market." He cocked his head to the side, eyebrows coming together as he considered. "Gildersnood during happy hour might come close. After you." He motioned to the door, which the end of his tail had already pulled open in readiness.

She made a small sound of surprise, followed quickly by another small, self-conscious laugh. She was adorable. *Grace is right. Fuck those Ketterling orcs. Get to her first.*

"So what brings you into town this morning if you're not moved in yet?"

"Oh, I have an appointment today. At City Hall, trouble with a permit. I'm *really* hoping it gets resolved, so wish me luck."

He placed his order, then sucked in a breath through his teeth as he felt her eyes moving down the long length of his tail as if she were caressing him with her hand. *This is not the place to get hard. You are forty-two years old and you should have more self-control than a fourteen-year-old.*

"I have a mobile order for Sumi!" Xavier, the dreadlocked owner of the coffee shop, called out, and Ranar watched as she waved the sheep-faced man down. *Sumi.* When he spotted Ranar beside her, Xavier's eyes narrowed. "Brother, now is not the time, but I need to have a word with you this week. A very concerning whisper I heard that you're going to want to get in front of."

He didn't like the sound of that, but Ranar was too distracted by the beautiful woman at his side and the weight of her eyes on him, the subtle jasmine and green tea notes of her perfume.

"Uh, yeah, sure. I'll pop back in the evening."

She had waited, he noted. Everyone in the world was in a rush at this time of the morning and she had an appointment to get to, but she had waited beside him as his order was prepared, taking in the insanity of the breakfast rush. He wondered if his neighbors would assume they were *together*, and not merely two caffeine seekers who'd accosted each other on the sidewalk.

"I wouldn't worry too much," Ranar assured her once he had his order in hand, gratified that she turned to exit with him. *Sumi.* Once again, he held the door open with his tail for her to go through first, and she turned to watch as he quickly serpentined out. "Anytime you're doing a new build or renovation they want to see all the plans for approval. Like I said, lots of codes to follow. As long as your architect is prepared to make some changes, you won't have any problem." *Are you going to shoot your shot? Or just slither home and curl up like the sad sack you are?*

Shut up, shut UP, he hissed to himself, not realizing he'd made any sound until she turned.

"Pardon?"

"Oh, nothing. Nothing at all. Just . . . snake thoughts." He smiled as winsomely as he was able, which he was certain wasn't actually all that winsome. *Here goes nothing.* "I was thinking, once you have a chance to settle in . . . if you want the grand tour, I'm an excellent guide. I've lived here my whole life and have the aforementioned panic attacks at the thought of leaving. I can show you all the hidden spots you won't find on the town's website."

To his relief, she laughed again, that musical little chime, rather than dumping her coffee on his tail. An auspicious sign. *Un*fortunately, her phone rang at that moment, her free hand scrambling to hold it upright, her eyes widening when she glanced at the screen. Ranar didn't know what to do. *Turn away? Give her privacy? What if she thinks you're ditching her? She waited with you inside, you should wait with her now. Right?*

"Hello? Yes, perfect. I'm still in the area, um, I'll be just a few minutes. Thank you!" She pulled a face when she hung up, looking petrified. "That was the receptionist; they're ready for me."

"Well, good luck. I'm sure you won't need it, but I'm giving it anyway." *You tried. Grace is out of her mind. That mothman has scrambled her brain.*

"Yes," she blurted. *Sumi.* "Ranar, right? I-I would love that. I mean, a tour. With you. I mean, *some*one has to show me what a Gildersnood is. I'd love to. And I'm taking a raincheck on that coffee. I need to be brave enough for the line eventually."

He was an adult naga. Formidable, regal-looking, completely in control of his emotions. It would *not* be okay to gather her in his coils and keep her there forever. As it was, she was fighting a war with herself, her feet already turning in the direction of the crosswalk, her adrenaline ready to carry her back to City Hall without her conscious approval, and her cheeks splotched pink.

"Um, I really should—"

"Go," Ranar told her with what he hoped was a reassuring tone. *She was beautiful.* "You know where to find me. Just give me a call at the shop and we'll exchange numbers. Please let me know if you need any help with the move. And knock 'em dead in your meeting! I'm sure it'll be fine."

"Thank you," she said gratefully, already moving. "For everything. I'll call you this week!"

It was annoying to admit that Grace was right. *You don't know that for sure.* There was still no reason for him to believe that this beautiful woman was actually flirting with him that day in his shop, but Grace had put the notion in his head, and that had been enough to buck up his courage.

Maybe she's just looking for someone to carry her sofa. Or maybe she wants a flower discount. Maybe she'll want to move in and stay forever. Maybe, Ranar thought with a small smile, he would send Grace one of her own fruit baskets as a thank you for being a good friend.

CTRL F5 Your Life

SUMI

"You'll find in the folders I provided the average city income taxes paid by four other Bloomerang subsidies. The business is sound. The parent company wouldn't be investing in our franchises if they weren't." Sumi forced herself to take a breath, swallowing hard. *Stop sounding so defensive. You're not administering a test to 7th graders. You're not here to make them mad.* "I've also included the certification that the parent company is a non-human business."

She hadn't discovered that part until long after she had applied for her franchise. Cambric Creek had a whole host of hoops she would need to jump through, she'd realized belatedly, including a stipulation that businesses in the downtown district be free of human ties. She had cried herself out the afternoon she read that particular detail on the zoning commission's website, laying crumpled in a heap at the corner of the sofa until the sun was low in the sky and her by-then empty condo left dim.

The condo had sold, the movers were scheduled, and she had already spent several nights in the new house, testing what it felt like to wake up there, in her whole new life . . . *And now you're back to square one with no job.* **So** *fucking Ohio.*

She had been clicking around on the Bloomerang website once she'd forced herself to get up, comparing the existing location with the map she had opened in another tab. There are other towns, the city is right next door. *So you have to commute, it's not the worst thing in the world.* She'd been checking to see if there was already a Bloomerang franchise in a place called Greenbridge Glen when her finger overshot the tab, opening the *About Us* section on the Bloomerang website instead. It had been right there, not hidden at all, merely a tab she'd never bothered exploring.

Two smiling faces, similarly featured but not identical, heads together. The photo was black and white, but it did not hide the tiny marks around their eyes, and she knew that if she could see the full color version of this picture, those markings would shine like the sun.

Pippa and Molly have always had a passion for flowers. "We used to love going to our grandmother's house in the spring, picking flowers with our aunts and great aunts, drying them with our great grandmother. We learned how to make herbal teas, how to use plants to dye wool. We learned what was edible, what was just for show, and most importantly, that a perfect bloom could brighten anyone's day. The tree in each of our stores pays homage to our Sylvan culture, to our grandmother and great-grandmother, all of those aunts, and everyone else who came before us. Flowers always make us happy, and we hope that Bloomerang can brighten your day as well."

She'd been crying again by the time she got to the end. *This is a gift from your mom.* It was, truly, in every way imaginable. A gift that solved all of her problems, for there was no need to look outside Cambric Creek if Bloomerang was Sylvan-owned.

Now she was here, before the zoning commission, desperately trying to keep her dream alive. *Advanced Rizzenomics: pleading for your life.*

"We appreciate that you've taken the time to put everything in such readable order for us, Ms. Trent. Our main concern is—"

"I've also have my business plan analyzed by a CPA, and you can see from year-over-year statistics provided by Bloomerang that—"

"You understand our hesitation at allowing a chain store, I hope." The speaker was a middle-aged fox woman, her ears barely visible through her mountain of teased-up hair. Her voice was pointed, but her smile was kind. *Like a switchblade hidden in a box of chocolates.*

"I do understand the concern," Sumi began slowly. *Just stay calm.* "I suppose I don't see it the same way. It would be a chain if there was a giant Bloomerang sign above the door. If the interior matched every other Bloomerang shop, all carrying the exact same product with the exact same uniform, but that's not the case." She took a steadying breath, reminding herself not to get sharp. "*This* is Pink Blossom. This is *my* store and I won't have another store anywhere else. It won't look like any other store. Yes, we'll be a Bloomerang partner, but Pink Blossom is the name above the door, that's the name people in the neighborhood will know. The flower shop just around the corner, when you're grabbing your morning coffee."

Her face was hot when she finished, the crescents of her nails biting into the meat of her palm. The fox woman's smile remained kind, but she looked unimpressed, as did the troll beside her. *Don't cry. You can cry when you're out of here. Not in front of them.*

"We also have a concern regarding two identical businesses within a very small square mile radius," piped up one of the two men on the panel, the thick-tusked troll. "Particularly as that business is well established in the community. There's no ambiguity on *its* status as a chain store."

He was talking about Ranar's little shop, Sumi realized. Her cheeks heated, her giddiness over the chance encounter with the handsome snake man resolutely put on the back burner of her mind until she emerged triumphant from this meeting. Surely in an affluent community, there would be room for two flower shops?

"I think we've established in our prior discussions over the financials regarding this matter that the issue of whether the community can support two identical businesses is one of undue concern."

The speaker was the other man, younger, in his early 30s at most. Handsome, dark haired, from a distance he appeared as human as Sumi. His voice was clipped, and *un*like the Fox woman, his face bore no smile for her. The troll huffed, but the dark haired man continued, ignoring him.

"My concern remains with the architectural plans. I'm not seeing a long-term root abatement system in place to ensure the sidewalk or neighboring sewer line incur no damage from this tree structure, Ms. Trent. What is the long-term water displacement plan for the rest of the roofline once your tree has surpassed the ceiling? Without those elements in place, I cannot in good conscience—"

Her tree. The tree that every Bloomerang franchise store had, the only design element that would tie her shop to its sister stores around the unification.

"Oh, the tree! Um, every partner shop has one, but it's a nod to the non-human ownership of the company," she quickly clarified. "And like the rest of the shop, it will be unique. But they all have them, so I'm sure all of that's been taken into consideration. I don't think that's really anything to worry—"

"I'm a structural engineer, Ms. Trent." A smile for her at last, although it was icy, with long canines. *Not that human after all.* "I assure you, it matters quite a bit."

Sumi felt her heart sink. *You can look somewhere else. There has to be somewhere within commuting distance with a space for rent. Figure out where Greenbridge Glen is after this.*

The young man had paused, just long enough to make her squirm before continuing. "But to your point, I have no doubt these concerns *have* been raised before, which tells me the plans exist somewhere. Your architect needs to unearth them. I'd also like to see the growth projections on the tree over the next two decades. Barring that issue," the young man went on, closing the folder before him, "I have no objections regarding the status of the business's individualism."

Her head raised, eyes widening. *No objections? Does that mean you're good?*

The troll at the center of the table sputtered. "Owen, I think this is worthy of a second look between—"

"We've taken a second look, Barth. And a third. I looked over the financials again this morning, and I still don't see a problem regarding the use. The Food Gryphon now has three locations in the tri-state area, yet you're not calling them a chain. Bloomerang is at the very least Sylvan-owned. That's more than we can say for the pharmaceutical company operating in the commerce parkway."

"The community perception, though . . . the Chamber of Commerce has already received quite a few calls—"

"Community perception isn't our problem." That sharp, icy smile from the dark-haired man once more, this time for the fox woman who'd objected, flashing to Sumi as he continued. "It'll be hers."

Wait, what? The fox woman clammed up, suddenly more interested in the front of her folder than in giving Sumi her kind, disinterested smile, but the troll, still sputtering, wasn't finished.

"Just the same, I think your father would appreciate you being a bit more circumspect with regards to—"

"My father wasn't voted into a seat on this commission, Barth. I was." The young man's tone was sharp, and even from where she sat, Sumi could see the glint of his canines, the silver flash in his dark eyes. The room went silent. "Ms. Trent," he continued several beats later, his voice still clipped, but not as icy, "this approval is contingent upon your architect submitting detailed plans to the city regarding root containment and a long-term abatement strategy to prevent damage to the municipal facilities, in addition to the other items we mentioned today. If you don't meet the deadline previously set forth , you will not be permitted to open your doors."

Her heart was holding its breath, the air in her own lungs non-existent, every cell in her body holding itself tightly as the dark-haired man signed the form on the table before him. A goblin who'd been sitting in the front row of the room scurried forward, nearly falling off her chair in her haste, carrying a lacquered wooden box. From it, the young man withdrew a long-handled stamp. The fox woman looked away as he stamped the document, and the troll fumed.

"If I may give you a small piece of advice," he went on, handing the papers to the troll, once she'd resecured the stamp. "This is a tight-knit community. You're coming in at a disadvantage. Get involved, and get involved quickly, Ms. Trent. If you follow Lolly, she'll ensure there's nothing else we need from you at this stage. Best of luck, and welcome to Cambric Creek."

"Hello?"

Sumi beamed when Meredith answered the phone, barely able to keep control of the fist that desperately wanted to pump the air in triumph. "Hey, it's Sumi."

"Oh my gosh, I was hoping you would call! Girl, you not only got out of this place, you slapped your ass all the way out of town! I was cracking up when I heard the news!"

She blushed, knowing too well that she had been likely the topic of every conversation in the teachers lounge in the weeks after her resignation.

"Well, buckle up. You're the first person hearing my big news and I just had to *tell* someone." She felt as though she might lift up into the sky, floating above Cambric Creek and all of its busy residents, up until she floated away. "I just got approved to open a business, here in the place where I moved. I'm opening my flower shop!"

Meredith squealed. "You know, I can't help but feel that *I'm* responsible for all of this. We manifested it all that day in your classroom. Now all we need is to find you the hot twenty-five-year-old to blow out your back."

"Oh, I already met him too!" Sumi was relieved that the sidewalk where she currently stood was empty, in between City Hall and the long community center. She knew that she was flapping around like a giddy teenager, bent over at the waist as she laughed, but it couldn't be helped. "He's not twenty-five, but he *is* gorgeous. Definitely has back-blowing potential."

She envisioned Ranar's thick serpentine trunk, wanting *desperately* to know how he would feel against her. She could tell even through the shirt he'd worn that morning that his back rippled with muscle. It made sense, for he likely needed a powerfully strong core to hold up his human-like upper body without legs for stability. *What do they say? 40% of our balance relies on our big toe?* She'd laid her hand over his arm that morning and she'd *felt* the strength in it, like a steel cord. Sumi had no doubt that he'd be able to blow out her back every day of the week and twice on Sundays.

"We met for the first time a few weeks ago. I bumped into him randomly this morning and he kind of asked me out? I'll keep you posted, but if he wants to make me his breeding bitch, I'm not gonna say no."

"Girl, say less."

She was smiling so hard her jaw ached. *When was the last time you were this happy? When you had something good to look forward to? Can you even remember?*

Seeing Ranar that morning had been an unexpected bonus to the entire day, only regretting that it had happened before her meeting when she was distracted and on a time schedule. *If you had run into him afterward, you might have offered to fuck him right then and there in celebration.* He wasn't especially smooth, which she decided was sweet and a definite green flag. *He's clearly not a player, or else he'd be better at this.*

He asked about her move, offered reassurances for her meeting, and gave her some valuable insight regarding the town's building codes. Sumi couldn't remember the last time Jordan had started a conversation asking about her, what she was doing, where she had been, how it made her feel. Not even their final conversation had begun that way. Jordan had been flummoxed to learn that she couldn't wait to quit her job, was appalled that she had quit at all, and was irate in his expected condescending–disappointed parent way that he had been the last to know.

Ranar did not seem to be in love with the sound of his own voice, a sharp and welcome departure from what she had grown accustomed to over the last three years.

The sight of his thick, brilliantly colored tail undulating out the door had nearly hypnotized her, and she wondered what his scales would feel like against her skin. Rough and jagged? Smooth and silky? Would he be heavy against her? Would he hold her in his coils like a constrictor? *And the tip!* He had pulled the door open with the tip of his tail, prehensile, acting like a third hand. *What else can he do with that tail?*

Sumi bit her lip, forcing herself to calm down. It was one thing to have had this sort of fantasy several weeks ago when he was just a stranger in a shop — *a rude, handsome stranger, you called him. Remember?* — And quite different now, when he had offered to show her around the town. *That's a date, right? We're going to be alone together. He's going to show you things like the waterfall and the coffee shop and maybe his bedroom.*

"Anyway, I literally just walked out of this meeting and I *had* to tell someone!"

Meredith squealed again. "I'm so glad you did! Give me a few weeks to get the kids settled into some kind of routine, and then you have to give me directions to this place. I'll come up and we can have lunch. I am *so* happy for you, Sumi!"

She had continued walking as Meredith spoke, impulsively turning up the pathway to the community center, pulling open the door. *May as well poke around while you're here. That guy said to get involved, right?* She had no idea what the handsome, dark-haired young man meant by her being *at a disadvantage*, and his remark about *community perception* being her problem to deal with was ominous, but she decided to take the advice. *Get involved and get involved quickly.*

There was a long bulletin board running the length of nearly the entire hallway, and the whole thing was full. Classes, workshops, continuing education. Intramural sports, children's programs, bake sales, ballroom dance. There was a wire rack on the ground, full of booklets. An outline of everything that was offered, Sumi realized, as she bent to take one from the stand.

If you want to get involved, there's certainly no shortage of opportunities. She *had* always wanted to take ballroom dancing. Maybe Ranar would be willing to take a class with her in his official capacity as her tour guide/future spouse. *How would a naga dance? Maybe something else.*

As she examined the calendar for a drop-in beginner's life drawing class, a tall, red-skinned woman shouldered her way out of the door in the center of the hall on the opposite wall. Burnished gold bumps rose from her black hair just above her temples. *An ogre.*

Sumi watched as the woman unlocked the glass panel of the bulletin board she stood before, swinging it open. She was replacing several of the notices on the cork board, leaning back to ensure they were straight before closing the glass once more.

The ogress moved further down the hall, and Sumi found herself drifting to the space the woman had just vacated, thinking maybe she could get the jump on a brand-new class announcement.

This month in the Nippon Club — Chadō — traditional Japanese tea ceremony.

"Shut the *fuck* up."

She jumped, realizing the voice had been hers, that her first action in winning over community perception had been to practically shout vulgarities in the community center. *They probably have toddler storytime going on. Senior citizen basket weaving. Wrapping teddy bears for needy children. And here you are, dropping F-bombs with zero abandon, uncaring of the delicate ears who might be listening. SO cringe.* Sumi turned, checking to see if the ogress had heard her. Sure enough, her head had swung around. *Are you fucking kidding? They heard you back at City Hall.*

"I mean . . . shut the front door."

The other woman snorted, shaking her head. "I try to catch myself sometimes. Or at least, I used to. Then I just decided it was easier to teach my daughter there are some words we use to express strong feelings, but they are at home words *only*. I'm just lucky cuntnugget wasn't her first word. Believe me, it was a nail-biter."

Sumi laughed, delightedly. Half of the teachers at her former middle school were of the holier-than-thou variety, and they never failed to keep the other half — *her* half — miserably in check. "I used to teach, so you'd think I would be better at this."

The ogress reversed course down the hallway, coming back to where Sumi stood, her eyebrow arching as she approached. When she spoke in Japanese, Sumi's face heated. *Nope, that's not gonna work. I was raised in a jar of mayonnaise.* The other woman raised an eyebrow, still grinning.

"Okay, nevermind. No language skills, but you *are* interested in the tea ceremony."

Deep breath. You're going to get involved. She nodded hesitantly. "My mother was Japanese, but she died when I was young. I-I was raised by my father's family. White. Human."

Another snort from the ogress.

"But I just moved here. I-I promised myself I was going to reconnect to . . ." She trailed off, raising a hand.

"Not white, not human?"

"Yeah. That part."

Despite her social inadequacy, the ogre woman softened. "I get it, it's important. That's why I do the club, actually, for my daughter. My brother and I emigrated together, almost a decade ago, and this is home now. But that doesn't mean it'll ever be *home*, you know? When I started volunteering here, I decided I owed it to her to bring pieces of home here. I don't want her to lose that part of herself just because she's growing up in the unification. It's important to be connected to tradition."

She probably needed to find a therapist, once she settled in, before the speed in which she seemed able to move from joy to tears gave her permanent whiplash. *Iced Grande Menty-B.* Sumi nodded, pushing her tongue into the roof of her mouth to hold back her tears.

She had tried explaining to Jordan what it was like growing up in neighborhoods where she didn't have the community, but Sumi knew he didn't understand. What she hadn't shared with him was that it only ever grew worse as she got older. Those little pockets of Asian friends she had in first and second grade broke apart, the singular tie that bound them growing brittle and thin, snapping as those other children grew up into their own culture and heritage. She had always been simultaneously too much and not enough, with no community of her own. *That's going to change here. You're going to find where you belong in this place.*

"Well, you decided to wander in today at the perfect time. I run the club, so I can get you all registered."

Her real estate agent was right, Sumi reflected as she followed the ogre woman into the office across the hall, registering with the recreation department and signing up for the Nippon Club, paying her full years' worth of dues on the spot. She *was* uncommonly lucky. Everything was falling right into her lap, and she might have felt guilty if she hadn't felt as if she were struggling for so long previously.

"I'm Yuriko, by the way."

"I'm Sumi, nice to meet you."

"Oh! We had a Sumiko in the club. She taught our ikebana class."

Electricity thrummed in her veins. "Oh, I've taken ikebana before! Just a short workshop, but I really loved it. Is that something that will be offered again?

The ogress, Yuriko, sighed heavily. "Unfortunately, she passed away recently. It's such a shame, she was the nicest lady. *Very* efficient. But once you get comfortable in the club, maybe you'll feel comfortable leading us through a class."

Sumi felt frozen, piecing together the other woman's words.

Someone in the community who practically shared her name, who passed away recently, who taught a class in the Japanese club. Heat flooded her face, the tears that lived so close to the surface of her composure these days rushing forward.

"Um, was-was she Sylvan? Did she live over on Poplar?" The other woman didn't need to answer, her eyebrows shooting up all the confirmation Sumi needed. "That was my great aunt. She's the reason I'm even here. She left me her house after she died." The tears overflowed, but before she could feel any mortification, she was wrapped in a too-tight hug, Yuriko practically able to lift her over the desk.

"There, there. I'm sorry for your loss. Like I said, she was a nice lady. It's kind of amazing, you just wandering in today. Almost like she was leading you here."

Sumi nodded, embarrassed that she was blubbering in front of the stranger. *Not a stranger. Your new community.*

"Will you be teaching at the school?"

It took her a moment to realize what the ogress meant. "Oh! Oh, no, I won't be. I'm not teaching anymore." She shook her head, wiping her eyes and snapping herself back. *Come on, get it together. You are being HIGH KEY cringe.* "No, I'm actually opening a flower shop. Just around the corner, off Main Street."

"Oh! That's perfect! Okay, forget what I said about getting comfortable. You're definitely teaching ikebana."

She sucked in a deep lungful of air once they were standing at the doorway of the community center. *Everything is falling into place here for a reason. This is where you belong. It's a gift from your mom.*

"If there's anything I can do to help you settle in, please just let me know. My cell number is at the front of the folder there." Yuriko nodded to the paper folder Sumi now carried. "I'll tell you now, this town fucking loves gossip and partying. In that order. Any excuse they can come up with to throw a festival, they do."

"Yeah, actually there is something." She thought of the dark haired man's words again. *Get involved and get involved quickly.* When she repeated the conversation for Yuriko, the ogress snorted in laughter once more.

"Oh, you came to the right person. I'll get you in good with the right crowd. Like I said, this town loves throwing festivals and street fairs. You're opening a new business, right? If you do a little table outside your doors and either give something away or donate all your proceeds to a local charity, you can basically write your own ticket. Don't worry, I'll get you there."

She left the community center with a bounce in her step. Everything was coming up roses. Her shop was going to open without a hitch. She had already been told by her Bloomerang partner that construction would move very quickly, and that the corporate goal for her shop was to be open as soon as possible. She was going to become a part of the fabric of this community, she was going to get in touch with her Japanese roots, she was going to learn more about Sylvan culture.

And you've already met someone! She would call Ranar that week, Sumi decided, make plans with him as soon as she was fully moved in.

Who knows? By this time next month, you might be in a relationship. New life, new love, a whole new you.

The Imminent Menty B

RANAR

ChaoticConcertina: *Today, my younger sister came over*
to have lunch with our parents.
I need to apologize in advance —
this is far and away my most self-pitying vent.
Please don't report my inability to take it on the chin
to the eldest sibling commission.
They'll revoke my membership card
and my buy-in is nearly vested.
Anyway, Doctor Sister picks them up.
Since she doesn't get a whole lot of time to herself anymore,
Mom made an appointment at the salon in town,
something she's been putting off.
Doctor Sister had very simple instructions.
Go to lunch. Stay with dad until mom is done.
ChaoticConcertina: *Bring them home.*

Isn't that simple? Is it just me?

Am I being unreasonable in my expectations?

An adult woman with an advanced medical degree.

She should be able to follow the same sort of instructions I

would give my nine-year-old?

I'm sure you can guess how this played out, right?

Of course she gets a call five minutes after my mother leaves.

Of course she brings dad home and leaves him.

Texts mom so sorry, gotta run, she's on her own to get home.

ChaoticConcertina: *So obviously I am the one*

who gets the call 40 minutes later

My father is on the other side of town arguing with a shop owner

Telling this guy he's wrong,

that he wants to talk to the REAL owner

Who is a troll my dad grew up with.

He moved to Boca like 15 years ago.

I get it, she's a doctor. I'm local.

Obviously I'm the one who has to leave work to get him.

I don't realize that my poor mom has been stranded

until after I'm already **back** *at work.*

At that point, I just closed up

because the whole day was shot at that point.

ChaoticConcertina: *Everyone is upset,*

I have to leave a message for his doctor that we had another incident,

and my sister is posting photos on social media

of their lunch like everything is fine.

The hardest part of being the eldest that no one tells you about

*Is that eventually you wind up being **everyone's** parent.*

Which makes you an orphan.

And I'm just so fucking tired.

. . . And I know that means nothing to an only child brat

My daughter will be here soon,

so at least I have that to look forward to.

You're going to want to be careful with your Pink Princess

in that south-facing window.

I'd maybe rethink that.

She's looking for something bright, sunny, and indirect.

If she needs a little pick me up every once in a while,

she can visit her southie friends.

I can't wait to see how beautiful they all look

once you have them all together.

Like a flamingo threw up all over the room, probably.

It's going to be glorious.

PinksPosies&Pearls: *As someone very empathetic and wise told me once,*

you don't ever have to apologize for venting here.

I'm so sorry that you're dealing with so much alone.

This is usually the point where I would play my dead mom card,

but I didn't have to watch her decline.

I miss her every day,

but the person I miss is make-believe.

I miss the mom I've created in my head,

I miss the person in the photos I have.

PinksPosies&Pearls: *But I didn't know her.*

You've known your dad your whole life.

I don't think you're feeling sorry for yourself

by mourning what you've lost.

I think that's the hardest part of

losing a loved one this way — you grieve twice.

You mourn the loss of the person they were,

the parent you had.

And then you grieve all over again once they're gone.

I hope your visit with your daughter is excellent.

And for the record, I have 2 younger stepsisters

PinksPosies&Pearls: *but they're a LOT younger so I don't know if it*

counts

I know there's nothing I can do to actually help anything,

*but I **can** distract you.*

I got approval from my new city to open a business

and construction started like 5 minutes later.

And! If that wasn't bad enough,

they're making me train with another location.

So when I'm not in someone else's business,

I'm driving to someone else's business.

PinksPosies&Pearls: *And if I'm not sitting in gridlocked city traffic,*

I'm meeting with the architect and contractor.

I've been here two weeks and I'm still living out of boxes.

I thought I was going to have a social life once I moved;

I barely get to sleep.

Eh? How's that? Need more distractions?

Have you ever wanted to learn the script

to the beloved 90's cult classic

Coming Gnome 3: The Grimening?

Because if so, it's your lucky day

It happened that first night Ruma was home. An inauspicious start for what was meant to be a great summer, and he was furious *she* had tainted the time with his daughter.

His mother had ignored him entirely, spending the day in the kitchen, but she'd at least capitulated to their normal hybrid of Western foods and Tamil dishes, including gulab jamun for dessert which Ruma devoured.

"Food is how I show you I care," she'd practically growled, whipping around with a wooden spoon and brandishing it like a weapon at Ranar's approach, shortly after he and Ruma had arrived.

"I know, Amma. And we appreciate it. Everything smells delicious." *Tragedy avoided. Misplaced accusations of raising a Westernized child – defeated for the day.*

He still wasn't sure how he and his ex-wife had managed it — he was an awkward extrovert, while Ruma's mother had always been serious and stoic — and yet somehow they had produced an absolute ray of sunshine, bubbly and full of chatter as she always was, the entire meal.

"And school?" his mother had asked, trying to clear the high table around Ranar's attempt to direct her back to coiling comfortably as he gathered the plates. "You're doing well? Lots of friends?"

"Of course she is." His father beamed, giving Ruma a wink. "Neja has always done well in school."

It was the black cloud he'd been waiting for, a constant tension he carried every day, wondering if it would be a good day or a bad day, a bad day or a worse day, if bad days *became* the good days once they outnumbered the good, and on and on. For the duration of dessert, his father referred to Ruma by the wrong name, making it clear as the conversation went on that he was referring to someone else entirely. His bubbly little ray of sunshine looked stricken.

"Thatha, it's *me*, Ruma."

"Everything was delicious," Ranar cut in smoothly, gently tugging the end of his daughter's long braid. He couldn't deal with another agitated backslide without snapping. "You didn't need to go through all this trouble, mom, but I'm glad you did. Five stars, my regards to the chef."

"Yeah, it was *so* good, Paati. Everything was bussin."

Ranar nearly bit his tongue, watching his mother's eyebrows drawn together as she undulated gracefully across the kitchen. Her gaze moved quickly from Ruma to Ranar, eyes narrowing, twitching when she settled on her son. She quickly looked around, and if there had been something appropriate in arm's reach to hurl at his head, he was positive she would have done so. *Never mind. Accusations of Westernization: full throttle, guilty as charged!*

"It's just so good to have you home. I'm going to teach you how to make this, so you can make it for *your* little one someday. But for now I'm going to make you a nice tea to help—"

"Actually, we have a date." If his mother had her way, Ruma would never leave. She would violate the custody order, refuse to answer the phone, and offer the arresting officers a comforting sambol as they broke down the door. He held up a hand to stave off the argument forming on his mother's lips. "Don't worry, Paati. You have all summer to feed her, I promise. But I need to hog her for a little while."

"But we need to go open the shop," his father said seriously, using the table for leverage to push himself up from his coil slowly. "I need to start the Gornish funeral."

"We will, dad, tomorrow. I don't think Mr. Gornish will mind." *Because he's been dead for nearly ten years.*

Once they were outside, he scooped up Ruma's hand. "I was going to suggest we get some fresh air and exercise, but I'm so full I think I would need to roll downtown at this point. However, I learned something *very* important recently. Kids apparently love coffee shops."

"Oh, bet!"

He closed his eyes, nearly choking on his laughter. "Let's stop home and then we'll drive over to the Black Sheep. But we're not getting doughnuts, so don't even ask. Sound good, baby girl?"

"Perfect. I need to change anyway. I wanna look super preppy for the town."

Ranar watched as she serpentined before him, taking a series of selfies as she moved along. He only understood every third word out of her mouth and he had a feeling she would be even more attached to her phone now than she'd been just a few months earlier, but this summer would end eventually. Ranar understood his mother's internal sentiment. He wanted to put his arms around this moment and hold it tightly, keeping all four of them locked in place forever, sealing out the outside world. *First though, you need to call in for reinforcements.*

ChaoticConcertina: *MAYDAY, MAYDAY, THIS IS NOT A DRILL!*

I know you're online.

Sitting there thinking about painting your ceiling pink probably.

But I need your help! This is an emergency & I only have a few minutes.

I don't know how to talk to my kid. I think she's been body snatched

She starts every other sentence with chat.

Are we chatting? Are you telling me? Is it an instruction? WHAT?

She just told my mother that the dinner she made was bussin.

It was the first time in 42 years that I thought my mom might hit me with a shoe.

WE DON'T EVEN HAVE SHOES.

PinksPosies&Pearls: *Stoooooop*

I'm crying. I'm laughing so hard you're going to make me pee myself!

I thought you said you talk to her every day!

How are you not already proficient in her native alpha tongue?!

ChaoticConcertina:

Don't be mean to me.

I only get little pieces of the slang when I call every night, it's not every other word!

It's not like this.

It's not skibidi, whatever the fuck that is.

PinksPosies&Pearls: *OMG*

Fear not, rizzly bear.

I gotchu.

I'd going to send you some pics of a cheat sheet my school gave us

You'll be speaking her language in no time.

This is so mindful of you, your vibes are max.

VERY sigma, and you can't shoot higher than that. That's elite.

Pinky to the rescue. Ranar grinned down at his phone screen, squinting at the screenshot she'd sent. *Ohio?* He wondered what she thought of kids, if she had any, if she wanted them. *Why would that matter? Are you just embracing the delusion with both arms now, giving up on reality altogether?*

It had been nearly two weeks since the morning he'd run into Sumi, and they'd still not found time to even share a single cup of coffee. He understood. Moving was chaos, and he'd contributed equally. They'd had an especially bad week with his father, the incident from the day his parents had met his sister for lunch snowballed into several days of extreme agitation and lashing out that Ranar knew would only get worse.

"Please don't be mad at me," Nisa had begged him days after the fact. "I had no idea my patient was going to go into labor. What do you want me to *do*, Ranar?"

"*Help* me!" he'd exclaimed, furious that his sister needed to ask, that it needed to be voiced at all. "Help me with them just the *tiniest* bit. I really don't think that's so much to ask."

He didn't know how it was that his sister was still able to quell any undesirable situation with her tears, the same as she'd always done growing up, but as soon he heard her sniffles, his anger faded, protective big brother instinct kicking on as it always had.

"I hate seeing him like this," she'd whimpered. "I feel like we already have to say our goodbyes and I just can't deal with it."

Ranar had closed his eyes, irritated that somehow he was meant to be unaffected by the same situation. "I know, Nisa. How do you think *I* feel every day? I'm the one here, watching it happen."

He and Sumi had traded numbers and promised that they'd get together as soon as their schedules permitted it, but it had yet to happen and he'd given up the expectation that it ever would. *Sorry, Gracie. She probably found the orcs. Or the orcs found her.*

He idly wondered what Sumi would think of their accommodative vehicle as Ruma curled into the passenger space, wondering if he would *ever* have the chance to have her ride in his. In place of a standard running board on a generic human SUV, his kicked down, forming a miniature ramp, easily manipulated with his tail, and a comfortable, open interior instead of seats. Hand levers for the brake and accelerator replaced floor pedals, safety belts on the side arms of the padded head supports.

They were halfway downtown before Ruma spoke, as soon as he braked at a light.

"Does Thatha not remember me because I moved away?"

Ranar was horrified to see the tears in her eyes, her miserable little voice. Her lip quivered, and beside her, the tip of her violet tail twitched.

"Baby, no. Of course not." He would have given anything for some of her nonsensical slang at that moment, anything to have saved them from having *this* conversation. He was never going to get a break from having this same conversation, Ranar realized, over and over, with everyone he loved. *Maybe you should start drinking.* "That doesn't have anything to do with it, Ruma, and I don't want you to ever think that. Thatha is sick. It's only going to get worse as the years go on. You living here or not doesn't matter. Sometimes he calls me the wrong name too, and he's with me all the time."

"I don't want him to forget who I am." The tears fell then, the weight of her misery dropping onto the already insurmountable load on his back with a thud.

How's your dad doing? You're all in our thoughts. I'm just glad my mom's heart gave out on her before her mind went. Every day was a new well-wisher, and Ranar sometimes wondered if his face might freeze into the rictus smile he adopted every time a well-meaning neighbor shook their head sadly and then walked off with an air of relief that it was him and not them on the other side of the counter.

"I know, baby. Neither do I. But here's the important part, Noodle. That name he was calling you tonight? Neja? That was his little sister. She died a long, long time ago, but they were close, everyone tells me. So he might've called you the wrong name, but he remembered the important part — that you're someone he loves, very much."

They were both quiet for the rest of the short ride, but the lively atmosphere of the coffee shop brightened her instantly. He had no idea how the pink, athleisure hoodie she'd put on over a white t-shirt was considered preppy and his mouth had opened to comment on her bag, what they'd called fanny packs in his day, but he'd had the good sense to abort the thought when she dropped it over her head, wearing it like a purse. *Maybe Pinky's cheat sheet covers clothes.*

If he had expected his tween to be a novice in the art of coffee ordering, Ranar would've been disappointed. *It's a good thing you were taught otherwise.* He'd not seen Xavier since the day he'd run into Sumi, his disastrous week subsuming his every waking moment. Neither the ram nor his sister and co-owner Xenna were working that evening, and once their drinks were delivered to the side counter, Ruma asked if they could stroll around downtown.

"We were barely able to come out at all when I was here for winter break."

Using the grass pathway, they made their way up Main Street, past the ice cream parlor and the jewelry shop, and accountant's office, and the marble entrance to the grand building in the center of the square, the golden domed clock tower looking out over the whole town, where Jack Hemming had his office.

"I miss it here sometimes," she confided unexpectedly. "There are lots of naga at my school, and goblins. Some humans. But not like this. We don't have grass sidewalks," she huffed, and Ranar chuckled gently.

"This place is pretty special. Although, there are more and more multi-species communities forming all the time. I'll bet that by the time you go off to college, this will be normal and you'll have your pick of where you live."

She nodded slowly. "Maybe I can go to college here."

His voice stuck for a moment, wanting nothing more than to agree with her wholeheartedly, assuring her that she could come back here whenever she wanted, custody agreement be damned. *But that's not what you agreed on.* "Sure, but this is a pretty small school. Maybe you'll want to try living in the big city for a while. But you can go anywhere you want, Noodle."

"Mommy's dating someone new."

She exhaled sharply after blurting the words, and Ranar wondered if she had been ready to burst, anxious to tell him from the moment the wheels of her plane touched down in Bridgeton. He waited for the hurt to come, the heartbreak that he was nothing more than a memory in his ex-wife's mind, but it never did. The only thing he was jealous of, if it was jealousy at all, was that she had managed to figure out how to balance it all, and he still couldn't.

"Well, that's good. Is he nice? Do you like him?"

Ruma shrugged, sipping on her overly sweetened ice cream drink. Ranar didn't think there was a single drop of coffee in it, but that was probably for the best. "He's okay, I guess." They had turned off Main Street, making their way down one of the narrow side streets in a concertina pattern, the sidewalk less forgiving here. "Is that comic book shop still open? I want to see if they have any of the MochiBunny merchandise."

"Yeah, it's right down this way—"

They had just reached the corner and Ranar turned, pointing down the crossroad when he saw it. His voice stuck, his jaw stuck, every muscle in his body stuck at that moment, frozen, rigor mortis setting in immediately. The windows were covered, hiding whatever construction was taking place within, wrapped with an advertisement that made his insides turn to jelly. Horror-stricken, slightly queasy jelly. The sticky sweet gulab jamun was in danger of making a reappearance on the sidewalk, he realized, swaying in place.

Coming soon!

The Pink Blossom by Bloomerang

It wasn't possible. They would never let a chain store open right off Main Street, practically under Jack's nose. It wasn't possible. But the sign is right there. Suddenly everything in his body seemed too high, his lungs inflating around his sternum, and his heart beating the back of his tongue. He was going to be sick. He was going to fucking set something on fire. *It's not possible.*

It had been their one saving grace, these last ten years or so. The safeguard he clung to in the endless winter months — they'd never have to worry about corporate competition in Cambric Creek, the bane of every small florist, the reason so many of his industry peers had shuttered their doors for good.

The entire floral industry hinged on one of two tent poles — online business and weddings. Funerals, though constant, were inconsistent in their needs. Perhaps if he was a florist in a human neighborhood it might be different, if casket sprays and cemetery pieces were more in demand, but as it was, many of his multi-species neighbors believed in committing their deceased loved ones to the flame. A small commemorative basket, perhaps a standing spray if there was an elaborate ceremony, but not enough for one to pay their mortgage reliably.

Weddings were a beast unto themselves. Ranar had often wondered if he could simply opt out of the online wire service altogether, reestablish himself as a wedding florist. It could be done, but as he'd told Sumi weeks and weeks earlier, that first days she'd come in to his shop, it required one working themselves near to death the entire bridal season just to keep the lights on during the winter months, when the entire industry took a long, chilly nap. *This is why brick-and-mortar is a liability.* The everyday online orders were essential to a daily operation like his, one that relied on an evenly dispersed workload, allowing him to pay his distributors and all the shop utilities during those months when the temperatures dipped below freezing. The wedding season paid for the winters and the online orders put food on the table, and that was the way it had always been.

Jack Hemming's distaste for chain stores had bled into his redeveloped downtown, the entirety of Cambric Creek seeming to embrace the mom and pop ethos. That was what it saved them, all these years. The knowledge that they were safe from one of these online outposts, that the money he had paid into the service all these years was worthwhile for the orders he received in return, that he could keep his doors open, keep a roof over his own head, and give his parents a reason to leave the house each day.

So what the fuck changed?

Ranar didn't know how he made it through the rest of the evening with Ruma. His smile felt plastered on, and he hated not being authentically present and engaged for a single minute of time with his daughter, but he would have been lying if he'd pretended that his brain wasn't somewhere else. *Somewhere else, throwing up in the bushes.*

It didn't seem to matter.

She was thrilled with her first day back with him — the visit with her grandparents, coffee, and a Squishberry — a squishy stuffed anime rabbit drinking its own expensive gourmet coffee, one she had crowed was a special edition she'd not been able to find at home. His hands were shaking once they were finally in his house, but Ruma seemed not to notice, and quickly settled in on the low, two-tiered sofa in his living room, finding a movie to watch.

Having the upper body of a human meant their furniture needed to address the physical needs of both snake and human torso, and the low, wide furniture with an elevated section was what most households like theirs preferred. The style was also popular with cervitaurs and other smaller hippocampean species, but nagas required heat, especially living in a colder environment, like theirs.

"Do you want the heat on, Noodle?"

"No, I don't think so. I have my blanket. But you should definitely make some popcorn."

He was glad she was so easily distracted, but annoyed that he had to share even a minute of his time with her thinking about literally anything else. Still, it gave him the opportunity to have a quiet breakdown, realizing he'd been remiss in keeping up with the neighborhood gossip, as he pushed his laptop open with shaky hands. Settling back on his coil, Ranar took a deep breath, tapping open the DiscHorse icon.

His conversations with Pinky had taken over nearly all of the time he spent online. How could they not? She was funny, she shared his love of plants, she was sharp and intelligent. *She knows the entire script of all four Coming Gnome movies. That's the most adorable thing in the world.*

It was his folly, however, ignoring the rest of his online communications. The business owner's server wasn't especially lively. After all, they were all local, and most of them saw each other in person throughout the month. Many of the older business owners in town had no use for the online social platform, while some of the younger members of the group tended to waylay every conversation into something that would've been best as a private DM.

Toggling over to the screen, away from his conversation with Pinky for the first time in months, Ranar held his breath. Maybe someone will have mentioned something. He hoped for at least one message, maybe two, anything to clarify this nightmare.

What he discovered, instead, was pandemonium.

His thumb began to tire by the time he got to the top of the back scroll, realizing with horror that the hundreds of messages he had missed — missed because he was busy flirting with a woman he would never meet — were all about him.

Where is he? Has anyone talked to him?

How could they let this happen?

I'd really like to know what Jack has to say about this.

Is this going to be what we all have to look forward to? A Blinxieburger on every corner?

Someone needs to tell Cal. If they're going to let in chains, the factory farms are next.

We're all going to starve at this rate!

I saw him just this morning, popped in to show our solidarity. Bought a vase for the desk.

That was the goblin from the laundromat, he realized, finally reaching the end of the litany of increasingly panicked messages.

He seemed to be keeping a stiff upper lip about the whole thing.

Ranar choked out a laugh, quickly covering it with a cough so as not to arouse Ruma's suspicion. Hardly a stiff upper lip. He realized now that this was likely what Xavier had wanted to tell him about nearly two weeks ago, what the kitsune had alluded to the previous night on his doorstep. *You should have taken a hand job at the very least.* The goblin from the laundromats, the two satyresses, clucking their tongues.

Tomorrow, Ranar told himself. Tonight he was going to curl up and watch a silly movie with his little girl. Tomorrow, he was going to City Hall to rip someone a new one, and if they weren't any help, he would sidewind his way up Main Street until he was standing in front of Jack Hemming's door.

They can't do this. I won't let them do this. Not without a fight.

When the next morning came all too soon, he felt as though he'd been run over by a truck. Ranar didn't know how it was that his head was so heavy, that sharp ever present pounding at his temple still going strong, nearly sleeping through his alarm, and yet feeling as though he hadn't slept a wink.

"Here's the plan, Noodle." He kept his voice light as they drove into work, Ruma nodding seriously at rapt attention. "You're to be the counter girl. Paati will run the register, but you say hi to people, ask them if they need help, so forth and so on. You know the drill."

"Chat, I can do that in my sleep."

Ranar grinned. At least someone was raring to go that day. "If Thatha calls you the wrong name, baby, just roll with it. He gets upset if he realizes that he's not remembering something, so think of it like a game. Like improv. It's not a game for him, but the rest of us have to play like it is. Just remember, he still loves you no matter what." She nodded again. "One thing he is still really good at is filling orders, so you can be his assistant and bring him flowers he needs. I have to go into town for a meeting this morning, but I won't be gone long."

After giving his mother a version of the exact same speech, with the added plea to *please* keep control of the situation while he was gone, he headed into downtown, bypassing City Hall altogether. There was no point. It didn't make a difference who sat in the mayor's office, who wore the magistrate's robes. It didn't make a difference if it was one of his sons or total strangers. As long as Jack Hemming drew breath, he would be calling the shots. The final boss, as it were.

Fortunately, he reminded himself as he slithered quickly across the cold marble foyer of the building, Jack was reasonable and friendly, wildly charismatic, and usually very fair. At least, Ranar thought that until he arrived to find the outer door to Jack's top story office was locked. *Fucking coward.* He cursed. He was going to tighten around this werewolf until his head popped off, at the earliest opportunity.

Ranar swayed there, listening to the clock in the hallway tick. Tick down the day, tick down the brief few weeks it seemed he had with his daughter. Tick down the two years that had gone by since he'd last even dated anyone, tick down his father's life. What was that he had told Pinky? It wasn't just a shop. It wasn't just a business. It had been his father's whole life, his grandfather's dream, both resting on that bridge he was expected to hold up. *They can't do this.*

He wasn't sure how much time had passed when the delivery person came down the hallway towards him, on the other side of the locked door. The goblin had their face down, eyes trained on their phone screen, barely paying attention to Ranar as he caught the door, slithering in behind them. He could tell the she-wolf on the other side of the desk was shocked to see him.

"Oh! I —there are no appointments this morning, I'm so sorry."

"I don't have an appointment," Ranar said flatly. "And I'm not leaving until I speak with him."

He wondered if she would call the police. He could tell that she was wondering the same thing, her hand reaching for the phone, whether to dial out or to dial into the office, he wasn't sure, both of their attentions caught by the sound of raised voices.

"This is my legacy, do you understand that? This downtown has *my* name on it. When something goes wrong, who do you think is the first person to get the blame? It doesn't make a difference what it is. A water main break, a faulty traffic light, a fucking dragonborn throwing up all over the parking lot on a Saturday night. They don't like the pattern of traffic, they blame me. They don't like a store that moves in, they blame me. Did you even think beyond the tip of your nose what the ramifications would be for—"

Ranar recognized Jack's deep voice, but he wasn't as familiar with the voice that cut in, younger, just as forceful.

"Of course I thought about it. Do you really think I don't agonize over every decision I make on that counsel, knowing how it's going to affect the rest of us? I understand this is your legacy, Dad, but what do you think *our* legacy is going to be? How long do you think your legacy is going to last if we keep propping up failing businesses just because we know the owners and they've been around a while? I'm *protecting* your legacy. Compare the projected annual revenue of the two businesses and the taxes they pay back to the community. There's no question. I made the best decision I could with the information I had, and I'm standing by it. There's room for both. You're the first one who's always going on about diversifying our portfolios. If he can't diversify his business and adapt, whose fault is that?"

The woman behind the desk closed her eyes, sighing quietly. She'd reached a decision at last, holding down a button on her phone. Her voice was quiet, but Ranar felt a shiver down his spine as if she'd screamed into his ear.

"*He's* here."

The voices on the inside of the long office went silent. Silent for a moment, at least, until Ranar heard Jack's dark laughter, devoid of humor.

"Sit your ass down. You made the best decision you could, I respect that. And now you stand on it with both feet."

Ranar simultaneously felt as if he had just been summoned to the principal's office and that he stood before a devil when the door swung open, the werewolf patriarch greeting him with bright eyes, and no sign that they had just been talking about him.

"Ranar, come in. How's your dad doing?"

How's your dad doing? We're so sorry to hear about his condition. Better you than us. "He's doing as well as he can. Day by day. But that's not why I'm here."

Jack Hemming moved the second chair before his huge desk as he went back around it, indicating the vacant spot for Ranar. The young man in the chair beside him hadn't yet met his eye.

"My son, Owen. He's on the planning commission."

At that, the younger of the two werewolves exhaled forcefully, turning to Ranar at last. To his credit, his eyes were, Ranar had to admit, full of compassion. "It's nice to meet you, and I am so very sorry that we are meeting under the circumstances. Look, obviously we know why you're here, and I don't want to waste any of your time, so let's get down to it. What questions can I answer for you?"

Across the desk, the elder raised an eyebrow, crossing his arms over his chest, and said nothing. Ranar had expected they would dilly dally, wear him down with niceties, and the younger Hemming's forth-rightness might've been refreshing under different circumstances. *Now's your chance.* Ranar swallowed, steeling himself, but when he opened his mouth, the words wouldn't come. *If we keep propping up failing businesses.* It was him, he was the failing business. Failing, in spite of doing everything right. Everything he had planned on saying, all of his vibrating anger and furious bravado seemed to fizzle away, leaving him mute, an impotent worm, unable to even defend himself or ask why. *Why?* That was the word his brain latched onto in the end.

"Why?" he croaked. "*How* could you let this happen? How could you allow this—"

"It's not a chain," the younger werewolf said quickly. "She satisfied the expectation that the store is run independently. It's not any more a chain than all the other flower shops carrying the Bloomerang product line."

She. "But it's—"

"Not human owned. I was a little shocked to learn that, actually. When we talk about non-human enterprises, very rarely are big national chains a part of the conversation, but this one should be. And again, since it's not a chain, the partner company makes very little difference."

Ranar closed his eyes, struggling to take even breaths without hyperventilating. *How can you do this to my family? We've been here for decades. Keep propping up failing businesses just because the owners have been around a while.*

"I'll be very honest with you, this was really a financial call, when it came down to it," the younger of the two wolves said earnestly. "I pulled the last few years of your city taxes, Ranar, and I ran them against the predictions for this other shop. Then I compared their business model with yours. I have to tell you, I truly believe there is room for both of you in town. You might need to diversify your strategy, but—"

"Do you know *why* this other shop is projected to do well?" He bit back, finding his words at last. "Do you know *why* she's going to bury me in profit margin? Because our entire industry is reliant on doing business with Bloomerang, and they make *every*thing expensive. I have to buy my stock from them. I have to buy my flowers based on their design specs. So if you're sending your girlfriend flowers for her birthday and you pick out one of their specials, I can't just put an arrangement together and drop it into a nice vase. I have to pull *specific* flowers, drop them into a *specific* vase, one that costs $1.70 more per unit even though it's identical to the one sold by the vase company that had to go out of business because they lost all of their accounts, a specific vase that I can *only* acquire through the Bloomerang catalog. I have to pay to be a part of their online service so that I can get Bloomerang's online orders. Do you know what's going to happen when this other absolutely-not-a-chain store opens, Mr. Hemming? I'm still going to need to pay my distributors. I'm still going to need to pay for my flowers. But *I'm* not going to have any orders, because Bloomerang is going to send all of them to this other store that *they* own. They're going to put me out of business; I hope you understand that. That's what you approved."

On the other side of the desk, Jack Hemming looked as if he were watching a tennis match, perhaps, or maybe just a slow moving train wreck, his eyes flickering back and forth between Ranar and his son.

Owen spread his hands. "So stop paying into that system. Leverage the rest of your business to do the heavy lifting. You do a really healthy wedding business; I know for a fact that you do. Stop paying that extra $1.70 for a vase. I understand you're upset, Ranar. I do. But put yourself in my position. I have a fiduciary responsibility to the taxpayers in this community. We approve businesses based on their potential to create revenue, because those tax dollars go straight back into the schools. If you were given the choice of the two businesses and told you could only pick one, what would you—"

"I would pick them," he responded woodenly. He couldn't blame the planning commission for making the choice that they had, his anger sliding away as the hopelessness of the situation enveloped him fully. They were right. His business was failing, the whole industry circling the drain, the corporatization that had begun several decades earlier finally achieving its aim. *And you're just as culpable for rolling over and lining their pockets all these years.* "I would pick them too."

"Have you considered selling the building, Ranar?" Jack's voice was low and steady, and not without compassion. "You'll receive double the market value, I can assure you. You're in a prime location with good parking. It'll go to a bidding war if you decide that's the route you want to take. I'll make sure of it."

He felt as if he were drowning, clawing at the surface of a spinning whirlpool that was sucking him down. He thought about selling the building every single week and had done so for the last five years. Jack Hemming wasn't wrong. He would be able to assure all of the business's creditors were paid back, see that his parents were set up comfortably for the duration of their retirement, pay off his house and still have a respectable nest egg for himself.

And then what? You're forty-two years old. You've never done anything but this. He had a degree in electrical engineering, one he'd never once put to use. That had been another expectation of him, the first baby born here, the good son. Get a good education in a respectable field, something his parents could write home about to relatives he barely knew. *You'll probably need to go back to school, learn all of the new technology that didn't exist twenty-five years ago.*

He could sell the building, and what would his parents do? What would his father do every day if he didn't have this routine, other than slip into this clawing oblivion even faster? *No.* No, he couldn't do that until he had no other choice. As he told Pinky, this wasn't like selling a used car. There was more to it, and it didn't matter if outsiders couldn't understand.

"She's going to put me out of business," he repeated. "So when that happens, I'll expect you to make good on that promise, Jack. I think that's the very least you can do for my father."

His muscles didn't want to cooperate as he uncoiled, shifting to the door in a herky-jerky concertina.

"I hope it doesn't come to that, Ranar. I know you think I'm wrong, but I really don't think you're going to have to shut down your business entirely. Maybe the brick-and-mortar end of it, because I appreciate that the property taxes are significant." Owen glanced back to his father. "But he's right, you'll make a pretty penny on that land."

His hand was clammy as he shook the younger man's hand, and then his father's. She was going to put him out of business, and he would have to figure out what to do next.

"You'll need to diversify the business, but based on the numbers I looked at, I think you can survive, Ranar. There's room for you and Sumi both. I'm sure of it."

Hatred & Disdain

SUMI

"We had four girls on staff, and me, of course. Well, that was for the design room. And then two girls who ran the counter, but they also had a big gift shop. If you're not going to have that and you're just doing flowers—"

"Just flowers," Sumi clarified quickly, hoping the troll didn't notice her gulp.

She hadn't counted on needing staff. Somehow, in her decade worth of daydreams of running her own flower shop, she was the only one present, standing in a warm ray of sunlight, surrounded by the soft pastel of her chosen interior, putting together an elegant vase arrangement with nary a single customer or other employee in sight. She was rather sheepish to admit that her long-held daydream of running her own flower shop was more akin to Meredith's living room bookstore than an actual frantically paced business.

At least, it seemed frantic to her.

She had been sent to a shop in Bridgeton, Urban Narcissus, to do her training. Training hadn't even occurred to her at all, but fortunately it was an automatic part of the Bloomerang partnership. Unfortunately, it meant she needed to cut her teeth in record time, and considering the first and only time she had ever worked a retail job was back in high school, everything felt brand-new. *It doesn't help that they sent you to the snootiest shop in the city.* Sumi didn't know that for sure, but she was willing to place a bet.

She had been excited at first, learning that the shop was nymph-owned, thinking she and the dryad might have something in common, but she was quickly dissuaded of that notion. The dryad who owned Urban Narcissus was as sleek as her shop. Cool and sterile, black and white with minimalist, box-like displays and stark lighting coming from tiny spotlights on a track. Even the tree exploding through the roof didn't soften the atmosphere. The whole thing gave Sumi the impression of a high-end shoe boutique, rather than flowers. *And this is why you're not a chain. Because every shop is different.* They specialized in orchids and tropicals, expensive architectural arrangements sprouting from black cubes and opaque white vases, given height with twisting sticks. It was the complete opposite of everything she wanted her own shop to be, right down to the arrangements they made. *But all of this looks expensive. Bet she makes a fuck ton of money.*

The dryad gave Sumi a fast up and down the first day she'd entered, sniffing. She had been told they had a dress code. All black. *I get that funeral flowers are part of the job, but this is ridiculous.* What *hadn't* been

communicated was that the staff wore sleek black trousers and match-
ing blazers.

She stood out in her black dress, but Sumi had decided, after the
second day of feeling self-conscious, that she didn't care. She wasn't
going out and buying a black blazer for a two-week training. *Look at
it this way, it's not like you would ever get a job here. She would never hire
you, you're too fat.* There were several other sylvans on staff that she had
met, a few other dryads, all of them just as sleek and reed thin as their
employer. *She clearly has a type, and you're not it.*

She'd never had a significant amount of self-consciousness over her
size. She knew that probably seemed counterintuitive to most other
women, but she had enough to be self-conscious about as it was. She
liked the way she looked, thought the face staring back at her in the
mirror was pretty, and if people disliked someone of her size having
self-confidence, Sumi had long ago decided that that wasn't her problem. This dryad wasn't any different.

Despite their owner, she found most of the staff to be friendly, even
if only superficially, but they all had one thing in common: frantic,
slightly panicked anxiety. Sumi understood, for she would be anxious
everyday with an employer like this as well, but there was more to it
than that. The dryad ran a tight ship, all of her employees knowing exactly what they needed to do each day. The most significant takeaway,
she had decided by the end of it, other than the fact that she was going
to need to practice making schedules and that she would probably cry
the first time she had to process payroll on her own, was that the orders
never stopped.

They never fucking stop. Every time she turned around, one of the girls would be scurrying from the office with a fresh printout, gathering up sticks and stems of expensive tropical flowers and colorful moss to place at the base of the arrangement. *Maybe it's because she's in the city. There's no guarantee you'll be this busy.*

"You'll need to accept orders hourly. I assign someone to the task each day, but we also keep the alarm set, just in case they are otherwise engaged with a client. We keep ours set to a specific dollar threshold so that we're not wasting time reading through the throwaways."

"What are throwaways?" She hated interrupting the dryad, who pursed her lips at the intrusion, but if she didn't, Sumi knew the woman wouldn't bother offering a more in-depth explanation.

"Orders less than one hundred dollars. Although," she went on in a clipped voice, giving Sumi another disapproving once over, "that might be too high for your area. You'll have to judge that for yourself. But *this* is a high-end establishment, and we don't need to waste time with forty-five dollar little vase arrangements."

It was a good point. Sumi had no idea what the average spend would be for her area. *One hundred dollars is way too high.*

"And I don't want my drivers disappearing all day for orders that will hardly cover the gas. You have to balance what you're willing to spend to make money, which is why we don't take the throwaways, and I don't leave on the automatic approval. Some people will try to slip in an order outside the delivery zone just to save on the higher charge, and once it's yours, you're responsible for eating the cost."

She had partnered with her Bloomerang area manager, once her training was finished, getting the appropriate job listings posted. She would need to hire a full-time floral designer. She was going to have to be someone's boss. Sumi couldn't conceive of it. Hedda was maybe ten years older than herself, had been working in the industry for more than two decades, and it was decided the troll would be the perfect hire to guide the rest of the business.

"How about this," Sumi said after a moment of contemplation, tapping the end of her pen against her lips, "when you go through this list today, pick out the six that you think are most promising. Then we'll interview them in batches. I'll talk to one, while you have the other two back here. We'll give them something simple, just a basket arrangement, but I want to make sure that you like them and that you're happy with their work."

Hedda smiled, nodding her agreement to the plan. Sumi liked the troll enormously, was thrilled for her experience and grateful that she was willing to take on the responsibility of head designer.

"Offer her ten dollars more an hour than she was making at her last shop," the Bloomerang manager had advised. "She'll be willing to take on more responsibility and she'll be less likely to quit."

She'd thought that last bit of advice seemed ominous, but Hedda was thrilled for the raise and ecstatic that she got to be in charge of the design room. "That's perfect. And two together is smart, that way we can get them talking. It only takes one drama queen back here to ruin everyone's week."

Sumi laughed weakly, not wanting to even contemplate the possibility of a drama queen to manage. "We'll hire two of them right off the bat, and keep the other names for backup."

It was as good a plan as they could come up with. It was nearly impossible for her to believe that they would be opening in just a few weeks time. Bloomerang had said the process would be fast, but she couldn't have conceived the construction moving as quickly as it did. *We don't want to waste any time in having you operational.* Hedda exited out the back door, and once she did, Sumi tiptoed to the front.

It was almost done. The walls were a dreamy wash of mauve and dusty pink, with slate gray fixturing and shelves, pink marble flooring, and bright track lights. There was lighting around the base of her tree as well, and its soft silver leaves lended their own impression to the color scheme she had tried to create. It was almost done, and it was going to be hers.

She had never in her life felt as on top of the world as she had in the past month.

Everything was coming together: the house, the shop, the club, and she woke each day feeling energized and excited, in a way she never had at the school. In a way she hadn't ever. She didn't feel as though she was ever going to be fully unpacked, particularly when she sat in endless gridlock getting out of the city for those two weeks she trained at Urban Stems, but now that was done with, she promised herself that she would empty one box a night.

She had already made a friend, Yuriko, who insisted that Sumi had dinner with her family, just a few days after they met that afternoon at the community center. She'd met Yuriko's husband and her adorable daughter, Mai. Her serious-faced brother, Kenta, had also come to dinner that night, and Sumi had collapsed from relief when Kenta's girlfriend Ava turned out to be human-passing.

"Just human-adjacent," Ava had joked cheerfully. "My father was a faun, but he skipped town right after I was born, so I grew up in human neighborhoods."

She had never had more in common with a group of people, and had needed to remind herself at several points throughout the night that if she broke down crying, they would likely not invite her back.

Her shop was going to open soon. Yuriko was fierce and funny and vulgar and would be a very good friend, Sumi was certain. She had joined the Japanese club, had met another half-human like her . . . There's only one thing missing from the recipe of her perfect life reset.

Sumi had taken care in dressing that day, pulling out her favorite dress, the dusty lilac making her skin glow like a fresh peach, especially once she applied a careful stroke of raspberry blush, high on her cheekbones. A soft, pearly pink for her lips, a touch of shimmer down her nose. She brushed her dark hair until it shone, clipping it out of her eyes and leaving it loose down her back. She wanted to glow for him.

She couldn't deny that she had spent a significant amount of time thinking about the handsome naga, slightly annoyed that all of her time was being eaten up driving back and forth to Bridgeton when she should have been having coffee with him, meeting him for dinner, letting him show her all around town, and then learn what kind of noise he would make when she licked the seam in his scales. There was a sex toy shop in town, because of course there was. Sumi already knew that the toy market could cater to any appetite, that porn existed of every species on the side of the veil, and although she was dying of curiosity, she had refrained from looking at any of it. She wanted to be surprised and delighted by him the way she had been delighted by the rainbow play of his vivid scales, his friendliness, and the delicious sparkle of his eyes.

Although, she would have been lying to herself to pretend that she didn't wish she had maybe been brave enough to stop into that toy store, particularly late at night, when she was in bed. Her vibrator got her there reliably, but it wasn't as exciting as wondering what his cock would be like. The only thing she knew about snake and lizard folk was that there was an enormous variety, there was no telling what his might be like. *Fringed, frilled, covered in spikes?* She had no idea, and with each day that passed without them having made good on their promise to get together, she lost a little bit more sleep and her vibrator got an even harder workout.

It didn't help that she didn't have any distractions.

Sumi didn't want to pry, but ChaoticConcertina had barely been online in the past two weeks, and she hoped that everything in his world was well. *I hope he's having a good visit with his daughter. I hope his dad is okay,* she thought to herself, turning away from the sight of her beautiful flower shop to carefully pick her way out the back entrance, following the same path Hedda had taken. The front of the building was wrapped in construction plywood. There was a door, but she didn't like using it, not yet.

She didn't have anything left to do that afternoon, not until Hedda provided her with the names of applicants to call, and she knew just how she would fill the time.

Glancing in her rearview mirror once she had arrived, she examined her teeth, ensuring they were clean and not spotted in pink lipstick. The Perfect Petal loomed before her, and there was no time like the present to put her love life on the same fast track as everything else.

There was a little girl standing in front of the register, filling in a box of envelopes, when Sumi came through the door, a clanging little bell announcing her entrance. Her dark hair was twisted up and clasped with a pink bow claw clip, one that matched the pattern on her oversized open cardigan, pink bows on white, over a simple T-shirt. There were more than a dozen beaded friendship-style bracelets interspersed with jelly bands on her slender, nut brown wrist, and on the countertop, her cell phone rested on a metallic stand, encased in a MochiBunny cover.

Sumi grinned. The girl was a few years younger than her former students, but clearly a budding fashionista with a clear understanding of the current trends. The hem of her pink and white cardigan was where her outfit ended, her violet scales taking over. She undulated as she filled the box, a soft sway, turning when she heard the bell.

His niece? His daughter? OMG, you are going to be the best stepmom in the world. After all, she had an excellent model, for her own stepmother had been wonderful. *You can go shopping together and go to the movies and have dance parties to the Epoch movie.*

"Hi," the little girl called out, grinning broadly. "Welcome to The Perfect Petal. Is there anything I can help you find today?"

At that, she couldn't hold back an appreciative laugh. "I don't think I need any help, but I have to tell you," Sumi motioned to the girl's outfit, "your drip is im*pecc*able. Super coquette." She would never let anyone claim fluency in slaying was an unworthy skill, for the girl beamed, her smile stretching from ear to ear, revealing miniature fangs.

"Thank you! I love coquette so much, that and berrygirl, but I don't see people here wearing it as much."

Sumi laughed again. It astounded her how fast this particular generation changed and adapted. Preppie now referred to expensive athleisure wear in bright, punchy colors and clear tote bags with varsity-style lettering. Then there was the wild of branching off of what she considered girly — ballet core, coquette, strawberry girls. If Gen Alpha did one thing well, it was apply labels to every little deviation. *And this is why representation matters. This is why human schools hurt more than just the non-human kids.*

"Did you get the bow tumbler?" She might not have been the most passionate teacher in her former building, and never referred to herself as an educator, but the one thing she had always done well was paying attention — who was friends with who, what girl grouped with bullies, noting it was frequently an overlap with the same group of girls who were another classroom's teachers pet — to what they were all frothing for.

Evidently, she had guessed correctly, for the naga girl threw up her hands, moaning as if she had just been stabbed.

"Nooooooo! It's sold out everywhere. I thought I would be able to find one here, but they don't even have the stores that carry them."

At that, Sumi huffed. *Yeah, because they're all terrified of chain stores for some reason.*

"I have my strawberry Simon cup, but it's not the same."

At the sound of the girl's dramatic cry, a man came lurching around the corner, the precise naga she had come to see.

"Are you okay?" Ranar demanded, his tail moving him so much faster than she thought it should have been able to. "Is something wrong?"

She had only a moment to admire the two of them together. Sumi could see that this girl was obviously his relation. She shared his thick fringe of jet black lashes and had the same angular face, although the scales on her tail were lighter, brighter, absent of the splotches of inky blue. *He wouldn't have asked you out if her mother was still in the picture.*

He turned a second later, his eyes landing on her immediately. Sumi held her breath, her face aching from the force of her smile. He was just as gorgeous as he'd been that first day.

At least, he was until his eyes narrowed, his entire face transforming into a look of abject hostility.

"Ruma, go in the back."

"But I'm—"

Sumi didn't understand the language he spoke, a quick susurration over his shoulder, little girl stiffening, doing as she was told a moment later. He kept his head turned, watching the girl slither away, waiting until the door had swung shut behind her. The little girl threw one last look back at Sumi, her eyes raised, before vanishing completely.

"You have a lot of nerve coming in here. What are you here to do, steal my car? You gonna ask me if I have tips on how you can drive it first?"

His words hit her like a fist, his displeasure to see her there dripping from every syllable, emphasized by his snarl. Sumi took a step back, feeling as though the bottom of her happiness had just fallen out. "What-what do you mean—"

"What do I *mean?*" Ranar looked at her incredulously. "Is this a joke? Is that what this is to you? A sick joke? You come in here and play coy and ask if I have tips about running a flower shop and you didn't bother mentioning that you were already under construction four blocks away? You know, you may have fooled the planning commission with your little claim that you're an independent store, but you don't fool me. Call yourself anything you want, but we both know the truth — you're running a bouquet sweatshop. It doesn't make a difference how many layers of pink paint you want to slap on it."

A lance beneath her breast, caught right in the ribs, making her suck in a breath, wobbling on her heel. Sumi suddenly remembered that despite her daydreams, she didn't even know this stupid snake, and she didn't owe him anything. She certainly didn't need to stand here and be insulted by him.

"Aren't you the one that said this is a terrible industry to be in? It seems like you should take your own advice if you can't hack it. You're a real asshole, you know that? No wonder this place is empty. Your attitude is scaring away all your customers."

Once again she was taken aback by how fast he was able to move, the push and pull of his muscles propelling him forward in the blink of an eye, his long tail seeming to fill the space, obliging her to take another step back. She watched as Ranar whipped open the cooler door, yanking out stem after stem, turning back to the counter nearly as fast as he had left it. She winced when he slapped the flowers down on the counter, pulling out a length of paper so roughly that the roll vibrated against its spindle.

"Here you go, Ms. Pink Blossom. My regards on your new store. I don't ever want to see you in here again."

Sumi wasn't sure why she hadn't already left, but she wasn't going to go quietly now. She grinned as widely as she could, showing as much tooth as she was able, accepting the bouquet. "I'm keeping this, you know. I'm going to press them so that I never forget. Just in case I get it into my head that we can be friends a few months down the road, I'll look at this and remember — no, that guy is a prick. Good luck, now that you're actually going to have some competition. You're going to need it."

She didn't look back. *You're going to put him out of your mind. This isn't that small of a town, you probably never even need to run into him again. You left all of the other worthless shit in your life behind, and you need to put him in that same box.* She nodded to herself in the rearview mirror, pulling out of The Perfect Petal's driveway for the last time. She wasn't going to let herself cry. He was an asshole and she could forget about him.

Looking down at the wrap of flowers, her lip curled back. Orange lilies and yellow carnations. *Hatred and disdain. Charming.*

She made it halfway home before her eyes began to burn. It wasn't even about him, not really. All she could think of as she pulled into the driveway of the house she had been left was the conversation she had shared with ChaoticConcertina.

What if you're the reason things are like this in the first place?

What if it's you?

The Art of War

The Day You Deserve

SUMI

ChaoticConcertina: *I have the most amazing kid.*
Have I told you that already?
Every day I'm astounded by her kindness & her perception for being so young
I have to stop and wonder where she learned it.
Because it sure as shit wasn't from me or her mother.
Neither of us were ever that good at reading people. Including each other.
Every night we go to the coffee shop together and people watch,
and every night she picks up on something that I ignore completely.
There was a minotaur sitting alone for the longest time, and that means
nothing to me. **ChaoticConcertina:** *You know, just some guy sitting alone,*
big deal.

She said no daddy, he's waiting for someone. You can tell that he's anxious.
It's probably someone he wants to impress, look at how nicely his hooves are
shined.

Who notices that? I pass 10 minotaurs a day.

I don't think I've ever looked at their hooves a single time.

Sure enough, a woman comes in and she goes straight to that bull's table.

See daddy? I told you he was waiting.

ChaoticConcertina: *I miss her so much when she's not here.*

And I'm only ever extremely cognizant of that when she is.

Isn't that silly?

When she's gone, my life is just this blur of work and responsibility.

making sure everyone is keeping their head above water.

and then she arrives and all of that noise just stops.

Every minute feels precious and priceless.

and I'm hyper-aware that we have far too few of them.

I have stuff going on right now professionally that's eating a lot of my brain space,

& I hate it. I hate it so much.

I don't want to think about anything other than enjoying every second she's here

Every day I have her within arm's reach.

ChaoticConcertina: *She asked why I don't have a serious girlfriend, LOL.*

I feel like she's my best advertisement.

I should start wearing a sign around my neck.

Questionable at relationships, but I make great kids.

That's sure to attract someone's eye, right?

"This is it! We are officially live, ladies!"

The gnomes cheered and Hedda lifted her water bottle. Sumi had been surprised when the troll had come back with the names of two middle-aged identical twins, but Hedda had been adamant.

"They were fast, like crazy fast. They've been working in the industry their whole lives, and we know they're not going to get into a knock down drag out fight because they're family and have to see each other over holidays. "

"Isn't that *more* of a reason why they would get into a knock down drag out fight?!"

The troll had just laughed. "Trust me. These are the two we want. If we need to hire more, the dragonborn and the goblin with the blue hair."

She had nodded, making a note to herself, but she was confident they were as staffed as they would ever need to be. Seff and her sister Doona would rotate between design and delivery, depending on the needs of the business. They had another potential driver waiting in the wings, a responsible-seeming troll whose youngest had just started primary school, but Sumi had a feeling they were adequate for the time being.

That was, at least, until she flipped down the computer, connecting to the Bloomerang wire system.

"I'm putting it on auto accept. At least for the first week or two, just to get our shop populating in the order queue, you know?" Her nerves were jangling. This was it. Her dream, her long held dream, finally a reality. *Who cares what that handsome jerk thinks. You worked hard for this.*

You had a deal with middle schoolers for years for this. You lost a tooth for this. What has he done?

Sumi was halfway across the shop, getting ready to unlock the door for the first time when she paused. Her head cocked, listening intently. There was something wrong. There was something wrong with the printer, the feed running and running and running.

"Shit. Fucking printer . . ." She'd fixed the printer in the school office on more than one occasion, she wasn't going to let this slow her down. She arrived back in the design room prepared to restart the damn thing when she stopped short, finding all three of her staff members huddled around the computer with wide eyes. The printer wasn't malfunctioning, Sumi realized.

It was *printing*.

Order after order, an endless stack. More orders than they have flowers, she realized, squealing. "Turn it off, turn off!"

Hedda fell forward, quickly tapping open the Bloomerang screen. She and Sumi huddled, each order that spit out ratcheting up her pulse a bit more, until she finally found the option to turn orders completely off.

She whirled around, staring at the stack of paper as though it might bite. "Holy shit."

"Alright girls," Hedda said, laughing weakly, "let's get to work! Are–are you going to unlock—"

"No," Sumi choked out. *So much for your first big day open to the public.* "No, I don't see how we can. I'm not sure if we'll even be able to—"

"You call the truck and tell them you need more. Don't worry, this used to happen all the time at my old shop. They're used to it."

"I-I'm sure this is just because it's the first day. It won't stay this way . . . Right?"

Seff pulled a face. "There are no other Bloomerang shops in town. I mean, Ranar, but he's not getting any of these orders, not now. There might be one in Starling Heights, but—"

"There's not," Sumi supplied, her stomach twisting over the gnome's words, at the sound of *his* name. She'd already looked in Starling Heights, back when she wasn't sure if Cambric Creek would work out, determining there was no Bloomerang branded partner store. *What did she mean about his orders?*

"Oh, well . . . Yeah, I wouldn't count on it slowing down too much. You're it. We're not going to get too much Bridgeton business, but we won't need it."

"What . . . What do you mean about Ranar's orders? How would we know what kind of orders he gets?"

The gnomes exchanged a fast look.

"Well, if this is anything like the last Bloomerang shop we worked in—"

"—And it is, they're all the same."

"The company sends their online orders to their branded stores first, as long as the system is on.

"But don't turn it off, because you'll get in trouble."

"Yeah, you have to make your quota. The other shops . . ."

She trailed off, not needing to continue.

Sumi nodded, turning away. *He won't get any, because they're sending them all to you.* She understood now. Understood why he was so angry with her. Understood what was going to happen to his compact and efficient little shop. Understood why her monthly repayment to Bloomerang was so fucking high. *They need you to be able to pay it back, and this is how they get you to do so.*

She could pay back the Bloomerang loan with the inheritance, she reminded herself, or with the money from her condo. She could expedite this whole process and cut them out of the picture entirely. After all, that had been her original plan, before she'd learned about the weekly shop quota for orders. *And then where will you be? Broke, with no guarantee this place is going to turn a profit without the system you bought into. He'll still hate you. How will that help anything? This is **your** dream too. This is your page refresh. You're not going to get another one.* Sumi pursed her lips, not liking the twist she felt, low in her belly. *It's fine. There's enough business for both of us.*

"It's a good thing there's enough business for us both," she voiced out loud, ignoring the way the gnomes exchanged another quick look.

Even though she attempted to push them away, Sumi turned Seff's words over in her mind as they worked that morning, over and over, and she had just about arrived at feeling horrible for what she had done to him, simply by existing, when there came a knock at the door.

Hurrying out to the sales floor, preparing an apology for whatever hapless customer was trying to get in, she arrived just in time to see the delivery driver leaving. The orc woman had placed the long, paper wrap on the pavement against the door, and was already loping away down the sidewalk when Sumi pulled it open with a frown.

The bouquet was beautiful.

Orange and yellow lilies exploded from the paper, long points of purple dame's rocket, yellow and white and purple striped carnations, big, showy daffodils with brilliant orange trumpets, and clusters of tight button tansies, like little balls of sunshine.

She recognized *The Perfect Petal*'s card instantly.

He really was a very talented florist, she acknowledged, looking over the wrap of flowers a bit closer. It was already arranged. All she needed to do was drop it into a vase and add water. Brilliant orange and yellow and showy purple, bright and cheerful . . . and strangely ominous.

"Oh, that was so nice of them," Hedda hummed, passing by Sumi to pull a bucket from the cooler. "That will look beautiful on the counter!"

She had already narrowed her eyes, examining the flowers closely. Dame's rocket and daffodil, yellow and striped carnations. Deceit and ego, disdain and disgust. The lilies' meaning was painfully clear — passionate hatred. The button tansies, so cute and cheerful, were a declaration of war.

Sumi flipped over the card with a trembling hand. His handwriting was bold and spiky, with a heavy downward stroke.

Have the day you deserve.

"Oh, he's such a pompous asshole rude motherfucker!" Her hands were trembling when she dropped the flowers into the vase, refusing to throw them away. *Let them remind you, just like you told him.* The promise she'd made him that day in his shop had been a bluff, but

173

now . . . now he was forcing her hand. Hedda raised her eyebrows at Sumi's outburst, while the gnomes were exchanging looks at the speed of sound.

"No, Hedda. I don't think it's meant to be nice at all."

Stomping to the printer, Sumi took a moment to compose herself, rolling her neck, reminding herself that this was a million times better than dealing with pubescent children all day. *Who cares how fucking handsome he is. He's ugly where it counts.* She didn't need to waste another second thinking about Ranar and his eyelashes, not when there were actually good men in the world, men like ChaoticConcertina, wherever he was. Not when she should have been more focused on burying *The Perfect Petal.*

She jabbed at the screen, keeping on the auto accept, but resetting the dollar minimum. *Forty-five dollars. It might not be good enough for Urban Stems, but it's good enough for me. At least for now.* "All right ladies, let's regroup. I'm going to call the truck for more flowers. We'll get the other two designers in here, I'll see if they can start today, and the other driver. Once we hit the halfway point of this stack, I'm turning the orders back on."

Hedda whooped. "You know, if it stays like this, we might never need to unlock the door! That really *is* the dream!"

Sumi walked to the front of the shop with a tight smile, lest any of them see the tears welling in her eyes. *Is that what you're going to do? You have this beautiful shop, and you're just going to keep the door locked all the time, churning out online vases and baskets?* She took a deep breath, attempting to steady herself as she picked up the phone to call the blue-haired goblin. Before she lifted it to her ear, Ranar's voice hissed through her head. *You're nothing but a bouquet sweatshop.* The tears overflowed.

It was someone's dream, maybe.

But it certainly wasn't what she had envisioned for herself.

PinksPosies&Pearls: *I'm so happy you're having a good visit with her.*

It's amazing how perceptive kids that age are, isn't it?

Sometimes students would be even more hooked into the staff gossip than some teachers.

Just based on body language and tone of voice!

They could tell who got along and who didin't and who was fucking the gym teacher.

And they were always right.

Fwiw, I would totally hit on you if you were wearing that sign.

It actually telegraphs a lot.

For starters, you love your kid, and that's the sexiest thing a single dad can do.

PinksPosies&Pearls: *It shows you have good self awareness*

Questionable at relationships isn't necessarily BAD at them

That's workable, women love a challenge.

And like, you made a kid so obviously everything is in good working order below the belt.

It shows you've had sex with another person before

That's more than some of these guys can say

so you probably have realistic standards.

I'd give you my number for sure.

Acceptance is the First Step

RANAR

"**S**he's going to put me out of business. It's not a matter of if, it's a matter of when."

Grace frowned, her blue eyes narrowing as she tried to find a hole in his logic large enough for her to stick her shot glass through, wrinkling her nose when there was none.

Ruma had been overjoyed when Grace turned up that evening, delivering a tote bag patterned with that same damned bubble tea-sipping rabbit and a discreet bottle of tequila behind her back. Ruma insisted her favorite human stay for dinner, and Grace's beaming smile and bubbly personality distracted long enough for Ranar to lean against the sink and close his eyes, resting his face for a few moments.

He was *not* going to let his daughter's summer with him be ruined by this, he'd promised himself. That meant putting on a cheerful, brave face each and every day — for her, for his oblivious parents, for the whole damned family, keeping every plate spinning without falter, and he was exhausted from the effort of smiling when all he wanted to do was sulk.

Once Ruma went to bed, Grace cracked open the bottle, her smile flattening out. The transformation was so swift, it might have been comical under different circumstances.

"Okay, let's strategize. How bad is this going to be?"

Ranar laughed, dropping back onto the sofa, letting his tail uncoil and stretch as he accepted a shot. "Well, I'm going to be closing soon. I don't know where *you* would put that on your disaster scale, but on mine . . ."

"Come *on*, I'm being serious! You can't catastrophize—"

He struggled to sit up enough to swallow without choking. "Gracie, I'm not catastrophizing and there's nothing to strategize. I had three orders today. *Three*. And they were all piddly little thirty-dollar vases; I can't even justify delivering that. She's going to put me out of business. That's not me being fatalistic. That's what's going to happen. I'm not sure how quickly, we won't be able to tell that until after the next few weeks, but it *is* an inevitability."

Grace opened her mouth to challenge him, but Ranar was ready.

"Do you remember, back in your hotel days? Did you ever have those big baskets of little ferns? The mixed variety?"

"Of course, all the time. We had a partnership with a local shop. We used to get those every—"

"That used to be a guy. That was a distributor we used for years. He covered the whole tri-state area, so every flower shop you called in all those years as you organized banquets and for weddings and proms and graduations, they all dealt with him. He was everyone's plant guy, which means, even though you didn't realize it, he was *your* plant guy too. Last time I talked to him, he was driving a school bus in Bingham. Do you know where all the flower shops get their fern baskets from now?"

She was quiet for a moment, dropping her head back against the single human-accommodating piece of furniture he had in his home, there for her alone. "Bloomerang?"

"Bloomerang. We used to have a different distributor for everything. I had a vase gnome. A basket guy. A company who did the boxes. Where are they all now? "

"Well, I'm assuming they're out of business, or else you wouldn't be telling me this particular happy story."

"They are all out of business. Every one of them. Along with more than a dozen flower shops just in the metro area. Do you know who's doing better than ever?"

She blew out an aggrieved breath, pushing to her feet to scoop up the bottle and top off his glass. "Let me guess." Waiting until she had filled her own glass, dropping into her chair once more, Grace rolled her eyes, kicking back her shot. "Bloomerang?"

Ranar raised his shot glass. "Fucking Bloomerang." He pulled a face at the burn, scowling at her once he had returned the empty glass to the table beside the sofa. "I hate tequila. You couldn't at least spring for the fancy elvish shit?"

"You're not going to have the budget for fancy elvish shit soon. I didn't want you to develop a taste for it."

Ranar dropped back to the cushion, rubbing a hand down his face as he laughed. He was fucked. There was no way around it. But at least he had good friends. *What do you have, Sumi? Other really sparkly eyes and great tits and a beautiful laugh? Hmm? Just a corporation pulling your strings.* He shook his head, pushing the thought away. *That's not helping.*

"Who's going to do my weddings if you go out of business? Like, that's *really* going to fuck me over. Thanks for nothing."

Ranar snorted. "That's the way it works. I rely on you, and you rely on me. We all rely on Xavier and his sister to get us through the week. Xavier ages his beans over at Enoch's winery, and Enoch relies on Cal to make sure the menu is supplied."

"And Cal relies on Rourke," Grace added. "He's a parts supplier, keeps all the machinery running."

Ranar raised a hand, emphasizing the point Grace was proving. "And I'm sure he has another small business partner that *he* relies on. It used to be easy. This all used to be easy. And then these big companies get involved and they fuck us all."

Grace poured herself another shot. "Seriously though, are you just gonna throw in the towel? You've been talking about selling the building for as long as I've known you." She paused, swirling her glass for a moment. "This is a good opportunity," she said slowly, at last. "Maybe that's the way you have to look at it, right? You know you'll get a ton of money for it, and I would really hold Jack's head to the fire on that. He owes that to you. *And* I would make him manage an investment portfolio for free afterward."

180

"I really don't think I want to trust these fucking werewolves with any other part of my life."

Grace snorted. "I mean, I get that, but making money is the one thing he's actually good at. Look at this town. Let him ensure you never need to work again. "

Ranar tipped his empty shot glass back, ensuring that there was not a single drop left. *This was a financial decision. Can't keep propping up failing businesses.*

"*Anyway,*" she went on dramatically, "this can be a fresh start for you. You could literally do anything you want! And as someone who started over again, I can tell you, it definitely has its perks. We should all get a do-over after we're thirty. We make all of our major life decisions when we're too stupid and young to see the long-term. When you start over again, you can be smarter. You have the benefit of experience that you didn't have as a twenty-four-year-old. Maybe you go back to court and get full custody. You and Ruma can travel all over the unification. See the biggest everything. The biggest ball of tinfoil. The biggest piece of cheese. All of that."

"You're starting to slur, Grace. And I can't wait to see the judge's face when I tell them I want to redo the custody agreement so that Ruma can have a childhood of roadside attractions instead of private school." He struggled to sit up as Grace laughed, pulling his tail in closer, hoisting himself up upon it, swaying as his head swam. "And I know I've been talking about selling, but that was different. I need to extend this as long as I can for my dad's sake. I don't know what's going to happen with him once we close the doors, this is all he knows. This is the only routine he's ever had. *Yes, I'm going to have to sell the building eventually, and I'm going to rake whoever buys it over the coals. But I'm not giving that up easily and I'm not going quietly. That's what they all want. She can put me out of business, but I can make her fucking miserable first."*

Grace laughed again, downing her drink and sinking low in her chair. "This makes me sad. She was flirting with you *so* hard that day! I thought she was gonna be perfect for you."

Ranar pursed his lips, the end of his tail thrashing in agitation, thinking of that morning at the Black Sheep. "Did I tell you I asked her out?"

From the arm of her chair, Grace's eyebrows shot up.

"We ran into each other outside the coffee shop. It was before the construction barrier even went up. She said yes, too. We were trying to make our schedules line up when—" Ranar cocked his head, pausing, remembering *why* Sumi was in Cambric Creek that morning in the first place. "Mother*fucker*, that was the day she got her permit. That's the only reason why we didn't set a date right then and there, she got a call from City Hall and had to get back to a meeting . . ."

She had looked so beautiful that morning, full of nerves, and he'd done his best to ease her mind. Ranar dropped his head back, groaning.

"She told me she was having trouble with a permit and I . . . I wished her good luck. You're right. I am just a stupid snake."

Grace was curled up on the seat of her chair, holding her stomach as she nearly convulsed with laughter. "*How?* How are you this unlucky? You finally meet someone, she's making eyes like she wants to fuck you on the spot, and it turns out she's the business rival who's going to put you under. Who else has luck like this?!"

"Don't throw up on my floor," he grumbled as she continued to wheeze in laughter. "I don't know how I'm this unlucky, it's not fair."

Grace gasped, still laughing. "Ranar, wait! Maybe *that* is how you get out from under this. What if she's still the one? Maybe you just need to fuck this out of your systems!" She looked incredibly pleased with the suggestion, nodding against the padded arm of the chair. "You should call her tomorrow and make the offer. I'll bet once she gets the double dick down, she won't even care about having a shop anymore. She'd probably be willing to work for *you*!"

"Shhhhhhhh!" He twisted in his seat, throwing a glance down the darkened hallway, feeling the room pitch as he did so. *Fucking tequila.* "Lower your voice! Gracie, I am begging you to see a doctor. That mothman has scrambled your brain."

"I think we're drunk," she stage whispered, still curled in the seat of her chair. "But this is a *very* good idea. You're just a silly snake, you wouldn't know a good idea if it slithered up and bit you." She sat up quickly, pantomiming his side-to-side undulation, both of her hands cupping the air around her thighs. "You just need to give her a taste of the stacked salami, and I'll bet this will all go away. Oh shit, I'm dizzy."

Ranar closed his eyes, willing the room to stop spinning. He would never drink tequila again. *You can't trust something made by centaurs in the desert.* He *wished* it could be that simple. If all he needed to do was pin Sumi down beneath his weight, the tip of his tail holding one of her legs open as he fed one of his cocks into her . . . *Who knows? Maybe she'd be up for taking both.* If all they needed to do was fuck this division out of the way, he would go knock on her door right now. He was certainly horny enough.

But you're not that lucky. And you were horrible to her.

It was a terrible character flaw, Ranar thought, that he was unable to be mean to someone and not feel guilty almost immediately. He had meant what he'd said that day, the afternoon she had turned up in his shop — or at least, he had in the moment. But he had wanted to bite his traitorous tongue out of his mouth the instant the hurt reached her eyes. Her words back to him were just as sharp, just as biting, but he had made the first strike, and everything that came after could be chalked up to defense.

If he could take that back, if he could smooth over this little tiny issue of her shop that would absolutely put his under, if they could tiptoe around the gulf that lay between them and put their differences to rest by fucking, he would. *Bury the hatchet. And then bury it again a little while later just for good measure. And then again in the morning. Just to make sure there's no resentment.*

But he wasn't that lucky. It didn't matter if the thought of her sparkling eyes and full lips made him hard, which they had, several times since the day outside the coffee shop, and it didn't matter if she had flirted with him once or twice. He was only attracted to her because Grace had put the notion in his head in the first place. It didn't matter if she had agreed to go out with him that morning in front of the Beanery's doors, that she'd actually seemed happy at the prospect. Didn't matter whatever possibilities had been there once.

They were enemies now. That was the way it was, and that was simply the way it had to be.

Poison the Well

RANAR

PinksPosies&Pearls: *So like, I know you have a lot going on right now,*

But I'm here with more problems that need solving

OR! Wtf, why didn't lead with this

I'm here to distract you from your problems...with problems of my own

ChaoticConcertina: *Hit me. I need ALL the distractions right now.*

Wait, it's the middle of the night.

Why are you even up?!

PinksPosies&Pearls: *problems*

I require the assistance of someone far less foolish that I am

Okay, so I met someone recently. I know this is going to sound stupid,

but right from the first moment, I felt like it was fate.

Like I was supposed to have met them,

that they were a part of this cosmic plan the universe has laid out for me.

186

Even though I had no real reason to think so, I couldn't shake the feeling they were

going to be this integral presence in my new life.

PinksPosies&Pearls: *I'm sure you can sense where this is going, right?*

I was SO wrong. The universe plunked them down to be my adversary.

And I'm so irrationally upset about it.

I've met WONDERFUL people so far! People who knew my aunt!

I started a class on Japanese tea ceremony and it was SO AMAZING.

I've been here 5 minutes and I'm already getting involved in groups, finding myself.

I should let this roll off my back, but I can't.

It's been weeks and I can't let it go. I can't stop thinking about him.

I need someone to tell me how to get over being HURT so that I can be ANGRY.

ChaoticConcertina: *I don't like this problem.*

Pass.

Can I have a different one?

PinksPosies&Pearls:

ChaoticConcertina: *Sorry. I wish I knew how to help.*

But that hits a little too close to home.

There's a person who has the power to completely turn my life upside down

right now,

And I keep thinking if I hadn't been such an idiot liking them in the first place,

I wouldn't be so upset about it now.

I should be strategizing how to keep them from wrecking me.

Destroying her reputation, starting rumors, letting the air out of her tires!

But all I'm doing is licking my wounds and nursing my hurt feelings and drinking tequila.

Like an absolute chump.

PinksPosies&Pearls: *Omg, ok reset.*

Here I thought I was up in the middle of the night so you could make ME feel better!

If there's one thing teachers excel at, it's gossip.

Did you think I was going to say teaching? Lol, a common misconception.

Teachers are SO GOOD at being fucking terrible to each other.

cutting each other down over the tiniest thing.

Your whole professional life hinges on the teacher's lounge & with the admin.

PinksPosies&Pearls: *I'm up tonight to help YOU, rizzly bear.*

You need to attack her where she lives, play an offensive strategy.

Defense is a last resort!

You don't want to have to defend your home turf, so take the shit talk to hers.

Poison the well, so to speak.

I WISH I could do that here, but this guy already has the home court advantage.

At the school, the well was the admin office. They're trapped at their desks all day.

And all they do is invent drama from something they hear in passing.

and then they pass it on to everyone who comes into the office.

PinksPosies&Pearls: *And seriously, fuck her.*

Whoever she is, get fucked, lady.

You need to figure out where or who your well is.

You don't even need to make something up, it'll distort as it's passed on.

Just sprinkle a little dissent in the well...

And watch the ripples grow.

·♥ · ♥ · ♥ · ♥ · ♥ ·

Anyone who had ever spent more than five minutes within the city limits knew precisely where the gossip well of Cambric Creek could be found.

The Black Sheep Beanery was the busiest business in town, from the moment they unlocked their doors at the crack of dawn each morning until the moment they were locked again behind the last straggling customers at night. Regardless of species, gender, or age, everyone in town passed through the Beanery's doors at least once a week.

It wasn't only that caffeine was a legal stimulant that the entire community was hooked on. It was a place to *see* and *be* seen. If one needed to catch up with someone else, one could likely find them eventually in the coffee shop; if one had good news to share and wanted it to spread as widely and quickly as possible — the Beanery was the site of one's celebration.

Likewise, it was the place to avoid if you were hiding your shame, which was why Ranar had avoided the coffee shop in those weeks after his visit to Jack Hemming's office and the subsequent disastrous encounter with the beautiful stranger to whom he had pinned too many of his hopes. Living in a town that was as addicted to the goings-on of the neighbors as Cambric Creek had its downfalls, and everyone being aware of his was not something he wanted to deal with, not them.

That morning, however, he arose with fresh eyes. Pinky was right. *Poison the well.* Play on the offensive as long as he was able, for he knew without question defense was impossible. Slither into the Black Sheep that morning with his head held high, a picture of tragic composure, the good son, just trying to care for his aging parents in the face of a corporate bully. And most importantly, allow his neighbors to see him doing so.

"Have you tried talking with anyone upstairs?" Xenna leaned over the counter, shaking her head sympathetically as a gaping goblin rang him out.

Ranar knew exactly what she meant by *upstairs*. "I talked with him as soon as the signs went up. He's sympathetic, but what's done is done."

The nymph who was working the espresso machine muttered something in response. Ranar was unable to make out her words over the *hisss* of the machine, but Xenna snorted, nodding her head in agreement. "Can't pay your mortgage with Jack's sympathy."

"What's most upsetting to me is the way she went about all this, you know?" he went on as earnestly as he could. *Remember, you are the victim.* "The other owner, I mean. She's positioned herself as an independent shop, but the corporation's name is above the door. You know, she came into our store, weeks and weeks ago. Asked if I had any tips. I didn't realize then that she was just scouting us out."

The sheep woman made a noise in her throat as Ranar re-coiled himself to the side, tail tucked out of the way, watching as the goblin whipped around to put their head together with the other cashier. *Watch the ripples grow.*

"Ranar, we heard the news."

He turned, tipping his head to meet the towering orc's eye. Magruh was the longtime chief of the Cambric Creek fire department, the same department where another one of Jack Hemmings's sons worked.

"My wife pulled out the headpiece from our wedding just the other night to show the grandkids. Your grandfather made it, not long before he retired. We just hope you'll be able to weather this."

Poison the well. He didn't need to act as he gave the big orc a sad smile. "I'm going to do all I can. I know it would be easier to just sell, but I want to hold on as long as I can for my dad. He still comes in for a few hours almost every day. We don't want him to lose that routine."

The big orc dropped a hand to Ranar's shoulder, patting with a shake of his head. *Watch the ripples grow.* He didn't know if this was specifically what Pinky meant, but he had a feeling it would be the most effective thing he could do. He didn't need to run a campaign of disinformation against Sumi and her shop — the reality was damning enough.

He felt cheerful for the first time in weeks as he left the coffee shop. He had a detour to make before heading to work, a special package to pick up from the refrigerator in his parents' garage, an idea inspired by Coming Gnome 3: The Grimening, ironically enough. Pinky to the rescue again.

His father was no longer able to drive, after too many episodes of forgetting where he was going mid route. That had been the first sign of how bad things would get, Ranar thought. When his father began to forget how to get to the flower shop, the place he'd spent nearly every day since he was a teenager, Ranar understood what the doctors weren't telling them. His mother only felt comfortable driving in the daylight hours, and parked in the driveway, directly adjacent to the door.

It left the garage the perfect place to store something undesirable, and he was hard-pressed to think of anything more undesirable than what he had waiting there. Transporting it was an aggravation. He knew it would be noxious — after all, that was the point — but he had forgotten in his planning that *he* would have to tolerate it long enough to make the delivery each week. *So you keep the window open and stick your head out like a werewolf. And if anyone asks what you're doing, tell them you're just trying to channel your inner Hemming. See what Jack says about that.*

ChaoticConcertina: *Do you want me to come kick this guy's ass?*
I mean, 'kick' is relative, but just say the word & I will eat his face off for you.
I get more annoyed every time you mention how badly this is messing with your head
*Frankly, I think me punching someone might be good for **both** of us.*
I'm not normally the violent type,
but with EVERYTHING I have going on and the way this dick is treating you?
I would love the excuse.
Seriously though, fuck this guy.
Just remind yourself what a pathetic, miserable weasel he probably is.
It's hard to stay affected when you see people for what they are
And he doesn't sound like someone worth affecting you.
You are brave and hilarious and an excellent plant mama. Fuck him for not seeing it.
I'm only half joking, Pinky.

Say the word and I'm on your doorstep with a baseball bat.

Let's break someone's arm.

Do you know what this is? FREE BONE MEAL

PinksPosies&Pearls: *OMG, stop it!*

I mean, don't stop, because this is the first time I've laughed in days.

Thank you. I needed that.

How do you always know what to say to make me feel better?

I tried explaining the situation to the one friend I made here, and she was zero help.

Like, actually NEGATIVE help.

FREE BONE MEAL

This makes us sound like some of those unhinged bee people.

You know what I mean? They find a swarming hive terrorizing a playground and they don't see hysterical children and anaphylactic shock. It's just FREE BEES!

Now that I mention it, the last time I laughed this week was from something you said.

PinksPosies&Pearls: *Thank you for putting up with me.*

Right from the beginning, I've been whining with problems,

*And you **always** make me feel better.*

Your daughter is really lucky to have you in her corner, you know.

The Language of Flowers

SUMI

There was a smoothie shop, off the beaten path, closer to the university and the hospital than the bustling center of town, and it had become her daily go-to. Sumi found it provided a welcome respite on the days she couldn't bear dealing with the staring eyes at the Black Sheep Beanery.

She didn't know how it was that half the town seemed to know her. She barely knew a dozen people, and half of that number were Yuriko's family. Not only did they seem to know her, Sumi got the distinct impression they disliked her. Is it because you're half human? Are humans not welcome here?! Discovering this smoothie shop had been a boon, and it was there that she found the answer to at least one of her unvoiced questions.

Join the local business owners coalition today!

She pounced on the flyer she found on the smoothie shop's long bulletin board, taking a screenshot of the web address, exclaiming in delight that the group had a DiscHorse server. *Oh heck yeah, you're joining that tonight. Finally make some friends.*

It was the first time she'd be using her account for anything other than chatting with ChaoticConcertina in months. She hadn't even checked in on the plant server that brought them together in the first place, nor on any of the other servers where she'd previously spent time scrolling. It was nearly embarrassing to admit that in place of an actual flesh and blood partner, her emotional and conversational needs were being completely met by a stranger online, but it was true.

The worse she felt about the situation with Ranar, the more she looked forward to ChaoticConcertina's messages, and Sumi had reached the point where something had to give. She wanted to meet him. She wanted to see if he really was as perfect for her as he seemed, and if it changed their relationship, they would either weather the storm or know for certain. Either way, she wanted to start living life offline, and knowing whether or not that meant with him or without was unavoidable.

For now, though, she needed to try making some local friends.

DiscHorse had a particular feature with its use of screen names that she appreciated. Different names could be applied to different groups one joined, allowing her to stay anonymous, unless she happened to share another group with one of the members. It was useful, as she had learned very quickly that much of the digital bullying her students dealt out occurred in private DiscHorse servers.

Even if it didn't appear she was doing anything other than typing on her classroom laptop, Sumi always kept an open ear, surreptitiously jotting down anything that sounded useful. She'd acquired the name of several of those private servers over the years, infiltrating them with one of her handful of sock puppet names. She had discovered a widespread test sharing scheme, in addition to identifying a handful of previously under-the-radar bullies. Anonymity was vital.

She had her finger poised over the button to join the business owners' server, doing so on her main account, but something tickled at the back of her mind, staying her hand. *Assess the vibes first. Some of these people are sus.*

She agreed with her inner tween, toggling over to one of her generic screen names, unconnected to her shop in any way. Sumi was shocked to have her suspicions proven right almost immediately.

Well, I certainly won't be using her for anything.

I don't care how nice she is, it's a point of principle.

Right! It's the principle of the thing!

AND she's brand new in town? Like I don't want to be that person, but . . .

*We all know you're **that** person, Skreeva*

Sumi scrolled back, and back and back, reading message after message of solidarity and support with the owner of *The Perfect Petal*. They vowed not to do business with her, vowed not to welcome her into the community. They *hated* her.

And there was Ranar, she realized. Not many messages, but just enough to engender sympathy, just enough to make it clear that *she* was the villain in his story.

It made her inexorably sad. She spent the entire evening curled up in the corner of her perfect, beautiful sunroom, sobbing into a pillow. *This wasn't the way it was supposed to be!* This was her reset, her fresh start. She was supposed to be happy. *Maybe it's you. Maybe you're the reason it's like this.*

No. She couldn't let them win that way. *Look around you! You have this beautiful house. You joined the Japanese club and have already made friends. The business is already doing great. This is like the school, it's just the hot gossip of the week. Give it a month and no one will care. Half of these people already don't care! It's not like all of your orders are for out of town.*

It was true. They could paint her as the villain in this story if it made them feel better, but every person who was choosing to order flowers on the Bloomerang website was just as culpable, weren't they?

He's not going to forget though. He's not going to get over this in a month.

Sumi couldn't explain to herself why she was so bothered by that. *He's one naga. You don't need to care what he thinks.* She didn't. She *knew* that she didn't . . . and yet she did anyway. She'd spent too much time looking forward to *him* in those first few weeks when she was training, spending her time in traffic, daydreaming about discovering Cambric Creek with him, taking it for granted that he'd be a part of her new life . . . and now she needed to let go.

Let it go and forget about him for good.

He hates you, He made that abundantly clear, so stop giving him energy. It's a big enough town. Your paths will probably never cross again.

PinksPosies&Pearls: *You'll be very happy to know that the Princess has settled in*

and she is living large in her new kingdom, surrounded by her subjects.

I managed to find a pink humidifier to accessorize her domain

and she gets perfectly diffused light all day long in this room, it's really

the dream.

I feel like we haven't talked about plants in ages. Isn't that wild?

That was all we talked about at all in the beginning!

Now we mainly talk about ourselves . . .

<u>ChaoticConcertina:</u> *but in a way, it's all the same.*

Things we're growing, nurturing, encouraging to thrive.

Pruning when necessary.

Holding our breaths when we repot, hoping the transition will be painless

for all.

Circle of life and all that poetic shit.

Sorry, I'm a day drinker now.

So you need to ignore at least a good 40% of my pontificating.

<u>PinksPosies&Pearls:</u> *Nope, I think your pontifications are perf*

I know to other people it probably seems silly, talking to a stranger

about houseplants.

But I don't know if I would've been brave enough for this repotting

adventure alone.

I have a confession. I keep thinking it's time we met.

See if we make each other laugh in person or if we're only funny behind

a screen.

Obviously not until after your daughter's visit, I don't want to take a single second of that.

__PinksPosies&Pearls:__ I know you're going through a hard time right now.
And I know you really don't want to talk about it Otherwise you would be.
And I know you're much more comfortable helping with MY disasters.
Just remember I'm here to help you through a case of root rot.
Whenever you need to unload whatever you're carrying.
And hey, we have the drop on some fresh bone meal, so things are already looking up!

There was something rancid outside her door.

She wasn't sure how long it had been there, because she and the rest of the staff used the back door, but now the day was here. She was finally opening *Pink Blossom* to the public. This was what she had envisioned, all of those days as she toiled away in the classroom. A beautiful flower shop, fragrant and feminine, cheerful customers and the even more cheerful chime of her cash register.

Nowhere in her daydream had there been this revolting, stomach-turning smell, like something dead. She gagged a little, fishing out her keys and quickly escaping into the eucalyptus and rose scented interior of the store.

Ugh, it's probably a dead squirrel or something. She peered out the window, craning her neck to see the unfortunate critter, but there was nothing visible. The clean sidewalk, the decorative, wrought-iron trash bin the city emptied weekly, the street beyond, still bearing the water marks of its early-morning cleaning. Sumi frowned. There was no sign of what could have been causing the smell.

You're right, it's probably a dead animal at the curb. The city department would likely dispose of it in the morning. *For what we're paying in property taxes, they'd fucking better.* Fortunately, the smell didn't carry into her shop.

Opening at all had felt like a hard-fought battle.

It was already *Pink Blossom's* third week in business, and she'd still not had the experience of her daydreams, her beautiful, dreamy-looking little shop unknown to all eyes but hers. They were simply too busy, the orders coming in a non-stop deluge each morning until she turned off the system. Sumi knew she could have stemmed the tide, set the minimum order amount higher, but she was too new for that, according to her Bloomerang managing partner.

"You don't want to start fiddling with the system too deeply, not yet. Get your shop's name out there first, that's the whole point. If a business has one of your arrangements on their desk and it starts to wilt, are they going to go online and start the whole order process from scratch? No, they're going to scan the QR on your card, and now you have a built-in customer. Trust the process, Sumi. I know it's overwhelming at first; your staff just needs to find their rhythm."

That was the goal, she'd told the designers the following morning — find their rhythm enough to unlock the doors. After the morning meeting, she'd gone to the front to pull from the coolers for the morning's first deliveries, baskets and vases that had been made at the end of the previous day. Seff and Doona had proved to be their most valuable hires, bringing along the experience of having worked in several Bloomerang-branded shops in Bridgeton.

The Bloomerang website, they'd explained, was built on a handful of base products. Four different baskets and four different vases, the basis of everything else offered. "If you have those pre-made, all we have to do is add flowers to bring it to value, depending on what they want."

It had been the game changer they'd needed, entering the second week of business with no slowing in sight. As she'd pulled the baskets from the cooler, Sumi had looked around her beautiful shop, understanding now why the footprint of her sales floor was barely half the size of the backroom. *You're nothing but a bouquet sweatshop.*

She was determined to prove him wrong, open her doors, let the whole of Cambric Creek see her beautiful shop. Near the front door was a four-foot section of wall covered in plants and live greens, the Pink Blossom logo rendered in glowing neon. Sumi had longed for the day when they would be able to turn the sign on, encouraging customers to take advantage of the social media ready photo op. Now the day was here, the rhythm found; a system that worked for them.

And isn't that what you want? To be successful? She did. Without question, she did. This was *her* dream. *But did you want to be successful like this? This isn't what you envisioned at all.* The question nagged at the back of mind, the reality of her shop so night-and-day-different with her naive daydreams that it kept her up at night, but she had reached a consensus with herself, at least for the time being. She would open the shop doors every morning, for just a few hours a day. It wasn't what she had envisioned, but it satisfied the inch beneath her skin.

The first customers through the door were a pair of shifters, gagging as they pushed the door shut behind them. "What is that fucking smell?!"

Sumi felt her grin falter as one of the women exclaimed, ignoring her cheerful greeting. "Something in the street, I think," she forced out, still smiling. "I hope they get it picked up soon. Fortunately, we smell lovely in here."

It proved to be a common refrain. She didn't have many customers come in, but each one that did mentioned the offensive odor outside her door.

"I didn't see anything in the street," an amphibious woman corrected her, nearly retching as she burst into the shop. "Maybe it's something in the trash."

Sumi nodded, cheeks burning. They were all looky-loos, just coming in to check her out, but that was fine. She didn't need their sales through the front door, but neither did she want the reputation of smelling like the dump. "Fortunately, the trash pickup is tomorrow."

Sumi watched with her own two eyes as the bin was emptied the following morning, breathing a sigh of relief. *Today's going to be a good day.*

That was, at least, until the very first troll through the door did so with her hand clasped over her mouth, just a short while later. "This whole corner smells disgusting." She peered around suspiciously, as though the source of the smell might be coming from Sumi's tree. "I really don't think it's sanitary for you to even be open."

Her smile felt frozen as she picked up her phone, once the troll left, hiding her face again, dialing City Hall.

"Miss, I don't know what you want us to do. It was picked up this morning."

Sumi glowered, wishing the bored-sounding voice on the phone could see her. "I understand they picked up the trash this morning, but obviously they left something behind. They need to come back and get it."

A long-suffering side from the voice on the phone. "Our trucks have very tight routes. We don't make repeat runs, because that would mean someone else doesn't get their trash picked —"

"I don't care," she interrupted, struggling to keep her voice from rising. *Do **not** let them make you the Karen. You are being unfairly targeted.* Hedda popped her head around the corner, eyebrows raised. "Can't you send someone to come out and check it? Call that guy from the planning commission, his name was Owen. He liked shooting orders, see what he's doing this morning. It smells like a dead body outside my door, and it's affecting my business!"

She was fuming when the city truck finally made its way around to their trash can, the *following* afternoon. Even opening the front door made the noxious odor suck into the shop, leaving her with no choice but to keep the *closed* sign in the window.

The orc driving the truck pulled a face as he approached the bin. She watched him pull up the nearly empty bag, knotting it and tossing it into the flatbed of his pickup before peeling off his gloves and turning for her door.

"Yeah, it was something in the trash. Just unlucky that someone dumped their take out right after pickup. The smell should go away now."

Sumi thanked him profusely, insisting he take a wrap of roses home for his wife on the house, waving as he pulled away . . . when her eyes narrowed. *Just unlucky my big bouncy ass.*

She walked back to her desk, after the truck pulled away, pondering the orc's words. *Unlucky* was having something noxious dumped in her trash in the first place. Having something dumped again, immediately *after* pickup, *after* the original something noxious was removed, was sabotage.

She stared at the shelf above her desk, where the most recent bouquet rested, her most recent reminder. Chrysanthemums, once again, bright and cheerful . . . and a single black dahlia at their center. She had retaliated, of course, not willing to back down from his intimidation, by sending him a dish garden of yellow hyacinths.

At least once a week a new bouquet arrived. Lilies and narcissus, carnations and even once a small pot of basil. *The fucking audacity!* Hedda and the gnome twins had watched open-mouthed as Sumi stamped around the shop, ranting to herself over the basil for a full afternoon.

As a response, she had sent him a beautiful bouquet of lush yellow roses and the gnomes had nudged each other, watching as she laughed wickedly, wrapping the flowers for delivery.

"Is all this supposed to *mean* something?" Hedda asked conversationally one morning, eyeing the collection of dried flowers from *The Perfect Petal*. "I feel you could both save a lot of money by just, I don't know, *not* sending each other a hundred of dollars worth of lilies every week. This is like, a *very* strange relationship you have together."

"Oh, *he* knows what it means," Sumi had assured her, cackling to herself as she prepared a bud vase with a single daffodil. "And we don't have a relationship."

This, though, was altogether different. This wasn't luck. This was biological warfare, and she wouldn't stand for it.

Calm down, it's done. Let the street air out, and then.

The following morning, Sumi came through the back door cheerfully, humming to herself. She had brought goodies from home, a beautiful flowering begonia to hang outside the front door, which she would prop open today, announcing to the whole town that she was ready to welcome them.

And for Ranar, something even more special.

Hollyhock wasn't the sort of flower you found in a shop. The old-fashioned bloom was common enough in gardens, though, and she had snipped several white stalks that morning, just for him. She would put them in an arrangement with pink hydrangea, female ambition, towering over his fragile ego.

Her good mood lasted all the way through the shop, until she reached the front door. She barely had pushed it open an inch before the smell reached her, the smoothie she had for breakfast threatening to make a reappearance on her shoes.

"Mother*fucker!*"

The echo of her scream reverberated through the shop. Hedda and the blue haired goblin both came running out from the back, probably expecting to see her laying on the floor in a pool of blood.

"I *know* this is him," Sumi raved. "I *know* it is! He has everyone fooled into thinking he's this sweet sap of a snake, oh, poor sweet Ranar, being put out of business by the big bad corporation. What they don't realize is that he's an asshole!"

She dropped her head back, forcing herself to breathe. *What did ChaoticConcertina tell you? Don't give him this much control.*

"I guess we're not opening another week. Fine, that's fine. Gives us more time to work on orders. Let's turn the system back on, Hedda. No reason to waste time up here. I'm going out for a bit. If the police call, someone needs to bail me out."

She felt positively unhinged when she pulled into *The Perfect Petal's* parking lot, practically wrenching the door off the hinges as she swung it open.

The naga inside was not the one she had come to see. The snake woman's eyes widened at Sumi's dramatic entrance, coming around from behind the counter with her brows raised. She was older, in the same age group as Sumi's parents, and she realized this was likely his mother or an aunt. "How may I help you today?"

Calm down. You can't act like a lunatic, you don't want to start yelling at this nice old lady. The crescent of her nails bit into the meat of her palm as she forced herself to breathe normally, gritting out a smile.

"Ranar. I'm here to see Ranar."

It was possible, the woman's eyebrows raised a little higher. "I hope my son has not done something to upset you, Miss." She called out in a language Sumi did not understand, before looking around conspiratorially. "And if he has, put him in order. We can't let them forget who is in charge in a relationship."

She knew her face was bright red by the time he came around the corner, eyes instantly narrowing when he saw her. His mother had turned, heading into the back room as he came out, pausing to swat at his arm with the stack of envelopes she carried. "Don't give her that look! Don't give *any*one that look, who raised you?!"

She bit down her laughter as he closed his eyes, exchanging hissed words with his mother until she disappeared. The glare was back instantly, and she met it with narrowed eyes of her own.

"I thought I told you I didn't want to see you in here again."

"I assumed that was personal business. I'm here with a delivery." She slapped the wrap down on the counter, ignoring the way the end of his tail swished about.

Ranar snorted derisively. "Let's see what tired tidings you bring today." He huffed as he unwrapped the flowers, rolling his eyes. "You know, I don't think pink hydrangea actually works the way you want it to."

"Yes it does," she snapped. "It works fine. This is your outsized ego, too showy for its own good."

She waited for him to say something snide about her hollyhocks, but he only squinted. "This isn't gladiolus . . ."

Sumi frowned. "No. It's . . . it's hollyhock. C'mon, seriously?"

Ranar looked at her askance. "A garden flower? Sorry, I don't know this one." He pushed the arrangement back across the counter, sliding it towards her as if he were rejecting a meal she had just served.

She balled her fists, shaking one at hand before slapping the counter. "It means female ambition!"

He snorted again. "I think you just made that up. I've definitely never read that before."

"Well, two seconds ago you thought it was a gladiolus, so maybe you don't know as much as you think you do."

Sumi was frustrated with herself. She was no longer trembling in rage, no longer felt the desire to hit him. *What is wrong with you? Punch him! You **want** to hit him!* She didn't, that was the problem. She never had. Biting her lip, she took in the sight of his rolled-back sleeves, forearms on full display like a slut, making her squirm. His disdain, she decided, was harder to take personally when it came fringed in his thick black lashes.

"Will you please stop putting dead body parts in my trash can? I know it's you, don't bother denying it."

The grin that slid over his handsome face showed he had no intention of denying it. *Not in any way that counted.* "I have no idea what you're talking about. Thanks for the nice flowers, I guess. This weed," he nudged the corner of her hollyhock, "means nothing to me, though. So this was just a nice gesture."

"Oh, you are the biggest dick."

He laughed, deep and musical, making her shiver. "Yes, I do. But I'm still not going to pretend this stick means *female ambition*. You're going to have to take the L on this one."

"I didn't say *have*, I said—" Sumi cut off, fuming, realizing he was still grinning. *You're letting him win! He's playing you like one of your fucking students.* "You know what's funny about that?" she countered, changing tactics. "I *wanted* to find out. I wanted to go out with you so badly, because you seemed so nice. I thought you were *so* handsome. You knew flowers! We would have something in common, right off the bat. I wanted to find out *everything* about you."

She looked pointedly down his body, her gaze moving beyond the hem of his button-down shirt, buoyed when he swallowed hard. They were practically touching now, she realized, not realizing that they had both edged closer as they spoke, keeping their voices low. Just another few inches and she'd be bumping his broad chest.

"But then you were so mean, for no good reason." She held up a hand, preventing the rebuttal she could tell he had forming. "I know *you* think it was a good reason. But I still don't get it. I have never, not a single time in my life, ever once lived in a place where there was only *one* florist. Only *one* drugstore. *One* grocery store. *One* doctor's office. It's weird, because I don't ever remember the owners of the two hardware stores putting bags of flaming dog shit on each other's porches even though they both sold hammers. Or the two different car lots setting each other's dumpsters on fire. Almost like they were able to coexist and be friends!"

She broke off to take a breath, swallowing hard. Ranar had averted his eyes from hers. *Please, please just hear me.*

"I know you want very badly to believe that I personally set out to get you, but that was never, *ever* my intention."

His mouth had flattened out, eyes dimming. He was quiet for a long moment, just long enough for her to let herself hope. Hope that they could get over this feud, and start over again as peers. They might never be more than that, but at least they could be friends.

"I'm not surprised you don't understand."

Sumi turned her eyes up, biting her lip. *Please let us move forward from this.*

"I don't know, you're right. Maybe if you had opened just another flower shop, maybe we could have been. Friends. More. But you didn't. Your business is *specifically* designed to crush mine. It may not have been your personal intention, but you're still part of it. So you didn't mean it personally, and you think all's forgiven? Am I supposed to thank you for blowing up my life? Because that makes you just another bottom feeder, preying on those of us who have put a lifetime into this industry so that you could stroll in and treat it like an assembly line."

She sucked in a small gasp, not expecting that he'd be able to hurt her feelings even worse than he did previously. *Don't cry in front of him. Don't give him the fucking satisfaction.*

"You're right, it was never my *personal* intention to hurt your family's business," she squeaked out, heat moving up her neck. Sumi didn't know if it was tears of sadness or rage, and suspected it was a bit of both. "But you've made everything pretty fucking personal since day one. I guess I dodged a bullet. I'm probably much better off stopping at that toy store over on Commerce, pick up the naga model. Get the full experience of fucking you while I'm fucking you over, right? Because you're ugly where it counts."

She was horrified with herself the instant the words were out, but it was too late. She didn't know what it was about him that brought out the worst in her. If she'd learned nothing else from middle schoolers, it was how to hurt feelings, and he made every rude thought that popped into her head bubble to the surface without a moment wasted for regret. *Here she is, the bitch you heard about.*

Ranar bent as his lip curled back, his face the scant inches from hers. "I've seen what they carry. It's a pretty poor imitation, if you must know. Definitely won't give you an accurate experience. But it's just a cheap plastic knockoff, so that's perfect for you. I'm sure you have puppies to kick on your way back to your sweatshop, so please, don't let me stop you from leaving."

Her nerves were jangling by the time she arrived back at the shop. She wanted to go home. She wanted to go home and cry, but home didn't actually feel like *home* yet. Nothing here in Cambric Creek did. The only thing that felt like home was sitting in front of her laptop screen with a glass of wine, giggling over whatever Chaotic-Concertina had to say for the day.

She was considering telling Hedda that she was just going to head out when she slipped back into the door, hearing their conversation carry out to the hall.

"His dad has dementia, but he still goes into the shop every day. It's probably good for him to have a routine."

Hedda made a sympathetic noise, agreeing with whatever Seff was talking about. "That's so difficult to deal with. My aunt had dementia at the end, and it was really hard on my cousin and her family. By the time she passed, I think it was nearly a relief for everyone. But then there's guilt added to your grief and it's just a mess. I wouldn't wish that on anyone."

In the hallway, her stomach flipped as Seff continued.

"Yeah, it's such a shame. They're such nice neighbors, too. I live on the other side of the development, but I see Ranar coming and going every day, he probably spends as much time at his parents' house as he does at his own. I know she thinks there's enough business for everyone, but we've worked in these shops—"

"—and they suck up all of the orders," Doona finished. "The only thing she's gonna have to work for is his wedding business. But I think there's a lot more sentiment attached there for customers."

Sumi stiffened. They were talking about Ranar. *And you.* She reached out for the wall, creeping to the front as silently as she could, tears burning in her eyes. She didn't know about his father. He had mentioned to her that very first day that his shop was a family business, but if she had known . . .

*What would you have done? Nothing different. What **could** you have done? Everyone everywhere has something going on at home, that doesn't mean you're responsible for all of it. This is where you live now. This is your dream too!*

Her little voice wasn't wrong, but neither was he for his anger, Sumi decided, not bothering to wipe away the tears that tracked down her face.

She stayed in front the next few hours, greening in baskets and vases until she was cried out, earning Doona's cheer when the gnome came waddling to the front.

As soon as she was home that evening, Sumi poured herself a glass of wine, swallowing several tablets of ibuprofen along with it before settling into the sofa with her laptop. She desperately needed something comfortable and familiar. She needed to talk with her friend.

But first . . . she couldn't help herself.

Checking the business owner's server was a punishment she couldn't stop doling out to herself. *Maybe it's one you deserve.* Just as she had suspected, the topic had already moved on. *Attention spans are short and there's always fresh drama brewing somewhere.* The current conversation was centered around a festival coming up. Sumi scrolled, looking for his name, but he wasn't there.

Instead, she scrolled back, back and back, delving through the back scroll until she found him there, accepting someone's well wishes, back when they had all discussed her shop.

Ranar_PerfectPetal

It was the required handle, she had noticed. Every other participant in the conversation had something similar — their first name followed by their business. *Ranar.* Sumi clicked his name wondering if he had bothered adding a profile. He hadn't. Username, He/Him. Nothing else. Sumi scrolled to the bottom of the page, expecting more disappointment. *Three mutual servers.*

She blinked. She had gone a bit of a spree after first signing up on the platform, joining more than a dozen different servers. A forum for sharing 90s pop-culture. Servers for plants, servers for teachers. A *Coming Gnome* server, hilariously. She tried to imagine the handsome naga as a fan of the movie franchise from her childhood, and couldn't do it.

She tapped the screen. *Which three could they be? Who are you other than an asshole, Ranar_PerfectPetal?* The Flower Market. Unsurprising, given his profession. She had joined the server months and months earlier, after learning that folks occasionally traded clippings of rare houseplants, in addition to heirloom flower seeds. The Vinery. She nearly choked on the sip of wine she had just taken. This was the houseplant server she had joined when her little philo was limping along, the server in which she had met ChaoticConcertina. The last server was, unsurprisingly, the Cambric Creek Business Owner's Coalition. *How?*

The sun went in and her automatic lights flickered on, as she hunched over the screen, squinting. She could figure this out methodically, she decided. Starting with the house plant server, she proceeded to tap on every member, assessing their profile. *She/Her, one shared server. He/Him, one shared server.* One by one, Sumi had made it through nearly the entire list, only finding a few people with whom she shared more than membership in The Vinery, and all three of them were only additionally in The Flower Market.

She didn't understand. *Is he covert? Is this just a weird glitch? This is just the app glitching, right?* So convinced was she that her phone was malfunctioning, that she stopped before even reaching the bottom of the server list, restarting her phone and checking to see if the app needed an update. Reopening DiscHorse, she quickly tapped back to Ranar's profile. *Three shared servers.* Sumi pursed her lips. Back to The Vinery. She was nearly at the bottom of the list, she realized, only three names left. Someone she had never interacted with a single time, herself . . . and ChaoticConcertina.

Something moved within her, a stone turning in her stomach, sitting heavily on her insides. She felt queasy, almost able to catch a slight whiff of that rotting, rancid smell from the garbage bin outside her shop door. Her finger was trembling as she reached forward, tapping on his name.

He/Him. Three shared servers.

The Vinery. The Flower Market.

And the Cambric Creek Business Owner's Coalition.

Sorry Is the Hardest Word

RANAR

ChaoticConcertina: *I hate being mean to people.*

I hate the way it makes me feel.

*Even when I think it's justified, and even when it **is** justified.*

I hate the feeling I get in the pit of my stomach,

the knowledge that I've just ruined someone's day.

And then I think I'm just being needlessly narcissistic.

ChaoticConcertina: *Because who am I? I'm a nobody!*

Why should my words matter?

*But then I see in the other person's eyes that they **did** matter, and I hate myself*

for it.

Even if I meant what I said, the second it's out, I just want to beg for forgive-

ness.

And I hate that too.

PinksPosies&Pearls: *I know exactly what you mean.*

Sometimes I have no ability to hold it the mean thoughts in my head

And I'm never mean first, at least, I try not to be.

I'm not a confrontational person.

There are just some people who bring it out in us, I guess.

People think the ability to say exactly what you mean the moment you want to say it

is a gift, but I think getting tongue-tied is better.

It gives you a chance to breathe & you don't have to live with the hateful thing you said.

*But for what it's worth, **I** appreciate that you don't like being mean.*

There are too many mean people in the world this week.

Don't be too hard on yourself.

Because even if you said something you regret, You're NOT mean.

You're one of the nicest people I know. "Know."

And if it makes you feel any better, I would forgive you.

I'm forgiving you right now, on their behalf.

He had been living under the delusion, those interminable weeks, that if he ever got the chance to tell Sumi exactly what he thought of her, he would instantly feel lighter. He had been positive that some of the weight he carried would magically lift, if only he was presented with the opportunity to unburden himself of the black bile in his heart, churning every time he thought of her sparkling eyes. Instead, Ranar thought miserably, it had only made him feel worse.

It didn't help that his mother and daughter were conspiring to gaslight him.

The conversation he'd had earlier that morning with Ruma had left his prana agitated, his nerves frazzled, and a gnawing restlessness beneath his skin that he was certain could only be assuaged by either finding her and apologizing for his unnecessary nastiness, or taking Grace's advice and fucking it out.

"Daddy, was that your girlfriend?"

He wasn't a young naga anymore and his body reminded him of that fact frequently. Ranar whipped his head around at Ruma's words, feeling a twinge go down his back as he did so.

"No! Baby, Grace is just a good friend. She and I have been working together since she moved here."

Ruma wrinkled her nose, a look of disgust crossing her face. "Ugh, no! Not Grace! I know *Grace* isn't your girlfriend."

He had never before had his feelings hurt by someone rolling their eyes, but his daughter's dramatic sigh, dropping her head back and rolling her eyes as if he were an empty-headed potato came close.

Ranar narrowed his own eyes in response, wondering why Grace was so obviously not his girlfriend. *What's wrong with Grace? She's pretty!*

"No, that other lady. The one you were arguing with."

His whole body had stiffened. *Who else were you arguing with in front of her?* He racked his brain, hoping against hope that he had picked a fight in the parking lot of the grocery store while he and Ruma made a pizza topping pitstop a few nights earlier, but nothing came to mind. Nothing other than that disastrous day Sumi had come into the shop, looking like some fertility goddess there to seduce him.

"The lady who came to the shop," Ruma had clarified, making it clear she was unimpressed with his slack-jawed response. "She was super nice, by the way. I talked to her the last time. She definitely passed the vibe check. Why are you fighting?" She glared suspiciously. "You shouldn't fight. Paati said any nag who tries to marry me should treat me like a goddess. You should be treating your girlfriend like one too."

Ranar felt his neck heat, twisting in the direction of the back coolers. "Your Paati shouldn't be worried about anyone marrying you for a long, long time," he called out, loud enough for his mother to hear.

"That–that's not my girlfriend. I don't have a girlfriend, Noodle. I am *too* busy with everything here—"

"Are you sure?" Ruma looked at him skeptically. "She sure seemed like your girlfriend. That's how you talked to each other."

"I thought you just said we were fighting?"

"Yeah, but you were *fighting* like she's your girlfriend." The look she gave him was almost pitying, fitting he thought. The closest he'd come to a relationship since the divorce was a stranger online. Being pitied by his fourth grader sounded about right.

"I don't know, daddy. Your rizz is *mid*. And it shouldn't be! But you should make up with her, I like her."

"Noodle—"

"You already said that you don't notice things," she pointed out, giving him the same scathing look he'd received from her grandmother his entire life.

"I hope you're telling him to make up with that pretty human."

His mother came slithering out of the back, serpentining around the counter at just the right moment, and Ranar refused to believe it wasn't a pre-choreographed move orchestrated by the two of them. *You really are an empty-headed potato.*

He'd pressed his tongue to the roof of his mouth, hands closing into fists as he swayed, forcing a smile after a moment. "She's sylvan, actually. Still not my girlfriend. I need to go pick up the wire racks from Grace for the weekend, so if the two of you are planning on inventing some new chapter of this pretend relationship while I'm gone, just remember that I've always wanted to go to the Amazon. So if the fictitious honeymoon is in the planning stages . . ."

"Is she related to Sumiko?"

His mother's voice stopped him in the doorway. Sumiko had been a good friend of hers, and he knew his mother had taken the sylvan's death earlier that year hard.

"I–I don't know, mom. She's new in town, she owns the flower shop off Main Street that's probably going to put us out of business by the end of the summer. Not my girlfriend. That's all I've got. I need to do this before it starts storming later."

He should have gone straight to the farm and avoided the rainy weather, but the Beanery beckoned and if he didn't crush the headache he'd been nursing since Sumi's visit with caffeine, he might expire before that weekend's wedding. It was a fine plan, he told himself, exiting the coffee shop, taking a long gulp before opening his umbrella.

At least, it was until he passed the printer on the way back to the parking lot. The door to the shop swung open and caught on the wind, smashing against the wall. Likewise, the person coming out only took a few steps before the lid to the box they carried was similarly wrenched on the wind, half a dozen printed flyers sailing out into the street, instantly turning into a soggy, mucky mess that littered the pavement. She yelped when they did so, the umbrella she was attempting to hold slipping on her shoulder, its delicate arms no use against the wind tunnel of Main Street, flipping backwards as she cried out again.

Of *course* it was her. Of course it couldn't have been anyone else in the whole fucking town. Of course he was going to be cursed to run into her over and over again, like the wretched eagle to his Prometheus, turning up each day with a smile to enchant him and peck out his liver.

Ranar wanted to smile at her misfortune; wanted to snicker at her distress. He wanted to go slithering past her with enough force to splash her ankles and dirty the hem of her dress . . . But as soon as all of those terrible thoughts occurred to him, he felt a twist in his chest and a flip in his stomach.

He couldn't. The mean, petty little snake on his shoulder may have wanted him to, hissing atrocities in his ear, but he couldn't even think it without feeling guilty instantly. *Would you want someone treating Ruma that way? Of course not.* There was no question of what he was going to do.

He had taken the box from her before even thinking through his plan, pushing his coffee cup into her hand, the umbrella he carried shifting from his hands to his tail, held over her and angled against the wind as he fixed the lid on her box.

Sumi gaped up. Her eyes narrowed, disdain filling them for the briefest moment, and he wondered if she was going to fling the coffee down and snatch the box back . . . But the look passed quickly. Her teeth sunk into that full lower lip, and he couldn't identify the expression in her eyes then. *Ruma probably could. She's right, you're hopeless.*

"You really are pathetic, you know that?"

His voice was rougher than he'd intended. He at least *sounded* like someone who hated her, even if his actions at the moment weren't quite lining up with that. *No. It's because you're not an asshole. And even if she's a backstabbing bottom feeder, you don't need to let her make you worse than you are.* She wore large gold hoops in her ears, their movement bringing his eye straight to the most kissable spot on her neck.

"Yeah, I know." Her voice was toneless in her agreement. "You didn't need to do that, but thank you for doing it anyway. I'm, um, I'm going back to my —"

"Obviously." He handed the box back to her, having closed the lid entirely. Their fingers brushed as she handed him back the coffee cup, a fraction longer than should have been necessary, like a bolt of electricity he felt shoot up his arm and straight to his groin. In their sheath, his cocks stirred. *No, absolutely not. Not now. She's the enemy.* "Keep your hand on the top of it, this wind isn't going to let up until we turn the corner."

Her dress that day was peachy pink with a deep V neck line, similar to what she had worn that morning outside the coffee shop. It was already dotted in raindrops from her brief sojourn without a functioning umbrella, marring the lovely effect. *It's fine, she'll dry.* Ranar kept his eyes trained on the sidewalk before them, not wanting to notice how the color made her skin glow, nor the way the draping fabric hugged her curves.

"I'm sorry." The words tumbled out in an unprepared blurt, not at all the polished apology he'd practiced in his head. "About the other day. I shouldn't have said those things to you. Even if I think some of them are true—" her eyes flicked to his, a ghost of a smile on her mouth, "—I shouldn't have said them. I'm sorry I did."

"I'm sorry too." Her voice was small, so different from her sharp brassiness. He didn't like it, preferred her with a bit of an edge. "For what I said. For what I didn't say. For the things I didn't understand. I'm sorry for all of it."

They continued for the next few feet in silence, and he wondered if he was meant to break it. *Your rizz is mid. That's humiliating, right?* Before he had the chance to draw breath, Sumi cleared her throat.

"Don't you get tired?"

Her voice startled him out of his thoughts, her eyes trained on his tail, watching his rectilinear movement down the sidewalk, her teeth once again finding her lip. He snorted, shaking his head. *Human raised.*

"Don't your legs get tired from walking? I have to imagine that it takes more muscle groups," he pointed out. "Left, right, left, right. I'm exhausted just watching you."

Her eyes flickered up to his, widening slightly, hand flattening over her mouth. "That was probably a really insensitive question, wasn't it."

"Yeah, that's the silliest thing I'm going to be asked today, without question. Nicely done."

From behind her hand, she began to giggle, hunching slightly, staying beneath the protective circle of his umbrella. Ranar tried not to notice how adorable it was.

"I don't know why it seems to me like you have to be so much stronger to move that way. Like, your core muscles and your back . . ." Her eyes flickered to him, voice trailing off as she cleared her throat. "Yeah, that was a real human observation. I'll take L on that one."

"You're going to have to. That was high key cringe."

There. Using the vernacular in the wild. He was rather proud of himself, having committed the entirety of Pinky's cheat sheet to memory. Ruma was less impressed with his attempts to use her slang, groaning and protesting every time he did so at home, but at least he had a slightly better understanding of what she was saying.

Sumi's head swung up, eyes meeting his again, only this time they sparkled, the corners of her mouth turning up in a wide grin. "It was. What is this called? The-the way you're moving now? Clearly I was never very good at biology. Don't ask me to name any of the lakes or rivers in the state either, they're all just Big Water #1 and Big Water #2."

He snorted. "Rectilinear. This movement, I mean. Not a river. You've probably seen this on a small scale in a caterpillar or inchworm. It's not what I prefer, but it keeps the end free." He motioned to the tip of his tail holding the umbrella over her and she flushed, nodding quickly. "Serpentining is the movement most people think of for nagas, that's the side-by-side, but we also use concertina and sidewinding."

Her head swung up, eyebrows raised, but remained silent.

"Basically any movement you'll find in larger snake species we use as well. And if you ask me if I get tired holding myself upright, I'm going to ask you the same thing."

Sumi laughed again, and he ground his teeth as a city truck drove by slowly. *How much poison do you think will stay in the well now that the whole town is probably watching you practically hold her hand all the way back to her store?*

"They're probably on their way to empty the trash. Some asshole keeps putting monkey brains in it or something."

"Fish guts, I think," he clarified. "Or so I would guess. Easier to acquire than monkeys. Did you have success at that place on Commerce?"

Her head whipped to the side, and the sparkle in her eyes made his chest hurt. "I decided to save my money," she huffed. "No sense in ruining my expectations with a cheap knockoff."

The pain spread through his lungs, making it hard to breathe. *Is this a stroke? Do you smell toast?* Blithely unaware of his inner turmoil, Sumi's eyes shimmered with the force of her smile . . . at least, until they trailed down, taking in the rest of his appearance. He could *feel* her eyes on his chest, taking in his sodden shirt, almost as if she'd pressed her palms to his bare skin. The weight of her observance seared him, and for an echoing moment, he couldn't remember if he was meant to be sabotaging her or taking her in his arms, scooping up and bringing her home. *You should treat her like a goddess.*

"Oh no, you're soaked! Wait! You should have this over both of us!"

Ranar stopped abruptly. *What the fuck is wrong with you? Do you even remember who she is, what she's done?* "It's not big enough for both of us," he snapped, heat burning his neck. "If you want to go ahead on your own, be my guest." *It's not big enough for us both and you know it.*

Her eyes filled with tears, nodding miserably. "I know. But I didn't then." She paused miserably, lip quivering for a moment before motioning to the building beside them. "We're here. I usually use this back entrance. I appreciate your help," she murmured, that sad, toneless voice returning. "I-I only meant that I feel bad that you're all wet now. I *do* feel bad, Ranar. I didn't know that it wasn't big enough for both of us. I understand now."

He looked away, unable to tell if it was rain or tears running down her cheeks.

"I-I have a bunch of promotional T-shirts, if you want to just change into something dry until you get back . . ."

"If you give me something that says Bloomerang on it, I'm taking us both back to Main Street and we're going to stand in the middle of the park until we drown."

Her musical laughter tinkled and chimed all around him, breaking the tension, and his stomach twisted again, although this time Ranar knew it was regret that ached within him. Grace was right. How could he be *this* unlucky?

"Okay, I mean, give me a *little* bit of credit. Even I know better than to do that. Do you want to come —"

"No, I don't."

Her mouth snapped shut, her head nodding quickly. He didn't want to go into her shop. Ranar had no doubt that it was lovely, as lovely as its owner, shiny and new and expensive. He didn't need to see exactly what would be replacing him in the community. Sumi nudged down the doorstop before disappearing inside. Ranar could see a tall, middle-aged troll woman peering around the corner at him curiously.

"It's actually from the company who makes floral foam," Sumi called out, returning a moment later. "I would apologize, but I think pink is probably your color."

He recognized the shirt instantly. There was a stack in his own shop, a promotional item sent once or twice a year by the company who made the floral foam. He idly wondered how long it would be until Bloomerang bought them out, one less player on the board. *Another one bites the dust.*

They were tucked beneath the overhang outside the back of her building safe from the rain, for the moment. Sumi stood before him, holding out the pink shirt with a look of uncertainty. The troll, he noticed, had moved her work juuust far enough down the table so that she could see out the door.

Ranar handed Sumi the coffee cup he still held, closing his umbrella and resting it against the side of the building. When he gripped the soaked edge of his shirt, her teeth sank into her lip once more. He wondered if she realized he was going to be completely naked in front of her. *If she didn't want to see,* he rationalized, *she can look away.*

But she *didn't* look away. She seemed glued to the spot, unable to turn and afford him a second of privacy, not even blinking. When he pulled the wet fabric up over his body, Ranar thought he could hear her soft intake of breath, his own eyes fluttering closed as he pulled the wet shirt up and over his head.

She was no longer biting her lip when he reached out to take the bright magenta T-shirt from her hand, another zap of electricity to his cocks as their fingers brushed. Her mouth was open in a soft *O*, and he was positive that lips had never looked as kissable as hers did just then. His eyes followed the movement of her throat as she swallowed hard, once again feeling the weight of her gaze like a brand as her eyes moved over his bare chest and down his stomach.

He had lied, technically. Nagas were well known for being incredibly strong and fast, owing to their enhanced core muscles. The ability to keep one's human half upright while engaging the necessary muscle groups to locomotor their thick tails into forward movement necessitated strength, back and abdominal muscles that were honed from infancy onward.

Sumi's eyes moved down his body slowly, coming to rest, as he pulled the bright pink T-shirt over his head, on his scales. Like his kitsune neighbor, she had landed a few inches higher than where his genital slit actually was. Ranar wondered what her reaction would be if he led her hand, as he had moved the kitsune's, to the right spot, if her fingers would stroke him just as adroitly.

Another soft intake of breath from her, her eyes snapping up to his, her cheeks spotting with color as she realized he'd caught her staring.

"Thanks for the shirt." His voice was low, completely absent of its earlier bite. He wanted to feel her hands on his skin, her nails scraping his nipples and over his stomach; wanted to feel the heat of her breath as he kissed her neck. He dropped his wet clothes into the bag she'd also provided, taking up his umbrella once more. "I'd say have a good day, but I think we both know I'd be lying." It didn't matter what he wanted. It wouldn't do to forget who they were to each other, *what* they were. It didn't make a difference what they might have been, if she had been someone different.

She choked out what was meant to be a laugh, and he tried not to notice the glossy sheen that still spilled from her dark eyes as he turned away.

"Ranar!"

That he did feel behind his groin, the sound of his name on her lips, the caress of her tongue over each letter, making his cocks vibrate within him. Ranar turned, holding his breath, willing himself to keep control.

"Your coffee."

Their fingers brushed again as she stepped out into the rain, arm extended, handing him the cup.

"I'm sorry."

"I'm sorry too," he responded automatically, unsure of what he was even apologizing for at that point. He wanted to taste her skin and determine what was the rain and what were her tears. *You are the unluckiest bastard in the world.*

"I know. I told you, you're forgiven. Have a good day. I *do* mean it."

Ranar grumbled to himself all the way back to his shop, irritated with himself for even stopping in the first place. He hated this war within himself. He needed to go in and have a conversation with his mother, at the very least. They needed to begin discussing what would happen next, which really meant *he* would need to decide what happened next, and then carry the emotional weight of the fall-out for everyone. *Fun times, good times. Love this for me. Maybe you should just sell the building now, call it early, move away while you can still salvage an ounce of dignity.* It was the last thought in his head as he pulled the front door open, hearing the familiar jangle of the bell.

Ruma was at the counter with his father, laughing uproariously as they played a fast-paced card game, one that originated on the island their family had left, one that he had grown up playing with his own grandfather at that same counter, what felt like a lifetime ago.

"Ruma, you have to keep up, you're never going to win that way."

"Thatha, you're too fast!" she squealed, slapping her card down against the glass.

Ranar turned quickly away, a fast sidewind out the door and around the building as he was sucked beneath an unexpected wave of emotion, gasping to keep from breaking down right and there. This wasn't just a used car he could sell off. His family had more history in these walls than they had in the house he'd grown up in, and it didn't matter how much Jack Hemming assured him he could get for the land or how much her eyes sparkled when she looked at him . . . but he didn't know how to just walk away.

One last steadying breath, opening his eyes . . . and meeting the gaze of the goblin from the laundromat, pulling into the lot slowly. Ranar raised a shaky hand, waving slightly as her lips pressed together, her head shaking sadly. He turned away, disguising his despairing laughter with a cough. *Well, you didn't even need to try hard for that one. You're pathetic and everyone knows it.*

She was beautiful and he loved her laugh, and maybe if their paths had diverged somehow, they would have been able to meet under circumstances that allowed a future. But they weren't and they hadn't, and Ranar was certain that was all that would ever matter. *Just watch the ripples grow.*

Take the L for the W

Delulu is the Solulu

SUMI

PinksPosies&Pearls: *Tell me about work. Unburden yourself.*

This is a bullshit-free zone.
You don't have to give me the can-do song and dance.
Tell me about it and make yourself feel better.

ChaoticConcertina: *Ugh, don't make me talk about it.*
I feel like it's the only thing I've talked about in two months.
It's certainly the only thing I've thought about.
If I didn't have all my plants on timers and water tubes, they'd all be dead.
The tl;dr is another business like mine opened just a few blocks from mine.
As it was very recently pointed out to me, that in and of itself **shouldn't** *be a death knell.*
But her business model is designed to eliminate competition.
Hi, it's me, I'm the competition.
She's corporately owned, tested and proven with a bottomless budget.

And her corporate business model is doing exactly what it is meant to.

ChaoticConcertina: *So that basically means the end for me.*

I'm trying not to take it all personally, but it's very hard.

Because what does that mean?

If you make a decision, you're basing it on what will be best for you, person-ally.

All "don't take it personally" means is "we didn't think beyond ourselves."

Pretty soon everything in our lives will be owned by corporations,

whose shareholders are most assuredly taking things personally.

They just won't bother considering anything past their bottom line.

Anyway.

I find myself faced with the unexpected prospect of starting over at my de-crepit age.

I've never done anything but this job.

I've never even worked for someone else before. I have no resume to speak of.

"How do you work on a team?" Don't know, never had to

I guess that was still pretty long for the tl;dr

PinksPosies&Pearls: *I know not giving yourself any credit is kind of your thing,*

But "self employed since the age of 10" is still pretty impressive.

You have skills you're not even considering right now.

Have you thought about what you'll do next?

ChaoticConcertina: *This is going to be incredibly whiny and self pitying,*

look away.

I don't want to think about it. I don't want to DO anything.
I want to stay home and make chili and help my daughter redecorate her bedroom.
I've been taking care of other people for more than half my life with no end in sight.
I've been taking care of this business my whole life.
I supported my wife, took care of our family while she did her surgical residencies.
And then she took my daughter from me and moved four states away.
Now I take care of my parents. My dad is only going to get worse.
ChaoticConcertina: *I'm **still** trying to take care of this business.*
I know this is oldest child syndrome and I'm not the only one, but why am I the ONLY fool capable of making a decision about any-thing?
About everything. All the decisions are mine.
So of course when something goes wrong, that's mine too.
I don't want to do ANYTHING next.
All I want to do is curl up in a dark cave and sleep for the next decade.
And learn to make chili.

PinksPosies&Pearls: *I'm so sorry you have so much on your plate.*
Taking some time off sounds like a good plan, you deserve it.
Although, I feel like you could probably video yourself going to job interviews.
And then monetize the views, because it'll be hysterical.
"If we call your last employer, what would they say?"

"That I'm extremely handsome and would be a good match for your niece.
"

Think of the possibilities!

*Mostly sounds like you need to find someone who will take care of **you** for a change.*

Get you a sugar mama.

> **<u>ChaoticConcertina:</u>** *Honestly, that sounds amazing.*
> *If you know how to find one, send me tips.*
> *Because I've been told my rizz is mid by my own flesh and blood.*
> *And I don't think that lines up the sugar mamas.*

I have a large extra hot honeycomb latte for Sumi."

She shifted through the press of bodies, making her way to the pick-up counter. The side counter Ranar used was much more convenient, she had to admit. *Well, you'll be using that one soon. With him.*

"That was really nice of you, Sumi." The sheep woman's voice was almost reluctant, her eyes flicking over to Sumi once she finally made it to the counter. After a moment, though, her mouth turned up with a hint of a smile. "To send something. That note was really nice. Thank you."

Xenna's mother-in-law had passed away unexpectedly, Sumi had learned from Yuriko. She sent the planter from Pink Blossom, an acknowledgment from one business to another, but the note she included to the Beanery's co-owner had been heartfelt.

"Of course, I'm so sorry for your family's loss. Is everyone doing okay?"

In any other coffee shop in the city, this sort of chit chat at the pick-up counter was unacceptable. Verboten. The line moved quickly and efficiently and chit chat was a deviation from efficiency. Here, though, Sumi had noticed this was where relationships were made and broken. Xenna and her brother Xavier were the arbiters of whom was worthy of conversation in Cambric Creek, and if they stopped to chat, you could hold your head up a bit higher upon your exit, knowing you were bestowed with a golden seal.

"Yeah. I mean, I am. My husband is upset of course, but our kids are taking it pretty hard. She wasn't my mother, but she was a really good grandmother."

"There's a book," Sumi said, fishing a business card and pen out of her bag. "It's called *See You In My Dreams*, it's really great for young children experiencing loss. Especially one that's close to them, like this." Xenna raised an eyebrow as she wrote down the title, able to envision the cover clearly. Sumi smiled wryly as she passed the card across the counter, taking her coffee. "My mom died when I was young, and it helped me a lot. I know it's still in print. Anyway, my condolences."

"Thank you *so* much, Sumi. Have a good day!"

Playing the dead mom card, she thought, holding her head a bit higher and she turned away from the counter, the recipient of Owner-to-Owner Chit Chat. That's what she would tell ChaoticConcertina. *Ranar.*

The revelation that they were one and the same had turned her world inside out. Sumi didn't know what to do. She didn't know what to say. She didn't know how she could go on casually chit chatting with ChaoticConcertina while she and Ranar were at war, couldn't listen to him make allusions to everything going wrong in his life fully knowing she was the reason why.

But neither could she give him up.

She knew there were some people who would roll their eyes at her placing too much importance on an online friendship, but it wasn't the 90s anymore, no matter how many Coming Gnome movies she still owned. It was a short leap from an online relationship to the real world, as evidenced by the dozens of dating apps, a relationship started by swiping left or right on one's phone screen, at dinner together an hour later, in bed shortly after that.

ChaoticConcertina was her rock. He was empathetic and smart, made her laugh and gave good advice and always knew exactly what to say to make her feel better. Most of all, most importantly, he was excessively kind. *The kind of man who would apologize to his enemy, after she had confronted him at his business, where she had been told not to come again.* Seeing him so shortly after her revelation had nearly upended her, but it had been cathartic, walking with him in the rain, her tears rolling down her face, washed away in the deluge. *The kind of man who would hold an umbrella over that same enemy, knowing it wasn't big enough to keep him dry. Knowing there wasn't enough business for them both.*

And then the icon indicating she had a new message had flared to life, and there was only one person from whom the message could be. It was him, of course it was him, telling Pinky — telling *her!* — how much he hated being mean to people, how much he disliked the way it made him feel. How he wanted to beg for forgiveness, even though he had meant what he had said.

Sumi was glad there was no expectation of video chatting, because she was a blubbering mess by the time she had read through his message, wheezing to breathe as she responded.

And of course she forgave him. Forgave for everything, because how could she not? *He* was apologizing to *her,* when she was the one who had ruined his life. But, she reminded herself, ChaoticConcertina didn't know that. She wanted to beg for his forgiveness in return, but he only thought he was venting to his friend, venting honestly and unselfconsciously.

That, more than anything, made up her mind.

She could not, *would* not give him up, and that made her decision on what to do crystal clear. She couldn't let go of ChaoticConcertina, which meant she needed Ranar too, to fold them together into the perfect partner. They would have to meet in the middle, find a way to meld the differing sides of their personalities. It didn't matter if he hated her now. She was going to make that snake love her if it was the very last thing she ever did. *And live happily ever after.*

* * *

Yuriko, at least, was sympathetic to her plight. Sort of. As much as Yuriko was sympathetic about anything, Sumi decided.

"Okay, remind me again who we hate? Because absolutely, fuck that guy. Who needs a conceited ass lick like that in their life? Nobody, that's who. Or do we *not* hate him now?"

Sumi hunched, laughing at Yuriko's casual vulgarity as they set up for the tea group. She would be eternally grateful to the ogress for welcoming her in with open arms. As soon as Yuri learned that Sumi had moved to Cambric Creek with no one, no family or friends or support system, she had practically adopted her, despite being nearly the same age. *Pink Blossom* was closed on Sundays, and she'd spent nearly every weekend doing something with the Nippon club or else, the ogress and her family.

"Why are you agreeing with me if you don't even know who I'm complaining about?!"

Yuri shrugged. "Hey, I'm just trying to be supportive. You were mumbling about some asshole, I just agreed." She raised an eyebrow as Sumi laughed again. "*Who* are we talking about?"

"Ranar. You know, *The Perfect Petal*?"

"That's right, your feud. You're the bitch from out-of-town corporate fembot drone dead set on ruining poor sad Ranar's life." Yuriko threw up her hands in self-defense. "I mean, obviously those aren't *my* words. What did he do now? He *seems* like a nice guy. A little oblivious. You know what I mean, my brother is the same way. Book smart but low perception. Need their hands held a little. Don't tell me he's a flasher in the park or something."

"No!" Sumi cried, shaking her head in amazement. "How would that even work, his balls are on the inside! No, I'm just . . . I'm done feuding with him. I've officially launched Operation Friendship. I just need to get him on board and he's making it so *difficult*."

Yuriko snorted in laughter, pulling open the folding table they used for practice. "I feel like that's a pie-in-the-sky dream, but it depends on what you mean by friendship?"

Sumi threw up her hands in exasperation. "I mean not enemies! We should be friends. We should start by being friends. I just need to get him on board with the idea."

"*Start* by being friends." Yuri gave her a look.

"Innocent friendship! Chaste camaraderie. A fond alliance. Bosom bonhomie."

"Keep going, you're just digging yourself deeper. You are *so* full of shit. Why, though? Why him? Leave the poor guy alone, let him lick his wounds in peace. Do you really think he's ever gonna be able to get over this?"

Sumi gave her a sour look as she wheeled in the chairs. "You know, just for the record, let me remind you, *none* of this is actually my fault. If Ranar wants someone to blame, he needs to look to his own neighbors. *They're* the ones choosing to place orders online instead of directly from him."

After all, Sumi reminded herself, she was paying her good fortune back into the community already, and she was barely unpacked. All of her floral designers, except for Hedda, were local, as were both of the drivers. They hadn't disliked her enough to not take the job, she thought to herself rancorously, had no problem depositing their paycheck every week. Their loyalty to Ranar only went so far.

"And you know, he's acting real innocent and sad now, but Ranar didn't have a problem with me when we first met. He asked me out! We could potentially already be a thing! It wasn't until I became his competition that he changed his mind and made everyone think I'm the literal devil. But that's what I'm saying, that should be *behind* us now."

At that, Yuri's eyebrows disappeared into her bangs. "He asked you out? Wait, when was this? Did you say yes?"

Sumi nodded, a little unwillingly. "Yeah, I did. But then my store started construction and it all fell apart because—'

"All because you're the big bad chain store that's putting him out of business," the ogress finished, finally catching up with Sumi's consternation. To her shock, Yuriko didn't offer her a sympathetic shoulder.

"Girlypop, this is so much deeper than 'I only want to be his friend.' You actually *like* him. I can tell. Otherwise you wouldn't be acting like such a mopey bitch about it. I don't know, I think you might be expecting a little too much from him. I mean, you're not only putting an end to a three generation family business, you're literally putting *him* personally out of work. He's not some dumb kid who can go pick up a side job at Blinxieburger."

Sumi heated as Yuri ticked off the reasons why Ranar would likely never forgive her. *It's not personal just means you didn't think beyond yourself.*

"*But* . . . he obviously liked something about you to pursue in the first place . . . " She threw up her hands. "You're all as bad as my brother! I guarantee half of this is just sexual tension. Gods, everyone in this town needs their hands held for every little fucking thing, I swear. Just fuck him and get out of the way! Ranar is *very* fuckable, by the way, if not a little dumb. You know nagas have two cocks, right? He can probably go all night."

"I know," she heard herself agreeing, dropping her face into her hands as the ogress laughed. "He's *so* babygirl. Look, I'm trying. Wait, are you sure? Two? *All* of them?"

"All the ones I know. Most of them can't shut up about it. Think about it."

You know they're probably spectacular. The rest of him is gorgeous, he's not going to have scrawny limp noodle dicks.

"I feel like I could bring him around to not hating me if he let me get a crack at them. I'm sure of it."

Their laughter was interrupted by the door swinging open, as the other members of their little study group filed in. Yuri's daughter, Mai, with Kenta's girlfriend, Ava. A kitsune from one of the developments and her two teenages daughters, a fox shifter, and two orcs who were planning a trip to Japan the following spring.

"Welcome back, friends."

Sumi grinned, forcing herself to focus. Yuriko's ability to voice switch was uncanny, her normal bossy vulgarity replaced with a serene intonation, as if she were a 23-year-old aesthetician with a trust fund, practicing professional mindfulness.

"This week our focus is on the chakin. The cloth we will use to wipe out our chawan, the tea bowl. We ask ourselves how something so seemingly insignificant and small can be so vital to our ceremony? But the smallest object is a venerated tool when part of the whole. We will be learning how to appropriately fold our chakin and when to use it, as we prepare our tea."

The Nippon Club met twice a month for their general meetings, but the members who had registered had been meeting for tea ceremony weekly, with the goal of hosting their own informal novice ceremony at the end of summer. They would be encouraged to invite friends and loved ones, practicing the main tenet of the tea ceremony — that the time enjoyed in each other's company was singular and should be cherished, a moment that could never be replicated again.

She wished she could invite Ranar and that he would say yes. She had envisioned it more than a hundred times by then. Bowing low before him, preparing his tea, sharing a moment together that could never be replicated, one of many she wanted to share.

She could invite ChaoticConcertina to this, Sumi realized. After all, he was the only one who fully understood how important it was to her, how much it meant. He would appreciate the underlying meaning of the ceremony, had practically voiced the exact same thing to her, in reference to the time with his daughter. He knew better than anyone, and would have been her first choice to invite to such an event, before she'd moved to Cambric Creek. *And maybe you still can.* First, though, she wanted to fix things with him. Fixing things with Ranar was her only priority, and she would take whatever opening she could find.

It was on a shelf at the supercenter in Bridgeton, of all places, that she found that opening.

Between Bridgeton and Cambric Creek, the superstore catered mostly to humans, and while that didn't especially matter to her, for she had grown completely comfortable shopping at the Food Gryphon, the selection did. Aisles upon aisles of choices, more choices than any one person needed to make over breakfast cereal or brand of cheese, but sometimes the plethora of choices was comfortable, and comfort was what she was seeking that rainy day, once she left the coffee shop.

Sumi was buying Hedda a new tumbler, for the model the troll brought into work every day had a faulty seal, and after the third leak of coffee had been mopped up from the design room floor, Sumi decided she'd had enough. She found a version on the shelf, the same size and color as the version Hedda owned currently, when she caught the flash of pink from the corner of her eye, at the back of a crowded row of blue cups emblazoned with dancing avocados. White with candy pink bows, the pink handle reminiscent of the medication one took for an upset stomach. *Perfect.*

If it was true that things came into one's life for a reason, there could be no mistaking what this reason was. *It's your perfect opening. You're not going to get a better one.* Searching the aisle, Sumi eventually found a pink heart silicone straw topper that would suffice, adding the peace offering to her cart. *He might not see it that way. But even if he doesn't, he has an adorable little girl who will.*

Sumi was aware that she had a fantastic amount of nerve returning to The Perfect Petal third time against his wishes. She could only hope that that moment they'd shared in the rain carried through long enough for her to make amends. *You're going to butter up his kid. Make him forgive you. Swallow his cock and suck his soul out. And then marry him. In that order.*

The familiar bell jangled above the door, and her stomach twisted at the thought of it being silenced forever.

"Good morning! Welcome to The Perfect Petal." Her dark eyebrows rose in recognition, smile stretching. "Oh, hi!"

Good, that's a good reaction. She's happy to see you. He hasn't poisoned her against you. Sumi half expected Ranar to have photos of her at his register, warning his family members from being polite to her, likely with instructions to call the police the second she stepped foot over the threshold.

That morning, his budding fashionista wore a pink dress with balloon sleeves, and behind her, Sumi could see a white cardigan tossed on the counter. Her hair was plaited in the sort of intricate braid one learned from watching step-by-step videos on social media over and over again, and the pleated skirt of her dress swished gracefully over her violet tail as she undulated in place.

"My dad's not here."

"That's okay, I'm not here to see him. And you look high key adorable, as always. That dress is not leaving a crumb. It's giving cupcake and it ate the whole thing."

The tiny Naga beamed, eyes crinkling with her smile as her shoulders came up adorably. "Thank you! It's my favorite."

Ruma. That's what he called her. "But I don't want to be a weirdo, so do you need to let your grandma know that someone's here?"

"Oh, it's okay, I know how to ring customers out."

Maybe when you're her stepmom, she can work at Pink Blossom. She'll fit right in with the aesthetic. Her dad can make us pancakes for breakfast after he's fucked me within an inch of my life, and we'll go to work while he makes chili. And then later we'll all do something together, like a real family.

The therapist she used to see in the city had loved delving into her hidden desire for a family, completely at odds with her choice not to have children. She had never wanted to be pregnant, had never loved anyone enough to be willing to have them in her life forever due to a shared child, and the thought of sleepless nights and potty training made her a bit queasy ... but the daydream of having a unit of her own and the security that came with it was one that she had never been able to shake. It was because she felt unconnected to her actual family, the therapist had said, replaced by her stepsisters. Sumi hadn't disagreed, knowing that it was actually only part of her loneliness. Cut off from half of what she was and isolated, and then replaced by her stepsisters. Her father had done his best and she couldn't have asked for a sweeter stepmother, but it had never mattered.

Here, though, she could be whole. She was positive.

She had always loved the idea of having a family unit of her own, simply wanting to skip ahead six or seven years past the messy pregnancy and baby stage, and Ranar and his daughter would fit perfectly into her little dreamworld.

"Are you still fighting with my dad?"

Sumi paused. *He told you she was perceptive, more perceptive than him.* He hadn't been lying.

"I hope not. I'm trying to make up with him. Maybe you can give me some tips, I'm sure you know him better than anyone. But actually, I brought something for you. I saw it this morning while I was shopping and I knew you probably wouldn't get a chance to find it before you go home."

If the girl had thought to question why Sumi seemed to know so much about her, it was washed away in the excitement in her eyes when the tumbler was placed on the counter, shrieking in excitement.

"That's the one! The one that sold out everywhere! Thank you sooooo much!" She had her arms around the cup, twisting on her tail gleefully. "I love it!"

Sumi had barely taken a breath to respond when another Naga appeared around the corner from the back room. She was reminded of Hedda popping out, catching her in emotional fits, every time Ranar sent her some mean-spirited bouquet. *You even have that in common. You both know the language of flowers, like two complete dorks.*

"Where's the fire, piya?"

This must've been his father, she realized, heart folding in a pile of guilt. *This shop is my dad's whole life.* She could see the resemblance immediately, despite the gulf of years between them. His warm brown skin was creased in age and laugh lines, his hair a perfect snowy white, but he had the exact same strong profile as he questioned his granddaughter. His eyes raised, seeing Sumi, white eyebrows shooting up.

"Sumiko! Good morning, why did you come out in this rain? Hold on, hold on . . ." He turned slowly, his slow slither resembling a shuffle. *Rectilinear. That's what it's called.* "Drishi, Sumiko is here."

When his mother gracefully slithered out from the back a moment later, it was with wide eyes, her hand at her throat. "I didn't expect to see her, but you can't ever be too sure. Welcome in again. You know Ranar isn't here?"

"I already told her," Ruma announced. "She said they're trying to make up, Nani."

Sumi almost swallowed her tongue. His family was full of perceptive women, it seemed. "Hopefully," she added with a small smile. "He can't stay mad at me forever, right?"

"He likes the color blue," Ruma said seriously, still clutching her cup, evidently taking seriously Sumi's request for help. "Even though he'll tell you he can't pick a favorite, but he says that about everything. And he likes to cook. He never lets us just make something from the freezer. He doesn't notice anything, you can't think he'll know what you want unless you tell him. He has, like, *negative* aura points when it comes to that, so if you want to stop fighting, you should just tell him that."

It was all she could do to keep from laughing. His daughter looked so entirely serious, and she was reminded again of his conversation online. *I've never once looked at their hooves.*

"But he's a really good listener," Ruma went on doggedly. "He doesn't ever get mad if you tell him things. And he'll do things he doesn't like if it makes you happy, and he'll pretend he likes them too so that you don't feel bad. I can tell, but it's still nice that he tries to pretend."

Like pretending he thinks it's a great idea for you to go to a fancy, out-of-state school, even though it broke his heart for you to leave. Like pretending he's cool as a cucumber carrying everyone's shit, even though he feels like he's ready to break. He was right. His daughter really was his best advertisement. Sumi thought her heart felt ready to burst, when his mother cleared her throat.

"Piya, will you please bring those white roses to Baba? That bucket is too heavy for these old arms."

Ruma ducked her head, beaming at Sumi a final time before doing as she was told.

His mother fixed her with an appraising eye as soon as they were alone.

"You know, I don't think I've ever seen Ranar so preoccupied with one person before, the way he has been preoccupied with you all summer. Not even his wife. So much agitation! I think you are bad for my son's blood pressure."

Sumi gulped. *You were doing better with the kid.*

"But that means you will likely be good for him in ways that a mother is meant to pretend do not exist. That's good, he needs that in his life."

Her smile spread, eyes twinkling, and Sumi almost choked.

"Can I ask, are you a relative of Sumiko Ito?"

Sumi was taken aback. She had been expecting to be asked about her great aunt, feeling her cheeks heat as she nodded. "She was my great aunt. She left me her house after she died, that's why I'm even here in Cambric Creek. But – but I never knew her, so I can't answer any questions."

His mother smiled, nodding, as if she had already suspected the answer. "She was a very good friend of mine. Such a wonderful lady. I did the flowers for her service myself, one last goodbye. You look like her, you know. That's why my husband . . ."

Tears raced to the surface before she had a chance to quell their movement. "I'm so glad. I'm so glad to know that she had good friends here. When I found out . . . I hated knowing she was alone at the end. I joined the Nippon club once I moved in, and I found out she was a member there as well. I feel a bit like I'm walking in her footsteps wherever I go. Everyone speaks so highly of her. I wish I could have known her."

"She taught a flower arranging class at the Nippon club for many years."

"I know," Sumi choked out. "I've been told *I* have to do it now."

They were both still laughing when he came through the front door. Ranar stopped immediately, eyes narrowing as the bell jangled.

"Are you familiar with the phrase 'turning up like a bad penny?'"

"Go!" His mother pointed to the back. "We are having a conversation that does not concern you." She waited until he quickly slithered past, grumbling under his breath and casting back one last, dark look in Sumi's direction. His mother rolled her eyes. "They are like little boys when they get their feelings hurt. But the answer is no. He won't be mad forever. I suspect he's not even mad now."

"He is," she corrected regretfully. "Unfortunately, he is. And it's justified."

"He's not. I know my son. His anger burns very fast and very bright and it is always very short-lived. He does not know what he feels, and *that* is what's making him angry. As I said, I've never seen him so preoccupied. You and I will have tea, and I will tell you all you wish to know about your Aunt Sumiko. Don't give up on him. You're very beautiful, and a beautiful woman needs a good man in her life. I'm biased, but my son is a very good Nag."

He was waiting in the parking lot, beside her car.

"Are you going to make me regret *not* being a dick to you? Is that what this is?"

Don't give up on him. He doesn't notice things. I hate being mean to people. Sumi knew she was at an unfair advantage, but an unfair advantage was an advantage just the same. She gave him her sunniest smile.

"Not at all. Your gallantry has already been noted. I wasn't even here for you, actually. But since you have accosted me at my car —"

"Accosted? This is *my* parking lot!"

"— this is the perfect time for us to have a chat and call a truce."

Ranar crossed his toned, well-defined arms over his broad, solid chest, his dark eyes narrowing once more. *I'm going to lick every inch of your body and find out what sort of noises you make.*

"When did I say anything about a truce?"

"You didn't. *I* did. Just now. It's high time for one. And you're going to agree to it. There's no reason we can't be friends, Ranar."

His nose wrinkled, lip curling back as he drew breath to decline her order, but Sumi didn't give him a chance. "Thank you for helping me. That day in the rain. You didn't have to, but you did. You didn't *want* to, and you still did. And that really shows the mark of your character, I think. So thank you."

She moved faster than he had a chance to draw back, dropping a hand to his forearm, still crossed against his chest, using him for leverage to raise up on her toes, brushing her lips against his smooth brown cheek. If he felt the way her breast pressed against his arm while she did so, all the better.

"I'm sure I'll see you soon."

He was still standing there as she pulled away, watching him in her rearview mirror grow smaller and smaller. He never moved away. *I've never seen him be so preoccupied with someone the way he's been preoccupied with you.* She had no real expectation that he would attend the open house she was planning, *Pink Blossom's* official grand opening, now that they had found their rhythm. He'd made it clear that day in the rain that he had no interest in seeing her dreamy little storefront, and Sumi accepted that he viewed it as likely a bridge too far.

...But she could try. She would ensure he received her invitation just the same, and hoped that he would see it for the olive branch and/or proposal of marriage that it was. And if not, she wasn't above using whatever tools she had in her arsenal to wear him down. *I'll see you again soon. I'll make sure of it.*

Mid At Best

RANAR

PinksPosies&Pearls: *Have I told you about the Nippon Club since I joined?*

It's become the highlight of my week.

The club itself only meets twice a month, but I signed up for this special tea ceremony.

Do you drink tea?

I know we've already established you have a caffeine addiction,

but do you ever diversify your drug of choice?

I am a tea drinker, but I drink coffee too.

I don't really understand the people who are either or & never the twain shall meet.

PinksPosies&Pearls: *Anyway — tea ceremony. It's very intricate.*

People study their whole lives to be able to host their own.

Because even the tiniest detail should be thought of as an art form, you know?

Little inconsequential things that are worth mastery.

But on the other hand, I wonder how many people get into something like this

and they never, ever host a tea for the people they love.

Because they're too fixated on those little details.

PinksPosies&Pearls: *I think it's beautiful and inspiring.*

It's also probably a damaging hobby for someone who fixates & has anxiety

Perfection is not attainable!

Right now we are learning to fold a napkin. That's it. Just a little napkin.

A little napkin that gets used in the ceremony. Inconsequential, right? Silly?

Not at all. A venerated tool, worthy of studying.

Because if something is worth doing, it's worth doing with your whole heart.

And I really love that []

I hope you're being gentle with yourself this week, friend.

You've definitely earned a bit of gentleness. [][][]

"We're going to this, right? I feel like we definitely need to go to this."

Ranar didn't need to turn to know what Grace was talking about. He had been waiting for her to pounce on him with the flyer from the moment he'd arrived on site that morning.

He loved the methodical progression of a wedding job: weeks of preparation, days of work, and then seeing it tangibly come to life, one wall of roses at a time. He was too busy for chit chat right now, placing arrangements and setting up the bridal arch, and he wasn't at all interested in the soft pink flyer he knew she held.

He himself had rescued those flyers from a summer storm, because he truly was, proven at every turn, just a stupid, unlucky snake.

Pink Blossom - Open House

Embrace your Flower Epoch!

Join us for an evening of refreshment, flowers and prizes,

As we officially open our doors to the community. .

He had received the same flyer, along with every other business in town. Ranar had let the pastel sheet of paper slide directly into the wastebasket, only to find it tacked on the wall later that same day, directly in his line of sight as he did billing for that weekend's wedding.

"I found this in the trash," his mother had pointed out cheerfully. "I didn't want it to be accidentally thrown away before you had a chance to record the date."

"Yeah, I don't think I'm going to be able to make it." He'd avoided his mother's eye altogether, refusing to turn as he pulled the flyer from the wall, wadding it in a ball, then dropping it into the trash once more. When he left at the end of the day, several hours after his parents, Ranar found the flyer again, smoothed out, and helpfully placed on the dashboard in his car.

And now Grace was getting in on the act.

"Why would I go? Did you ask yourself the answer to that question before those words bubbled up to the surface, Gracie? 'Why on earth would Ranar want to attend this, when of all the things in the world he doesn't want to go to, he doesn't want to go to this thing the most?' Did you ask yourself that?"

Grace only rolled her eyes. "Actually, smart ass, I did think about the answer to that. Perception. Public perception is why you should go. Do you want people to think you've been beaten by this?"

"I *have* been beaten by this."

He felt something strike him on the back, but didn't bother turning, too engaged in fitting together the pieces of the arch, his tail holding up the side arm.

"You have *not* been beaten by this. And that's what you want people to see. You are unbothered. Moisturized. In your lane. Ready to bounce back. Like, the worst thing you can do is *not* go."

"I can think of plenty of worse things."

"No, because you're not thinking about the fallout of not going. Do you really want to be the source of sad gossip? Like, right now you have the benefit of sympathy on your side, Ranar. But do you want people to think you're pathetic? There's a *very* fine line between *sympathetic* and *pathetic*, and once you cross it, there's no going back. You have everyone's sympathy right now. It's a family business, your dad is sick, big corporate bad guy. Everyone feels for you! But if you don't put in an appearance at her open house, that sympathy is going to turn ugly. 'Oh, he's probably at home. I wonder if he's going to lose his house. He's probably not going to be able to take care of his parents. He should have closed years ago and turned it into a barbecue joint. If it wasn't already a failing business, she wouldn't have shut it down so quickly. I heard he's never even been on a date before.' You don't want any of that, believe me."

Ranar did turn, finally. "I don't know what I'm supposed to do with any of that, Grace. With friends like these —"

She threw another roll of tape at him, this one bouncing off the front of his shoulder. "No, don't give me that. You know I'm right. The people of this community love nothing more than talking shit about each other. Don't give them ammunition. You *haven't* been beaten by this. You are going to clean up really nice, you're going to slither into her shop, drink her free champagne, take one of her little flower seed packets or whatever the hell she's giving away, and your going to laugh and smile and look like you're having a grand old time without a care in the world. You let everyone see that *you're* the bigger person and keep their sympathy."

He hated admitting that she might be right. Gossip was the lifeblood of this community, and Ranar didn't want to find himself on the wrong side of it.

Ruma was overjoyed that he was going out, even though it was decided that she would stay home. He had considered bringing her along. Even Grace had to give it serious thought, admitting there was no better way to engender sympathy than showing off his adorable, bubbly daughter, reminding the whole town that he was a single father being put out of business.

"I don't know, I feel like it punches the wrong button. It would be different if your ex was dead."

"Grace, for fuck's sake!"

"I'm just saying! Everyone loves a widower! Widowers are hot, we would be beating women off of you with a stick. But a divorcé? Ehhhh, what's wrong with him? That's what they're going to think."

"What's wrong with me right now is that I am friends with you. You're acting like I'm brand new to the town and everyone is forming their first impression of me just this week."

She shrugged, giving him an unsympathetic look. "In a way you are, Ranar. First impression after tragedy. You've been here your whole life, but that means you sort of become part of the town, like a light fixture. But now you've been the source of hot gossip these last few months, and you're coming out the other side of it *not* the victor. People will be forming their first impressions all over again."

"You know what I think? You spend too much time with Tris."

Ruma would be staying home for the event, removing the buffer of her youth and charm, which he had no problem admitting that he had been planning on using as a security blanket. She had still been excited that he was going out, and Ranar suspected that was the most damning indictment of his social life possible.

"You need to mog every other guy there, got it? Let me see what you're wearing."

He admitted he hadn't given it any thought at that point. Ruma had dropped her head back, arms opening wide, as if she were silently imploring the heavens for an answer on what she had done to deserve him.

"Daddy, it's a *theme*. You can't go not dressed to the theme!"

She had bitterly lamented his lack of a baby pink dress shirt, fighting a war with herself over whether or not he ought to wear the very light purple or the soft dove grey she had decided were a satisfactory showing of *being in his flower epoch*, in lieu of the pink.

When Grace showed up to collect him, Ruma had still been giving him a critical once over. "What's the verdict, little miss?"

"I did the best I could. He wasn't even going to follow the theme! Look at Grace! She understands!"

Grace wore a billowing pastel floral dress with huge puffed sleeves, the skirt an avalanche of organza ruffles. Her mountain of blonde curls spilled over her shoulders, pinned back from her face, and she carried a shiny, beaded clutch.

"Are we going to a flower shop open house or the prom?!"

"Calm down. You heard her, it's the theme. We're in our flower epoch!" She twirled, letting the skirt of her dress swing. "Do nagas even go to prom?"

"They do when they go to high school a mile down the road. I don't know what the two of you are so worried about," Ranar added testily. "My plant friend told me I'm sigma. I thought that was good."

"That's the best," Ruma promised, accepting his forehead kiss. "Is *she* going to be at the party? Don't forget! Gag her with rizz!"

"This kid has made it her life's ambition to set me up," he grumbled once they left his parents' house, his mother and Ruma both waving from the window. "Look at the two of them. Conspiring against me. You should hear them. They think I need to ask Sumi out, forgive her for everything. They're practically planning our future together now."

"Well, I think they're right," Grace laughed. "If you remember, I was in favor of meeting you here, specifically to facilitate you getting laid tonight. You are your own biggest enemy, babe."

The shop was beautiful, as he knew it would be.

A wash of dusty pink and grey-backed lavender swirled the walls, with bunches of flowers tied and suspended from the ceiling. a long wall of cooler cases, shelving holding bases and small planters, and there in the corner, lit with twinkling lights, stood a strangely majestic tree. It looked like something from an old growth forest, and Ranar wondered how much they spent on its care and transport in the delivery to its new home here. *An obscene amount of corporate money, just for effect.* He couldn't hold back a somewhat disgusted snort of laughter at the social media ready backdrop, complete with a neon logo, just at the front door. *Ridiculous.*

Although, he couldn't help noting there was a line before it.

Obviously this flyer had gone out to more than just the other local businesses, for the coltish young women lining up to pose together before the wall of greenery in short, voluminous floral dresses certainly weren't any owners he recognized. Selkies and shifters, kitsune and a beautiful cervitaur, harpies and mothwomen. Everyone, it seemed, understood what the *flower epoch* theme entailed. These young women had gone all out dressing for a flower shop open house, and were posing as if it were the social event of the season.

"Oh, she's good, Ranar. She's really fuckin' good."

Grace nodded her chin in the direction of the work counter, which was serving as the bar for the evening. Signature cocktails, three to choose from, all pink in color with different flowers floating on their surfaces. Beside the work counter, several dozen tiny, iridescent gift bags waited, and in front of that, several trays of hors d'oeuvres and crudités.

"*This* is how you throw a work event. Get it online. She knows exactly who she's marketing to . . . She might have put you out of business even with*out* the corporate money."

He turned sharply, giving Grace a poisonous look. Somehow she had already acquired a cocktail, holding a self-defensive hand up, blue eyes sparkling as she sipped it.

"Oh, this is di*vine*. I'm going to have at least four of these. You don't need to worry about me getting home, I already told Merrick I would probably be calling him. So you're off the hook as the official DD. Have a drink, loosen up. Go find her. And maybe give her your own big double-D tonight."

He had already spotted her, his eyes scanning the crowd for her as soon as they stepped in the packed space. She looked as beautiful as she ever did, even more so in her airy floral dress, her cheeks flushed and her eyes bright.

Grace is right. Go over, say hello. Be pleasant. Let people see you saying hello and being pleasant. We're all friends here, one big happy community. Ranar shifted. He was keeping himself tightly coiled, not wanting to take up any more space that he absolutely required, which was still more than the average bipedal citizen. There was Xenna, standing beside Sumi, he could say hello to her as well. The sister of the ogre who did his taxes was talking, and all three women laughed.

He was just about to make his move, when Sumi turned, her smile wide as Kenta's sister introduced her to Sandi Hemming, who had also apparently understood the dress code. He watched as she and the werewolf leaned in, air kissing on each cheek, the whole floofy, floral group laughing together at something that was said. This was her place, in the community now, with friends. She looked happy. In her element. This was *her* night, her moment. And he had no desire to detract from that.

Ranar knew that he would be an uncomfortable pause, an awkward silence, and once he quickly took his leave, a *fucking yikes*, as Pinky would say. Grace had miscalculated. He should have stayed away.

He was carefully navigating his way through the packed press of bodies, trying not to inadvertently trip one of the giggling young women waiting in line for the photo op and was nearly to the door, when he heard his name. She had even ruined that, for his name would never again sound right to his ears, coming from anyone else's mouth.

"I'm so glad you came. I had wondered if you would and I-I was worried you weren't going to."

He turned as much as the tight space permitted, coiling back on his tail. She was right there, standing very close, gazing up sparkling eyes.

"Everything looks beautiful. It's a gorgeous shop. Congratulations." He hated himself for being the reason why the light in her eyes dimmed, each of his short utterances making her wince ever-so-slightly. "Really," he added in a gentle tone. "It's beautiful. All of it. It suits you." His eyes were locked on her lips, and he watched almost as if in slow motion as her lip caught behind her teeth. "This, I mean. This is all perfect. You're going to be very successful, Sumi."

He turned, uncoiling enough to push himself forward towards the door, when she caught his wrist. Once more, her fingertips pressed into his skin like a brand, searing him.

"Please don't leave."

Ranar turned back slightly, just enough to see her eyes, which looked glossy with unshed tears. Hoisting his coil up, he twisted fully to face her again. "Don't. Don't do that." He was only vaguely aware that it was *his* hand cupping her jaw, thumb smoothing over the apple of her cheek. "Put all that away. This is the fake it till you fucking make it crowd. This is *your* night. Everyone is here to see you. Go show them that you know how to throw a party."

"I don't want you to leave." Her hand was still locked around his wrist, and he couldn't tell if it was his imagination, but Ranar was positive she had tilted her head slightly, pressing to his hand.

"I kind of need to. It's *tight* in here and my tail is very in the way. I'm gonna wind up tripping that cervitaur, she's gonna fall through the cooler, and you're gonna have a lawsuit on your hands." He grinned. "Actually, now that I've said it out loud, it seems like a pretty good plan."

"This is the only part I was allowed to show anyone." The brightness had returned to her eyes, her rose-pink lips turning up. "The sweatshop is in the back. Promise me you'll come back and I'll show it to you. I'm throwing everyone out at eight, come back then. I have something for you."

Cambric Creek seemed designed for couples after dark. Ranar didn't know why he was making circles around the streets instead of going home. Instead, he was shifting from the grass sidewalks to the pavement, cutting up alleys and through parking lots in an effort to continue moving downhill, knowing if he kept shifting at a diagonal, he would never need to traverse any of the steeper streets. There were couples holding hands on the towpath beside the waterfall, couples walking in groups on Main Street. Couples standing outside one of the pubs, obliging him to sidewind across the street to move around their laughter, a solitary figure, uncertain in what he was doing or what he was waiting for.

Why are you going back? Just because she asked doesn't mean you need to listen to her. He didn't, but neither did he have a good reason to just go home. After all, he'd already made plans for Ruma to spend the night with her grandparents, having no idea what time Grace was planning on keeping him out until the first place.

They hadn't arrived right at six, deciding fashionably late was the best entrance to make, and so he didn't have terribly long to wait before he was making his way back downhill, tracing the path they had taken that day in the rain, until he arrived at that tiny back lot where she and her staff parked.

Ranar waited. Most of the attendees who had dropped into her open house were gone at that point, and he watched as the mobile bartender wheeled out the back door, packing up his truck before pulling out. One by one, each of her employees came out the back door, full of adrenaline and good cheer from their successful night. Sumi held the door open, talking to a tall troll as she stepped out, the last car in the lot aside from her own. He saw the moment she stared past the troll, spotting him there on the other side of the street in the shadows. Without breaking her conversation, she made a small motion with her index finger, motioning him to go around to the front.

You should leave. You should just leave now, what the fuck are you doing? What are you thinking? None of this is smart. Your life is in disarray because of this woman. And here you are, letting her lead you by the nose, still. It didn't prevent him from doing as he was bid, pushing forward, moving downhill in long glides, turning the corner until he waited before her windows.

When she appeared at the back of the shop, Sumi beamed at the sight of him. *Just a stupid snake.* She hurried to the front, moving as fast as she could at her towering heels, throwing the door open for him.

"Oh, good. I was worried you weren't going to come back."

Ranar slid through the doorway, slithering past her as she re-locked the door. He wanted to ask why she was so worried about him coming back, why she had wanted him there in the first place. "It's a very pretty shop," was what he said, instead. "I'm assuming they built up around the tree?"

She nodded. "That's one of the first things they do. They bore down and make the hole and then they bring the tree in on this huge truck. Everything else gets done from there, the flooring, the walls. None of the steel beams were even put in on the front of the building until they finished with that piece of it."

He nodded. *Frivolous corporate money.*

"Come on, let me give you the tour. I didn't understand why the square footage of the storefront was so small during the construction phase. I questioned it a few different times. Now I get it." He followed her around her back counter, down a short utility hallway, a door leading to the same small lot he had just stood watching, and on the opposite side, an open doorway that led to the design room. "Here we are. Sweatshop central."

He couldn't hold in a short burst of laughter. Her design room was nearly double the size of her sales floor, with two long centralized work cables, a perimeter counter, the utility sink with cabinets, a half-size refrigerator, and a mobile flower cooler. It was gray and sterile, like an operating room, utterly joyless. It bore no resemblance to the front of the store, of which the fanciful feminine color scape matched so well with its owner.

Nor did it resemble the work room in his own shop, the doorway of which was notched with his and his sister's heights, as well as Ruma's. Their work room had a wall of windows and was always full of sunshine, or else the gray patter of the rain outside, running in rivulets that they could see. Ranar could tell her employees would work beneath the fluorescent hum of the overhead lights, with no clue of what the weather or time of day might be outside their gray cinder block prison. There was nothing personal here, nothing colorful or bright, nothing but a reminder of what they were. A soulless corporate sweatshop, rolling over the same businesses that had trusted them for decades.

"This is more like it," he laughed again. "Yeah, this is exactly what I was expecting. You threw me with all of the cotton candy fluff out there."

"The cotton candy fluff is who *I* am," she said pointedly with a laugh. "This is . . . yeah. Exactly what you said. Nothing has been what I expected."

Her voice trailed off slightly, her eyes dropping to the floor.

"The front is beautiful," he heard himself saying, unsure why he was trying to make her feel better, "and your coolers are full."

"Yeah, that's all for tomorrow. Two of the girls are assigned to work on replenishing the cooler, that's what they do every afternoon. They just make everything to the general spec and we go from there."

"Two of the girls. How many employees do you have?"

"Seven. Although, two of those are drivers. I might have to bring on a counter person if we ever pick up in the front, but as of now it's not necessary."

Ranar chuckled to himself. Seven employees, and she'd barely been open for three months. He supposed it wasn't fair to compare that piece of his business to hers. Mira was his only employee, but he and his parents could do the work of five floral designers with their eyes closed. *Still. Seven!*

"Well, it sounds to me like you're crushing it. Yeah, it's pretty fucking ugly back here."

Sumi laughed, taking a tiny step closer as she did so.

"But you're doing great. Honest. It might not be exactly what you envisioned, but . . ." He trailed off, motioning vaguely to the room. Motioning vaguely at his life, for a decade ago, he'd never would have guessed that he'd be starting over again at this point. "They rarely turn out the way we expect."

She kissed him.

That was what he would cling to, after.

He glanced back down to her, after his hand dropped, and suddenly there she was, catching his lips with her own. She was taller in her heels and gripped the front of his shirt for leverage, catching him unexpectedly in a kiss, soft and tentative.

That he kissed her *back*, he would simply have to live with. Not only kissed her back, but deepened the kiss immediately, his hand dropping to her hip to hold her close, angling his mouth to slot against hers fully. She was warm and her lips were sweet, tasting of the sugared rims of her fancy cocktail glasses, whimpering into his mouth as one of his fangs caught in her lip.

When she dropped down from her toes, Ranar was breathing hard. Her mouth was still open, lips parted and plump, her eyes wide, as if she couldn't believe her own audacity . . . When he closed the distance and kissed her again. Another little kitten whimper, her un-sharp teeth taking its turn to graze his lip, before her tongue slid against his. She sent a shock down his spine when her hand pushed into his hair, her long nails scraping against his scalp.

Sweet like candy, he thought as she dropped down again, mouths parting. When she took a tottering step back, Ranar forced himself to swallow.

"I-I have something for you."

She turned from him, carefully crossing to the side counter before rooting through a large, pink floral tote bag on one of the countertops. "I brought this for your mom. I started going through some stuff at the house and I found all these pictures. I thought this was a nice one."

It was a photo in an intricate, gold wrought frame, one of his mother and her late friend from some years back, who was evidently Sumi's great aunt. Both women were smiling, holding teacups, with their heads together.

"I was going to bring it to her, but . . ." She trailed off, an adorable flush moving up her neck. "Well, I wasn't sure how serious you are about me staying away. I didn't want the police to be called."

Ranar laughed again, forcing his blood to cool. *That's that. And it was a mistake in the first place.* "Are you kidding? All I've heard for the last week and a half is how she's having you over for tea and the two of you are going to have a grand old time, and she's going to take your flower arranging class at the Japanese club. I hope you have a sweet tooth, because she's going to ply you with desserts until you have rose water and coconut coming out of your pores."

Sumi laughed, delighted. "I am *so* looking forward to it. I had a rose-water dessert for the very first time just a few weeks ago. Strawberry Rose daifuku. Maybe I'll try making some for her to try. Your family is Indian?"

Ranar smiled wryly. It was hardly the first time he'd heard a variation of *so where are you from*. "*I'm* from Cambric Creek. I was born at Healers', just a few miles away, over by the university. As I said once before, I've lived here my whole life. But my family is Tamil."

The flush had spread up to her ears. "You just need to be aware now that I'm going to ask *so* many silly questions. Because not only was I raised *very* human, I was raised almost painfully white."

Ranar chuckled. "I'll let mom know to use a light hand with the spices."

She teetered on her heels as she laughed again, burying her face in her hands. "Okay, wait. I have something else. This is for Ruma. Well, she gets a bag too, you both do. But this is especially for her."

She pulled two of the iridescent little gift bags from the shelf. A frequent shopper punch card, a voucher for a free single rose, a five dollar off code, various gourmet candies, a tea candle, organza wrapped and smelling of gardenia, and a pothos clipping, secured in a water tube. "Grace is gonna love this."

"Are you together?" Sumi asked the question suddenly, whirling around to face him, grabbing the counter for balance as she did so. "I – I mean, you came together tonight. And that day at your shop —"

"Grace is the event planner over at Saddlethorne. She sends a lot of her brides to me for their wedding flowers, and she does my fruit baskets. Well. She did. But no. We're not together. Not like that. Her boyfriend is a mothman, he works over at the University. If you ever need to know anything about moths or bats or hummingbirds, I suggest you look it up yourself or ask literally anyone else, because you will never escape the conversation with him. That is how you will die."

She was laughing again as she pulled a small pot from the same tote bag. "Okay, good to know. This is for Ruma."

Ranar examined the small plant, feeling his heart do an odd somersault that was surely not normal. This was more than a clipping. This had started as a clipping and had been nurtured to its current state, which would continue to grow into a full size plant, if nurtured. The pink princess philodendron wasn't an especially difficult or needy plant, but it had a cult-like status online, thanks to its splashy pink and green variegated leaves. This was Pinky's namesake. His stomach swooped, and Ranar couldn't tell if what he was feeling at that moment was guilt or not. *How can you be guilty? You've never met her. You've never made plans to meet her. You can't cheat on someone you've never even met, right?*

"I know she's a pinky girl. I wanted to make sure I got it to you before she leaves. I figure her visit is probably winding down, right?"

"How do you know that?" His voice was a hair sharper than he intended, Sumi's eyes going wide. He had been lamenting earlier that same week to Pinky, his heart already feeling a bit heavier, knowing Ruma would be leaving soon.

"Oh, um, she – she mentioned something about it the last time I was in the shop. You know, when you yelled at me outside my car. And told me never to come back."

He let out the breath that had been building in his chest. "Right, of course. Well, she'll love this. It's funny, I . . . I have a friend who cultivates philodendron. This variety is one of her prized possessions."

"It's a real beauty," Sumi agreed, humming lightly. "Well, again. I didn't want to make it burst a blood vessel in your eye or anything, so."

He laughed again at her audacity. "Don't worry, my mother and daughter are completely enamored of you, I hope you'll be happy to hear. They'll be over the moon to know that *I* came tonight, and *they* received gifts."

She made her way back to him slowly, carefully. His stomach muscles jumped when she gripped a handful of his shirt, tip of his tail thrashing from its coil. "Well, I have something very different in mind for you."

This time, Ranar was ready. His arm came around her as their mouths met, groaning when she scraped the back of his neck. Her giant, soulless flower factory assembly line was so well provisioned, that he had his choice in which way to turn, twisting on his coil as he gripped her, lifting her easily to sit atop one of the work tables. He wanted to taste that spot on her neck, that enticing, kissable spot that her earrings drew his eye to like a beacon.

Ranar tried to pay close attention to her every response as their mouths moved over each other. Her fluttering intakes of breath, her soundless little whimpers, the thrum of her pulse beneath his lips as he kissed over her jaw and down the delicate column of her neck, his tongue finding that spot just beneath her ear, gratified when she shivered against him.

He wasn't sure when she had begun unbuttoning his shirt, only realizing she had done so when it was parted, and then her hot hands were everywhere, her nails scraping over his stomach, catching on a pebbled nipple, her palm flat against his heartbeat.

She had her legs open, straddling his thick trunk, her ankles hooked behind him, rubbing against his scales. Ranar could feel his core beginning to heat, his cocks vibrating within their sheath, begging to come out. *No. That's not what this is. Not until she makes it that.* The tip of his tail wrapped around her ankle, and was stroking her leg with a slight pressure when she pulled back, gasping.

"Is – is that your tail?"

He didn't know how to answer, his mouth hanging open from where she had pulled back, nodding.

"What else can it do?"

She had him at an unfair advantage, he thought, returning his mouth to her throat, sucking her pulse point as her head dropped back to give him better exposure, as if he were a vampire. He wanted to kiss down her chest, bury his face in the soft mounds of her breasts, suck her nipples to hardness and not worry if his cocks slid free... But he would have to make do with his tail for the time being, for this was no place to undress her, here in her gray cinder block sweatshop.

Sumi whimpered as his tail moved up her leg, slipping beneath her dress. This woman had ruined his life, he reminded himself as the pointed tip of his tail stroked against her inner thighs, seeking entrance. She was his enemy, that hissing little voice on his shoulder rejoined, as he learned the feeling of her silky panties, tracing against their front, back and forth, and down until she whimpered into his hair. She was careless and hadn't thought beyond her own ambitions, he couldn't help but remember as he began to stroke in the spot that made her jerk against him. He would hate himself in the morning, a likely reality as his tail found its way beneath the hem, dragging through her slickness.

Sumi's mouth was open, her breath thready as he kissed his way back up her throat, scraping his fangs on her jaw, that's the tip of his tail moved in circles around her clit.

It was ironic, he thought, following her subtle little cues, the way she trembled, the way she gasped, tickling over the exposed pearl and making her jump, before resuming his tight circles around her, pressing into the side of her hood. She claimed this was something she had in mind for *him*, and now her head was thrown back, both hands over his shoulders, gripping him tightly, her eyes closed and her mouth hanging open, as he teased her ever closer to coming against his tail.

"A little faster. Right...right there. *Fuck*, right there. Just against the underside."

She now had her arms looped around his neck, the pretense of her doing anything other than enjoying herself gone. He chuffed about a soundless laugh against her hair, grateful for the instruction. Ranar continued to kiss her neck and her shoulders, hating himself as he loved the feel of her in his arms and the way she trembled against him.

He felt the moment when her orgasm hit, her hips bucking slightly against the counter, panting against his bare neck. When it was clear she had already tipped over the edge, he moved his tail, removing the pressure from her spasming clit, pressing into her heat to feel the rhythmic squeeze of her muscles. Sumi moaned against his skin, her thighs trembling. When she slumped against him, her muscles going slack, he just held her for a long moment, rubbing her back as his tail withdrew.

"That was amazing." Her voice came out a laugh, shoulders shaking against him as she sat up slowly, taking his face in her hands. "I'm sorry, Ranar. For all of it. I hope someday you can forgive me."

He didn't fight her when she pulled his face to hers, meeting her lips and another soft, sugar edged kiss.

When her hand moved down his chest, he expected her to begin buttoning his shirt. He wasn't as ready for the hand that slid down, past his skin and into his scales. They always stopped just a few inches short, he thought, taking her wrist and moving her hand to the right spot, knowing she could already feel the swell of him just inside. The end of his tail came up over his shoulder, allowing him to suck the tip clean, his first taste of her, but hopefully not the only one.

"Okay, that's like, stupid hot. I need you to understand," she murmured gently, scratching behind his ear with the hand still cupping his jaw, "that I'm going to fuck you unconscious tonight. Okay? I hope you're ready. Your place or mine?"

Things We Won't Regret Tomorrow

SUMI

"Can I lick your slit?"

The words were out before she could even decide whether or not it was an appropriate thing to ask him. Beneath her, Ranar shuddered, a strangled sound lodging in his throat. Sumi couldn't tell whether or not the question was well received.

"Who asks that?!" he finally choked out, making her push to a sitting position.

"It's an important question! What if you don't like that? I don't know if you do or don't. I just wanted to get your consent. It seems like an important thing to get clarity on, I don't know how sensitive you are or —"

"Sensitive," he gritted out, his teeth gnashing as she scraped her nails down his chest. "And yes."

" . . . Yes, what?"

"*Yes*, you can lick my — I can't even say it."

She collapsed in giggles against him, resuming her mouth's journey down his body, gratified by his rumbling groan as she did so. "Good. I was hoping you were going to say that."

The amount of times she had envisioned having him stretched out beneath her — his bare skin a warm brown expanse, surrounded by the rainbow brilliance of his long, heavy tail; what she would do to him first, how she would touch him, what she might say — hadn't left her any better prepared for what she would actually do when it happened.

Sumi couldn't stop looking at him. He was beautiful. She loved the long line of his neck, the almost elegant musculature of his back and shoulders, the way his heavy black lashes fanned out against his cheek like a bruise every time his eyes fluttered shut, which they did every time she leaned forward to press her lips against his sternum. *He really is so babygirl.*

She had promised herself that she was going to lick every inch of his body, and now that she had the opportunity to do so, she was inclined to take her time. *He needs someone to take care of him, put his needs first. And this is how you can start.*

Her mouth had already made it down his neck, soft sucking kisses following his jaw and down his throat, grinning when it bobbed against her lips as he swallowed. Her tongue and teeth made the journey across his shoulders and clavicle, kissing down the center of his chest, pausing to circle his firm pectoral and suck a brown nipple into the hot wet heat of her mouth. She had a hand pressed flush to his belly, liking the way his muscles jumped and danced when she did so. When her teeth closed over the pebbled tip, the sound that pulled from his throat made her pussy clench.

He had told Pinky that he'd not been in a serious relationship since the end of his marriage. *That doesn't mean he hasn't dated. That doesn't mean he's not getting laid. He's too handsome not to, doesn't make a difference how awkward he claims is, which is not at all.* Still, she thought rationally, even if he dated casually, even if he had regular hookups, she was willing to bet there hadn't been anyone who truly took their time with him in ages. *If ever. He said he and his wife were never really in love.*

She wasn't pressed to rush, wanting to pay attention to every patch of skin, every muscle and sinew, every bit of him that had been so overburdened for so long. She knew it was an unfair advantage, but it was an advantage all the same.

When her mouth made its way to his other nipple, Ranar groaned, sinking his fingers into her hair. She had taken note that pulling her hair free was one of the first things he did upon arriving at her house. It had been bound up in a high, bouncy ponytail for her party, sleek and unserious, and he had carefully pulled it loose, raking his fingers through her long tresses gently once they were free. *Good to know.*

"I don't think this is very fair," he whined from the pillow, attempting to pull her up to him, not the first time he had tried.

Sumi only laughed, flipping her hair back over her face as she grinned up his abdomen, dragging her teeth over his ribs. "This seems completely fair and even to me." A sucking wet kiss, more tongue than teeth, moving a trail down his belly, smiling against his skin when his muscles jumped. "I was completely selfish just a little while ago. And you didn't seem surprised at all."

"Yeah, not one bit."

She laughed in outrage, nipping at his skin, enjoying his sharp intake of breath when she did so. "I'm getting close to the danger zone. For all intents and purposes, you have to treat me like a dumb human. Is there anything I need to know before I go any lower? You're not gonna, like, jizz venom in my eye, are you?"

"If you keep going this slowly, I can't make any promises," he huffed in a strained voice.

"I'm serious!" she laughed, smacking his stomach lightly. "Is regular lube fine or will it make your scales fall off?"

Ranar shook his head, eyes still clenched. "No lube necessary. Self lubricated and ribbed her pleasure."

"Oh wow, that's a very nice perk," Sumi murmured to herself, running her nails lightly down his groin. "Do you know kids today probably have no idea what that means? Or they probably have some silly word for it."

"Like mogging. That was my instruction tonight. I had to mog harder than the other guys. I still have no idea what it means."

She dissolved into giggles against him once more. He was adorable, and her alter ego was exactly right in her assessment. He needed someone to take care of him for a change. *And it just so happens that I have a successful business and plenty of room in my bed.*

"You succeeded. *So* babygirl. What about protection?"

He shook his head again. "Not unless you're less of a dumb human than you think. Our biologies aren't compatible. No chance of pregnancy."

"Aww, that's so sad."

He lifted his head, dark eyebrows drawing together as his eyes fluttered open to peer down at her. "Wait, do you want to have kids?"

She blew out an aggrieved breath. "Are you joking? I'm more than halfway to menopause. I don't want to start going backward!"

His laughter was a vibration against her lips as she resumed kissing her way down his body. His scales were smooth and dry, like little armored plates, and from the way his muscles tensed and tightened and jumped, Sumi could tell they were very sensitive in this area. She didn't need him to direct her this time. She could already feel the bump in his skin, the hot heat of him just behind this protective wall of muscle, and she was looking forward to seeing what kind of noise he made when she licked the seam that held him at bay.

Ranar did not disappoint. The groan that pulled from his throat was startled, as if he hadn't expected the sensation, and she wondered when was the last time anyone had done this to him. He was incapable of being quiet, another strangled moan as she lapped against his skin, caressing the seam of his opening, feeling like she had won a victory when the tip of her tongue was able to breach the resistance ever so slightly. She was patient and wouldn't be rushed, and it would take as long as it took for him to open for her fully. The thought had barely crossed her mind when her mouth met fresh resistance, the tip of his cock crowning against her lips.

"Wait." His voice was a croak above her, his hands scrabbling against the covers. On the floor, his tail twitched, jerking and thrashing, as if he had only the most tentative grip on his control.

"*Please* come up here. I haven't even had a chance to—"

"We can take as long as it needs to take! I already told you, I'm not in a hurry. You don't need to feel like we have to rush through a checklist—"

"*You* can take your time," he corrected through gritted teeth.

Sumi regretfully pulled back, climbing up his body slowly. *Remember what you used to teach. Consent can be withdrawn at any time.*

"I don't have that luxury," he grumbled, his hand dropping immediately to her hip as she settled beside him. "I should have spelled out the mechanics better," he admitted, palming her ass. "I'm not like a human, flopping around. There's no inflation lead up. We get hard inside first." He swallowed with some difficulty as she lightly scratched his stomach. "Once they're out, it's go time. I won't last long."

Sumi grinned. "That's okay. You don't need to worry about that. Not unless you're planning on this being a one and done deal." Her grin faltered when he remained silent.

"I didn't say *that*," he said at last, turning her until she was on her back and he was above her, his mouth descending on hers in a kiss that curled her toes. She whimpered when his hand cupped her mound, two long, strong fingers stroking into her heat. "But I don't even know if I've changed my mind about you as a person yet," he murmured into her skin, kissing down her chest and groaning against her breasts.

He had two fingers inside her, stroking her inner walls, his thumb rolling over her clit as he sucked her nipple, but he hadn't decided if he liked her as a person yet. All she could do was laugh into his hair. *You deserve that.*

"Oh, I don't know. I think I'm changing your mind." She writhed beneath his ministrations, but when his mouth left her breast and his body began to shift lower, Sumi stopped him. "What do you think you're doing?"

His smile would stop her heart until the day it stopped beating for good, she was certain.

"Sorry, you're right. I should get consent." He nipped at her skin. "I want to lick your pussy until I'm close to drowning."

He would make her laugh until that day as well, another bone-deep certainty.

"Oh, *that* you can say."

Ranar frowned when she struggled to push up from the mattress, begrudgingly allowing her to reverse their positions once more. "I guess that's more of a universal concept," he laughed, seeming satisfied being under her when Sumi resettled herself over his chest, her thighs stretched wide on either side of his shoulders.

Using her padded headboard for leverage, she leaned forward, just far enough for him to dart his tongue out, flicking her clit.

"I've never had a partner ask if they could *lick* my *slit*."

His hands cupped her ass, pulling her forward, and Sumi obliged, lowering herself enough that Ranar was able to drag his tongue though her folds, delivering the same sort of toe-curling, sucking kiss to her clit as he had to her mouth.

"Sounds like you need to be fucking a better class of women." Her voice was breathy and her eyes had fluttered shut as his tongue began to set a rhythm against her, using her previous direction to focus his attention to the underside of her clit, licking upward, pressing the point of his tongue into that spot that made her see stars, punctuating his licks with a sucking pressure that made her cry out. "You seem to be doing pretty well with your mortal enemies."

Sumi made herself gasp when she lifted from his mouth, her thighs trembling.

"I wasn't done." He glared.

"What is it that you want?" she asked, still breathy, wanting to do nothing more than sink down on his mouth and ride his tongue until she was satisfied, whether he drowned beneath her or not. *If he dies, he dies.* But she wanted to hear him say it first. "What do you want to do?"

Ranar glowered up at her, and the pissed-off look on his face coupled with the way his lips and chin glistened with her slick, made her positively gleeful. She loved him. Loved him with her whole heart, and she would spend the rest of her life learning the specifics of his every mood and emotion, tiny details that made up the whole, the most worthy discipline she could ever master.

"I want to make you come against my mouth." She let him pull her back down ever so slightly, close enough for her to feel the heat of his breath against her. "Is that better?" he asked snidely, making her squeal when nipped at her inner thighs. "I want to lick my mortal enemy's pussy until she falls apart against me. How about that?"

"Maybe you just can't bear not being in control."

Her head dropped back, a sigh escaping her mouth when he flattened his tongue, delivering a long, slow lick up the whole length of her cunt, his lips fastening over her clit once he reached it. Sumi dug her fingers into his hair, losing herself in the pleasure as he nursed on the exposed bud of nerves the same way he'd sucked on her nipple, his groan vibrating through her body when he broke off.

"Maybe I just want to make you feel good," he murmured against her thigh, his hands releasing her without protest when she raised up to her knees, swinging her leg back over him.

"*That* I believe," she said softly, once she was stretched beside him once more, her body turned just enough that she was able to hitch her leg around his tail. "Because it's like you can't help being just the *best* guy, all the time." She tasted herself on his mouth, relieved when he sighed into the kiss, his fingers walking down her spine. "And I would be thrilled to have the honor of having the best guy take me to pieces with his tongue," she breathed into his hair as his mouth drifted to her neck, just below her earlobe. "Every day for as long as we both shall live." Sumi pulled back, not giving him a chance to react. "But first, *I* want to take care of *you*."

He groaned as if she'd gotten one over on him as she reversed course down his body, until she was once again in the slit-licking zone.

"Are you nervous?" she asked suddenly, the thought only just occurring to her.

Ranar's laugh was a scrape of shaky breath, his muscles jumping again as she caressed him with her fingertips. "Maybe? My anatomy is very much *not* human. If you run off screaming and leaving me twisting here with my dicks out, we will *never* mend fences, just so you're aware. I will *never* run out of fish guts for your trash. Maybe I don't want to take that risk."

She was laughing before he'd even finished. *He's always made you laugh, right from the start. Don't kill for bone meal unless it's a really nice plant.* "Don't worry, I ask dumb questions, but I don't scare easily. And I understand the assignment. Once they're out, it's go time."

He groaned when she licked up the seam in his scales once more. Sumi was relieved that her previous work hadn't been undone by his little detour down her body. It was only a minute or two before she was able to close her lips around the tip of his cock, dark pink with a spiraling depression, giving his head the appearance of a rosebud. *How fitting.* Ranar's back arched off the bed when she sucked it into her mouth, tracing that spiral with the tip of her tongue.

Sumi felt caught between divided excitements demanding her attention — his moan was a rumbling vibration, groaning out of him like like a slow-moving eruption, one she could feel against the fingertips still pressed to his abdomen, and then below — the steady press of his cock against her lips, quickly followed by its twin just below, pressing out together, breaching the wall of muscle as if he were giving birth. She didn't know how she was meant to choose which to suck first.

The meat of his top shaft curved upward, while its brother below moved straight out like a club, each possessing a fist-sized swell just a few inches below that rosebud tip. They were each covered in tiny spines that she quickly discovered were soft against her tongue, while his underside was ridged, nearly resembling his scales. *That's going to feel fucking amazing.* A thick vein that ran through the center of each gave off a hint of blue, ribboning through the pink flesh like a core, and at his base, the spiraling line that started at his rosebud tip opened into frills, like little wings. She had never before seen so much texture in a penis, could never have pictured *this*, and realized she had maybe done herself a disservice all those years dating human men.

It took her a moment to realize that what she first thought was Ranar's inability to keep still was a different movement entirely. Sumi gasped. That thick vein at their core was shared, she realized, and as blood pulsed back and forth through them, they retracted and ballooned, those little spines inflating with blood before going soft again, a repeated push-pull, promising to drag against her inner walls. As the blood pumped back and forth like a valve, his shafts distended, one at a time, a delicious game of tug-of-war. *He's going to be like fucking a sex toy.*

"If this is the start of the human freakout, can you give me a head's up so I can make a call for backup?"

"Oh, you are so *impatient*!"

"Because I'm not going to last that long," he insisted peevishly, earning a fresh round of her laughter as she straddled his tail. *Giddy-up, cowgirl.* "You've had me wound up all night, I'm *dying*. I've been hard for hours. We could have been fucking a lot faster if you hadn't been so determined to take the scenic route, probably on round two by now, but now I am ready to burst, so—" He cut off on a hiss when she pressed one of his pearling rosebud tips between the lips of her sex, sinking down on him slowly.

"At least I know there's one way to shut you up," she wheezed, her body tensing when she arrived at the swell in his shaft. A *huge* disservice to herself, she realized, in more ways than one, for she'd never encountered anything like this.

When Ranar's hands landed on her hips, Sumi braced herself for the inevitable pain as he pulled her down. Instead, his palms slipped back, cupping her ass again, rocking her gently.

"Nice and slow." His voice was low and soft, no hint of demand to be found, despite his words only a few seconds earlier. "You're doing great. Just take it nice and slow. You can do it, just let yourself loosen up."

Her eyes slipped shut, placing her palms flat on his, belly bracing herself as she rocked against him. When one of his hands moved, his thumb nestling into her clit, rubbing slow and steady circles against her, her head dropped back.

He really is incapable of being anything other than the best guy.

Her hips began to move with more insistence on their own, mewling as he worked her clit in just the right spot, loosening her muscles and making her honey flow. Sumi felt the vibration of his groan when she sank down at last over his swell, feeling her walls stretch as he slid all the way home. "Is this okay?" she asked in a shaky voice.

"Perfect. I want to feel you squeeze me tight."

Now that he was seated within her, his other cock was at the perfect position for her to grind against, once she began to move, earning another one of those throaty groans from his throat. Sumi was able to feel that pulsing push-pull within her as she began to rock against him, the flex of those little spines tickling her inner walls, his rosebud tip kissing the edge of her cervix. A direct hit would have been agony, but this angle had her eyes rolling back, her core tightening on each bump, making her quiver.

When Ranar began to buck up into her, her moan came out as a wail. His tail thrashed, pushing himself up, meeting her hips with a crash on each thrust.

"Is this everything you thought it would be?" he groaned, bringing his thumb back to her clit.

Sumi was gasping on every downstroke, a high pitched noise leaving her mouth whether she intended it to or not. "Is *what* what I thought it would be? Your cock? No, I could have never —"

"Fucking me," Ranar clarified, bringing her down hard against his base. "Fucking me while you're fucking me over." He didn't give her a chance to answer. "I'm going to come. Can I finish inside you?"

All she could do was continue to squeak as he redoubled his efforts against her clit, propelling her to the finish line alongside him. "I want you to squeeze me so tight you milk me dry."

Sumi had no idea if her cunt lived up to his expectations, but he far surpassed hers. When he erupted inside her, she could feel him surge, all those little spines ballooning, pressing on her inner walls as he filled her with molten heat. She was able to feel the precise moment when he was finished, like an immediate deflation, then she remembered why a heartbeat later. *Because he still needs to come from the other one.*

"Fucking you is everything I hoped it would be," she confirmed, raking her nails over his chest. "I never really wanted to fuck you over.

But I'll gladly fuck you again. Have any requests for weird snake dick number two?"

He was gentle and kind and made her laugh and would never hurt her, as evidenced by the way he gently eased her body into accepting his . . . But he could if he wanted to, she was reminded, flipping her and reversing their positions with a speed and strength that left her breathless.

"Fast and dirty," he admitted with a laugh. "You've got me going cross-eyed here."

She loved the way he made her laugh, the way he always knew what to say to set her at ease. She loved talking about plants with him, talking about her fears and her dreams with him, talking about silly little nothings with him. And now she knew that she loved having sex with him.

"Hold me down and take what you want. You've had me horny over your forearms for half the year."

He was solid muscle, and when he fed his second cock into her — easily, as she still gaped from its brother's withdrawal — she could feel the strength in his back, the pure muscle of his tail, and knew that he could probably crush her. Sumi led his hand to her neck, the light pressure as he pinned her down everything she'd wanted all those months ago, when ChaoticConcertina had first responded to her message on the plant server. Ranar pulled her legs around him and she hooked her ankles, likewise wrapping her arms around his back.

Fast and dirty sounded like the fucking of her dreams, and she had no doubt that he would prove to be the best guy in that as well.

·❤·❤·❤·❤·❤·

"Hedda, I was struck by inspiration on my way in this morning."

Her blood thrummed. She was on cloud nine. She was sex sore and probably bow-legged, but she had fucked that naga into her mattress by the time she'd finally let him leave in the middle of the night, grumbling that he was too old to not get at least a solid six hours of sleep. *You're going to marry that snake.*

The troll raised her eyebrows. "*More* inspiration? We've barely cleaned up from last night!"

Sumi was amazed how much she suspected she loved the business piece of it all, once she removed her guilt over *The Perfect Petal's* owner from the equation. She was driven by something that had never possessed her in the classroom, a giddy desire to succeed, to push higher, to aim bigger. Unlike those first few months, when she mourned her success in *spite* of Ranar, now she was determined to be successful *for* him. *You can't be a sugar mama if you're barely clearing six figures before taxes, and he needs a Kiss the Cook chili apron.*

Urban Narcissus had, if nothing else, been an excellent model for her. A business aiming high, elevating both their product and clientele, and reaping the reward. It was the dryad and her sleek black suit Sumi had thought of that morning.

She did a double take once she entered the design room, as Hedda guiltily slurped coffee from her leaky cup. "First of all, get rid of that fucking menace before it spills all over the counter again! I *literally* bought you a new one!"

One of the gnome sisters dropped her head against the worktable, shoulders shaking in laughter as Hedda sniffed, begrudgingly carrying her cup to the sink, and removing the brand-new tumbler from the cabinet.

"Throw it away! But I was thinking, remember what I told you about that shop I trained in? *Urban Narcissus*? You liked that mothman guy, right? He lived in the apartments off the highway, I believe . . . I say we call him back, he can be the Bridgeton driver."

Hedda pulled a face. "I don't know if that's going to be worth it. You've got a *lot* of shops in Bridgeton to compete for the business."

"Oh, but that's where you're wrong. I'm not worried about the other shops in Bridgeton. How much competition does *Urban Narcissus* have?"

The troll cocked her head as Sumi grinned ferociously. It turned out she had quite a knack for the art of war in business. She had never wanted to direct any of it at Ranar. The only thing she wanted to do with Ranar was pull him into her arms and kiss him until he forgot about the past few months, but *that* was a different plan. *This* plan was fueled by spite, born out of a conversation she'd overheard at her party. Two selkies, comparing notes over recent weddings they'd attended, and how expensive everything, including the flowers, had been.

"That's the kind of stuff my boss likes on the front reception desk," one of the girls had added.

Weddings were a beast she didn't want to touch with a barge pole, but arrangements for offices were a different story. *That* she could do. Do it easily and do it well. *And upcharge in the process.* All she had to do was click a few boxes on her Bloomerang partner portal. She had already checked. Tropicals and other high-end flowers and botanicals, orchids, bonsai . . . they could elevate the offerings and the price point commensurately.

"If we were to start buying the big tropicals and expensive shit, don't you think we might get a piece of that business?"

"We might, but they'll still have the edge of being closer in distance. If you're setting the minimum price point to be the same as theirs, I don't see how —"

"Oh, but we're not going to match their minimum price point. We're going to set *ours* two dollars lower."

The grin that spread overhead Hedda's face was diabolical in its dawning, and the gnome sisters cackled in unison from the other side of the table.

"You're going to Showcase Showdown them."

"We're going to fucking Showcase Showdown them."

"You are both evil," Seff hooted. "But I love it."

Sumi grinned. "The difference between being evil and being shrewd is in how you choose your victim. *This* is just good business." She turned away still smiling, humming to herself. She had a future naga husband to keep, the best guy without exception, and he deserved only the best in return.

The UnFriendzone

RANAR

"So that's it. I need to pull the plug before I start throwing good money after bad. You know the weddings will start to dry up by mid-October. I'm going to quietly put it on the market by the end of this month, and hopefully I'll be able to move any stock we're sitting on by the time it goes to escrow. We're done."

Grace nodded slowly, not bothering to challenge him.

He'd already had the same conversation with his parents that morning. His mother understood, insisted it was for the best, that she wanted him to get as much money for the property as he could without sacrificing anymore to the taxes. She *said* that, but as she left the room, Ranar watched her pause, reaching a hand out to touch the notched door frame, marked with their heights.

A short while later, he had been in the design room with his father, organizing himself for that weekend's wedding. "I used to put Ruma in her swing right there, remember? Every afternoon while we worked. I used to tell her this place would be hers to worry over ... We'll need to get you out of the house every day after this place is gone. Figure out a new routine. Okay, Appa?" Ranar knew he was as much talking to himself as he was to his father, not expecting an answer.

His father looked up, fixing him with a look, shaking his head. "You worry too much. You always worry too much. Let your mother and I do the worrying."

He smiled sadly. It was bittersweet that the fact that his days of worrying about this place were nearly at an end. "I'll try to do that more."

"Ruma needs to be a doctor, not run any of this. Sell it and send her to a good medical school. And you don't need to worry about this place so much either. Focus on school. Then you get a good job that doesn't keep your hands in water all day."

Ranar laughed, turning away as his eyes burned. *Where the fuck was this lecture twenty years ago?* "Okay, if you say so. You're the boss."

"Don't forget it. Why don't you go call that pretty girl and stop worrying so much."

He left the room laughing again, having no idea what his father was talking about, because he surely didn't know about Sumi or any of the goings-on with her shop, but he had been thinking of doing that exact thing all morning.

Now Grace was here, insisting that she had business to discuss that couldn't wait.

"Can I make a suggestion without you biting my face off?"

Ranar rolled his eyes, turning to face the bubbly human, but said nothing, silently holding out a hand for her to continue.

"I think we all agree that you have to sell the building, that's the best choice."

"Gosh, Grace. Thanks for weighing in with an opinion on that decision that has absolutely nothing to do with you. I'm glad I have your approval."

"But moving past that," she continued giving him a sapphire glare, "I think you should keep paying your business taxes. Don't dissolve your LLC. Dump the property taxes, for sure, but the business . . . Ranar, you *can* make this work. The weddings alone —"

"The weddings aren't enough, Grace."

"Will you *please* let me finish? I know you think this means you just have to throw in the towel and start selling peanuts on the side of the road, but you're actually being kind of ridiculous." She glared.

"I was actually going to sell little journals bound with my molted skin. I was going to call it the Necronagacon."

"*Anyway.* You know I have the contract for the Fall Festival. This coming year I was going to try to get the summer carnival as well. Cal is like a shark. He got a little taste of blood in the water, now he's on a feeding frenzy. This is between you and me, no one outside staff knows anything yet, but we've already broken ground on an indoor facility. It's going to be *beautiful.* Log cabin style, with a wall of glass that looks out over the hills and the lake."

She paused for maximum dramatic effect, and Ranar crossed his arms, wishing she'd get on with it.

"He wants to be able to compete with Enoch over at the winery for the winter events. That's my focus this year. He wants me to hire in someone to run the CSA so that I can put all my energy into building the wedding business."

"Congrats. That's amazing. Did *every*one I know conspire to make me feel like a failure this week, or is it just a coincidence?"

"Oh my *gods*, Ranar. Just think of allll those winter weddings and banquets. This is what I do. This is what *you* do. Having an in-house florist would be a huge win for me, and it would be a win for you, too. I know bitching about them is one of your favorite pastimes, but I also know that you secretly love doing weddings. You don't want to admit being a masochist, but I *know* you love them. We can put together packages, pre-designed based on your specs to streamline the workflow. And what have you always told me? Wedding season pays for the winters. Think about it. You've already been working your ass off every summer, it's not like that would be something new. Let's say it takes a year or two for our winter business to solidify, even though I promise that won't happen. You can take the winters off until I start booking, actually get to spend time with Ruma when she comes home for vacation. The two of you can take a trip together, not worry about work."

She was playing dirty. There was nothing that he would like to do more than escape the cold winters in Cambric Creek, even if only for a week or two, and Grace knew it. And he *did* love doing weddings. The work was methodical, and he loved having one singular concept to unify.

"Please think about it. And we would keep the name! The name recognition is half of what I want — special events at Saddlethorne Farm, flowers by The Perfect Petal. Two multigenerational family businesses, born and bred right here in Cambric Creek. You know people love shit like that."

"So I'm going to have to, what, work in the rain next to the pigpen putting together table arrangements?"

"You work at home. In the design room."

They both turned at the sound of his mother's voice, serpentining around the corner. Her hands were tightly clasped in front of her already, swaying from side-to-side in excitement, and he knew he was beat.

"You know we don't even use that big family room since you and Nisa moved out. What is it doing? Just sitting empty. We can turn it into a workroom for you to do these events. You need to start thinking about yourself, Ranar. I know it's easier to take care of us, but you need to take care of yourself as well."

You need to find someone to take care of you for a change. If only it could be as easy as Pinky made it sound. Grace was right. It would be a huge win for her not having to contract in work for her events, and an all-inclusive wedding package including flowers would be a desirable bonus. ***And*** *you won't have to learn to be a short order cook at the diner or sell peanuts on the side of the road outside Cockatrice games. That's a plus.*

The business was barely worth the property taxes, but the property itself would ensure his parents would be taken care of for the rest of their years. The building would ensure that he had a paid-for roof over his head and a few years to fuck around and figure out what was next without depleting his savings. *This is what's next. You don't need to burn money fucking around if you're doing this.*

Instantly, the wheels began turning. "We can set it up exactly like this place." All three of them looked around, as if they were committing the space to memory. As if he would need to. He had spent more time in this room than he had probably in any other room in the world. "Mom, we could make it look exactly like this. The same layout. I can have this table brought over, with the same cut marks that have always been here. We can put the extra coolers in the garage."

"The zoning —"

"Fuck the zoning," he slapped his hand down against the counter to make his point, wincing when his mother smacked him with a rolled up newspaper.

"Language in front of a lady!"

"The zoning won't be a problem," Ranar went on. "Jack wouldn't dare give me an issue about anything else, and if he does, I will deny it to his face. 'What are you talking about, this is home therapy.' We can do this. We can make it so that dad still has this place to come to every day. And, you know, I'll be able to feed myself. That helps."

"And if you need extra space for really big events, I can figure something out on site—"

"He can borrow space from his girlfriend."

Both their heads swung to his mother, who looked entirely too pleased with herself over the bomb she had just dropped into the conversation. "She has that big shop. Plenty of space. And she would never say no to you for anything."

He could tell Grace was giving him a *look*. Ranar refused to make eye contact with her, refused to acknowledge his mother's fictions, but he could feel her look the same.

"Perfect. I think it's gonna work out great for everyone, I really do. I've been thinking about it for weeks. And we can help you with the space, the boys from the farm can flip it in a weekend. You should see the magic they work on the barns. If someone will be home this week, I can have Brogan and Zeke —"

"If you're sending handsome farmhands to the house, I can leave right now."

He was going to remind his mother of this afternoon in two weeks, Ranar decided as she swished triumphantly from the room, when she needed his help resetting the television remote.

Grace waited until they were alone, almost visibly counting. When she got to five, she pounced.

"If you don't tell me everything right now, and I mean fucking *every*-thing, I'm going to call Tris. And *he'll* find out. And he'll root out every-thing you think you're hiding plus the shit in your past you've already forgotten about, so unless you want your sex life to be front page news, you'd better spill."

Ranar scowled. Tris was a gossip columnist, an absolute menace wherever he went, and was one of Grace's longtime friends. She had known the sneaky satyr for more than a decade, and she clearly wasn't above using him as a weapon.

"That is so low of you —"

"I will call him right now, don't test me. Why was I not the very first person to hear about this?"

Ranar blew out a breath in aggravation. "Because she doesn't exist! My mother and my daughter have decided to spin yarns together as a bonding experience, I guess. They saw Sumi in here one time and they both decided —"

"Sumi? Pink Blossom Sumi. Whose party you ghosted like a fucking loser, ghosting *me* in the process, after I worked so hard to get you there? The one I said literally from day one was flirting with you? *That* Sumi?"

There was nothing he could say. Ranar already knew the conversation wasn't even worth continuing. Grace would proclaim victory, would insist that he ought to be indebted to her forever, and he wasn't willing to give her the satisfaction. He rolled his eyes, making a dissenting noise in his throat.

"I didn't ghost, I stepped out for some air. Those social media girls were tripping over my tail, there was no room! But I didn't leave. Sounds like you indulged in a few too many of those cosmos and didn't know whether you were coming or going."

"Oh my stars, you fucked her didn't you? You did! I can tell, don't try to deny it!"

"Oh, *how* can you tell?"

Grace was practically crowing. "Because your ears are turning red and you're not actually a very good liar, Ranar. You fucked her. Did she actually pull down her dress and ask if you wanted to squeeze her boobies?"

Ranar slouched into his coil. He didn't want to have this conversation. He didn't want to think about the things they'd done that night and how much he'd enjoyed it. Wanted to think even less about the way she'd turned up two days later, bringing him coffee and lunch with instructions to keep his strength up, kissing his cheek before she sped away, leaving him dumbfounded in the parking lot. He most especially didn't want to contemplate the way he'd replayed the events of that night on a near constant loop, practically needing to wear an apron twenty-four hours a day to disguise his arousal.

"I'm pretty sure she fucked me, actually. She didn't ask me to squeeze anything. But she *did* ask if she could lick my slit, and I blacked out after that. I don't remember what happened the rest of the night."

She was a heap of blonde curls, face down on the table, shaking in laughter. "I feel like I deserve a monument in the park for this. I knew she was perfect for you! Asked if she could lick your slit, fucking hells. Thank the goddess one of you is willing to make the first move. You know you love bossy women, hurry up and marry this one."

"Again, how do *you* know that?"

Grace was still laughing as she pushed up from the table, checking her cherry-red lipstick in the mirror before turning to the door.

"Because I've been bossing you around from the day we met. I'm going to be proud of myself over this the rest of the week, I really am."

Ranar squirmed once she had left. He could still feel the heat of Sumi's mouth, the drag of her tongue over the most sensitive spot on his body. Grace was right — she was bolder than he'd ever been, had been right from the start. She was ruining his life, throwing his entire existence into shambles, and had been brazen about it from the beginning . . . but she had an audacity that took his breath away, and he would have been lying if he pretended it didn't turn him on. It was turning him on right now, feeling the slight vibration of his cocks in their sheath.

This was going to be a stressful few months, this transition, and what was that she had told him? *Please let me know if there's anything I can do to help you. Anything at all.* His hand operated with a mind of its own, tapping open his phone and scrolling to her name.

Hi

He groaned at himself. *Hi, really? What are you, ten? Mid at best, on your luckiest day. Pathetic. A pathetic worm.*

Hey! What's up? Something you need?

Every time he closed his eyes he could see her there above him — dark hair hanging around her face, her cheeks splotched pink. The second time they'd had sex, she'd been fully in control. Her head had dropped back as she rode him, her rosy lips parting in a moan he heard rattling through his brain every time he attempted to focus on anything else.

She hadn't waited for him to be smooth, hadn't waited for him to make the first move, hadn't waited on him for anything. *She'd still be waiting.* She had taken what she'd wanted from him, straddling his body, riding one of his cocks as his hands roved over her body. She had been the one to reverse them, requesting a repeat of *fast and dirty*, had instructed him to hold her down once more, pinning her beneath his muscle and weight. He still had marks on his back from where her nails had scratched against him. *Was there something he needed?*

I don't know if need is strictly the right word.

Ranar closed his eyes, breathing slowly, in and out. He still wasn't sure if the situation was mortifying or if it *was* exactly what he'd needed, something he'd not even known he'd needed.

Something you want?

He swallowed hard, gulping down the mortification and his pride. He didn't have much of that left anyway. Then he paused, body vibrating in anticipation as she typed another message.

Give me an hour. My house. The back garage door is unlocked.

Ranar frowned. He didn't like that. Didn't like it, and was going to give her lecture over it . . . in an hour, when he saw her. *When she leaves her thriving business in the middle of the day to come take care of your erections, just because you made a vague hint at needing some relief.*

That he *needed* her mouth, her tongue, hot at his slit. She would suck the tip of his cock as it began to protrude from his sheath, nursing on the button of slippery flesh until his tail was thrashing and it slid out fully, quickly joined by its brother. He would bury himself in her heat and she would ride him until he came, first from one, then the other, until they were both satisfied and he was limp, a giant worthless worm.

And then he would s her about her door again. Because he might not have been very good at asking for what he wanted or even thinking about his own needs ahead of anyone else's, and hadn't run a spectacularly successful business, even though it was handed to him . . . but he *was* a good dad. And he would never *not* lecture Ruma over leaving her doors unlocked.

An hour later, he nearly had a heart attack with her garage door opened, with him lurking inside.

Sumi was laughing as she stepped out of her car. "Sorry about that! I didn't think about you being in here until I'd already hit the button."

"I guess I should be happy the actual house door wasn't unlocked as well, but do you see what just happened? Some creeper lurking in your garage, because you didn't let the door do the one thing a door is for."

"Yeah, but you're a creeper I'm happy to see."

He followed her uncomfortably into the house, unsure of why he was so uncomfortable in the first place. She turned once they were both in her kitchen, stretching up on her toes, hooking her arms around his neck to meet his lips. She hummed into the kiss, and his stomach flip-flopped.

She kissed him like someone she cared about. Someone who was more than a secret fling, more than a former rival. *Current rival? Defeated rival?* It was a deep kiss, long and warm. It felt unearned to him, for he wasn't someone important enough to be the recipient of such a kiss. She kissed him as if he were someone she loved. Ranar swallowed hard at the thought.

"I do have bad news, unfortunately. One of the girls is a bit under the weather so we're a little shorthanded. I can't stay too long. I hope fast and dirty will suffice."

Neither was he in a position to pick and choose what scraps he was thrown. "That's perfect, actually." They were fucking. Right? That's all they were doing. Getting some of the hostility and aggression between them out of the way by fucking.

That didn't fully explain why he took so much pleasure in undressing her, kissing his way down her neck and over her full breasts making the journey down the soft swell of her stomach and across her round hips, pulling her legs apart. He would fuck her fast and dirty, but he needed her wet and warm enough to take him.

He hadn't been with too many bipedal women in his lifetime. Hadn't been with many women at all, if he were being honest with himself, but he enjoyed this. He especially enjoyed doing it to her. The heat of her, her responsiveness, the way she rocked her hips up into his face, chasing her release against his tongue. He especially loved the moment when he brought her over the edge — her breathy moans, the way her fingers would tighten in his hair or at his shoulders, pulse of her and the hot rush of heat coating his tongue. Her eyes were heavy and her arms languid when he finally came up for air, his victory glistening on his chin.

"On your back, please."

Ranar grinned. Grace was right. He *did* like bossy women.

It didn't take long for Sumi to tease out his cocks, having a better understanding this time of he liked and how he responded. When she pressed two fingers to the skin between his shafts, however, Ranar almost turned inside out.

"What was that?" She did it again, pressing her fingers to that in-between space, circling with just enough pressure to make him wheeze.

"Oh my god, are those your balls? Is that what I'm doing? Am I rubbing your balls right here?"

She was not letting up, and for the first time in his life, at least since he was a teenager, Ranar was worried he was about to spray from both shafts at once.

"I don't know, but I think you should stop."

"What do you mean you don't know? How do you not know?! I'm just a dumb human, you can't expect me to —"

"Because I've never taken a magical trip into my cock slit," he said gruffly. "I don't have balls, not the way humans do. But yeah, I guess that's probably what you're pressing on."

"Does it feel good? Or am I hurting you?" She had stopped by then, her eyebrows kissing her hairline.

"It feels good. A little too good."

"How has no one done this to you before? What about your wife?! You know what, never mind. Forget about all of them. Okay, let's put a pin in this. I don't have time to explore this as deeply as I would like to today, but the next chance I do, we are going to find out just how sensitive your little snake taint is."

The next time. Ranar didn't know why it was that he couldn't simply enjoy this for what it was. Casual sex between two people who barely liked each other. *Why does it feel like more?*

"You've spent so much time distracting yourself with my *little snake taint* that we're probably only going to have time for one fast and dirty. I'm going to need to jerk the other one off in your bushes like a pervert." He raised himself up, remembering. "Speaking of your bushes, *why* are you leaving your door open? What's wrong with you? Do I need to have a talk with your parents?"

"This is when I would normally play my dead mom card but I would rather you just shut up and let me fuck you."

A tickle at the back of his brain, but too much of his blood was rushing for it to penetrate.

Sumi bit her lip, turning to stare at her bedside table for a moment. "Can we try something? It's gonna require a little bit of prep, but I think you'll be happy with the results."

Ranar held his breath when she coated his hand in the lubricant she pulled from the bedside table, using another generous blob on her own fingers to slicken herself.

"I need you to stretch me open a bit. I don't think I'll be able to relax my muscles enough to take you on my own."

Her ass was like a full, ripe peach, thick and juicy. He liked gripping it, liked bumping into her from behind, feeling the roundness of her pressed to his tail. He tried not to lose too much of the lube to her skin, working a finger into her tight hole as she squirmed. He began to play with her clit as he worked in the second digit, enjoying the way she whimpered and jerked against him. She was close to coming again by the time he had a third finger inside her, choosing to curl his body, leaning in to suck on her clit until she came against his tongue for a second time. By the time she was coming down from the second orgasm of their afternoon, Sumi decided she was ready to take him.

He couldn't remember the last time he had a partner willing to do this. The kitsune from up the street had taken one look at the swells of his shaft and said no, not that Ranar had done anything more than wave to her from his driveway in months.

Sumi gripped his front shaft tightly, instructing him on the back as she lowered herself slowly.

"Nice and easy," he crooned into her hair. She was beautiful and brave, so much braver than he was. "You're doing so good. You take my cocks so well." He was several inches into her by then, his twin swells making her pause, breathing heavily. "You're so beautiful," he murmured, rocking up slowly, feeling her breath catch as he did so. "Brave for even trying. If this is all you can handle, this is fine, Sumi. This is all I need."

At that, her eyes popped open. "No, it's not. Stop selling your own needs short."

The world went white as she dropped her weight, allowing gravity to force her body down on his cocks, crying out as she did so. Ranar gasped, wheezing. She felt incredible.

"Holy shit, it's *so* much."

Her voice was thin and strained and it was all he could do to keep a tight grip on his control.

He *needed* to keep control, for her sake. She was doing this for *him*. Why, he had no idea. Couldn't explain it to himself if he tried. He was nothing to her, not really. The pathetic sap she had put out of business. If all this was a pity fuck, it was still more than he deserved.

"You feel amazing. You're squeezing me so tight, I can barely move, you're squeezing my cocks so well." It was true. Ranar rutted against her, his tail coiling around her legs, holding her close.

She was breathing hard, her breath a forced wheeze, squeaking when his tail slipped between her thighs, nestling in beside her clit. Sumi began to gasp, her clit still swollen and sensitive, her arm reaching back to wrap around his neck. His mouth was drawn to that spot below her ear like a magnet, feeling her thighs tremble, his fangs grazing her skin. He wanted to bite her, mark her as his, which was the most foolhardy and inappropriate thing he'd considered in a summer full of bad decisions, but when she cried out, tightening around him, he was gone.

He had joked to Grace that he had blacked out the first time he had spent the night in Sumi's bed, but this time was less of an exaggeration. Both cocks spasmed at once, clenched in the dual vise grip of her body, his fangs bit sunk into her tender flesh, and the lack of blood in his brain nearly sent him sprawling to the floor.

When he was able to see straight again, he was flat on his back in her bed, with her tucked against his chest. They were both breathing hard.

"That took fast and dirty to a new level. You almost got me there."

Ranar laughed weakly as she gingerly fingered the bite mark on her neck. He had pitched sideways, managing not to break the skin, but it would leave a bruise. *Because that's just what you want her neighbors to whisper about,* he thought wretchedly, gently raking his fingers through her hair.

"I always knew this big ass was going to be the MVP someday," she went on. "Someday, I knew it would happen. I never would've guessed it was to provide more cushion for my naga lover's pushin', but I'll take it. My students," she went on with a laugh, "they used to say *gyat!*

That's what I had to put up with. This is so much better. And you're a lot cuter."

"You're a teacher?" Something moved within him, a slithering in his chest, constricting around his lungs, making it difficult to breathe for a moment. That tickle again, something nestled in the folds of his grey matter, a connection he couldn't quite attach.

Her head tilted up, eyes meeting his, her lip catching in her teeth. "I used to be. But I'm not anymore. I have something I wanted to ask you. I'm going to send you a nice invitation, don't worry. This isn't being prompted by the hot dp action, by the way, I was going to invite you anyway. But the club I'm in, we're having a little ceremony. It's nothing formal, just a way to celebrate everything we've been learning with friends and loved ones. I'd really love for you to be there. You're the only person I'm asking, so if you don't show up, I'm going to look like a real loser. Just putting that out there if it helps you make up your mind."

By the time he was back in his own shop, Ranar couldn't focus on anything. His lungs felt flipped inside out, something gnawing at the back of his brain that he couldn't quite make out the shape of, one that left him discomfited just the same. He had agreed to attend her ceremony, and that, too, left him feeling ill at ease. He didn't know why. He hated not knowing how to categorize his feelings, and she had left him feeling that way since the instant she had walked through his doors, months earlier.

Months ago. Not half a year ago.

And yet. The thought of blocking her number, of ignoring her presence entirely, shutting her out, left him despondent. She kissed him as though he mattered, and despite what Grace and his mother and daughter might think, Ranar couldn't come up with a single reason why that should be so.

And yet. Turning to his laptop, once he was home, made his insides bunch, that constriction around his lungs growing tighter. *But why?* The ongoing chat with Pinky had been his solace. So why, then, did it now leave him feeling stricken?

Too many little things, too numerous to be inconsequential.

He sat there, leaning back on his coil, staring at the screen until the room had gone dark, not shaken from his reverie until Ruma came bursting into the room, showing off the sweater she'd bought while shopping with his mother. Ranar forced his attention away from the black screen, forced himself to be present where it mattered, and pushed aside the slithering worry in his mind.

. . . For now. Put this aside for now. And then figure out what's going on.

ChaoticConcertina: *I've been giving this a lot of thought. A **serious** amount of thought.*
I just want to put that out there so you don't think I am being an impetuous creeper.
I think we should meet.
After all this time and after everything we've shared,
I don't think it's so completely inappropriate to consider.
I made a really important decision today.

I am closing my business. I've already reached out to a listing agent to sell the property.

ChaoticConcertina: *I even had a meeting this afternoon with one of my business partners*
on what potential next steps might look like.
There's a chance I'm not going to wind up working at a car wash, which is great.
And then after I had all these important conversations today,
I met up with someone.
Someone I think I might have a future with.
Or at least, someone who could have a future with a version of me.
But I didn't tell her about any of it.
I'm telling you.

ChaoticConcertina: *I realized once I got home today & opened my laptop*
that it was a foregone conclusion
that I would tell you immediately,
because I trust you implicitly.
*I don't know if I trust **her** the same way.*
I don't want to enter into another relationship if there's a possibility here.
If there's actually something here at all.
There's a lot of stuff swirling in my mind right
now that I can't make heads or tails of
With all the uncertainty in my life I've been dealing with,
I need to know where I stand
With you. With her.
With whichever version of myself this is.

I hope that makes sense.

To Have and To Hold

SUMI

PinksPosies&Pearls:** *My dearest friend,*

I had planned on sending you an invitation.
It had been in my head for weeks to do so.
After all, who else would I invite but you?
You have been here for me through every step
of this mad leap into the unknown.
You've been here with a supportive ear
and a wise word or two of advice from the start.
You always know what to say to make me feel better,
and you always, always make me laugh.
I told you once before that I was very sad
for the version of myself that I had been,
PinksPosies&Pearls: *because she wasn't very happy.*
And it took me a long time to realize how unhappy she was.
You were part of that.

You didn't know it at the time,

but I don't think I ever would have realized how unhappy I was,

if I hadn't had someone in my life

who made me feel so completely opposite of that.

I'm sure you thought you were simply giving me advice on plants,

but what you were really doing

was encouraging me to care for and nurture myself.

You know, alongside my philodendrons.

PinksPosies&Pearls: *I don't think I would've ever taken this leap*

if it hadn't been for your encouragement.

I told you about my Japanese club,

and how wonderful it's been.

Those tiny details that we master in an effort to make the whole.

Little, inconsequential things,

but they have their place in the world,

and that makes them invaluable.

That's how I have felt about our friendship.

Sometimes we talk about little, inconsequential things,

but all of those little things,

those seemingly meaningless conversations,

have meant so much to me.

PinksPosies&Pearls: *My club is hosting a tea ceremony,*

And we're inviting our most treasured friends

and loved ones to celebrate with us.

And of course I had a mind to invite you.

But I did not.

I invited someone else,

someone I want to be a part of my life.

Someone I can see myself with for the long haul.

How could I not?

He's always known what to say to make me feel better.

He's always known how to make me laugh and how to lend a supportive

ear.

And even though he thinks he's not brave,

*he encourages **me** to be brave.*

PinksPosies&Pearls: *I love him.*

And now I want to be there for him.

He's been my rock & I want to repay that in kind for him,

now that he so desperately needs someone to care for him.

I couldn't have done any of this without him.

And so I hope you understand.

If I can only choose one of you,

I have to choose him.

She was a nervous wreck. Sumi peeked from the edge of the partition that separated their guests from the staging area, her eyes bouncing from head to head, mentally cataloging all in attendance. The small space was full, with guests both young and old, some familiar faces and many more strangers.

She didn't see him anywhere.

"I think I have everyone in order," Yuriko announced, coming around the corner from the back. "Are you ready?"

"More like you've put the fear of assorted gods in them," Sumi laughed, hoping her voice didn't sound as forced and brittle to Yuri as it did to her own ears.

"What's wrong?" the ogress asked flatly. *Dammit.*

She shook her head, willing the tears not to fall. "He's not here."

Yuriko groaned, not needing more than that. Sumi's eyes burned as she was pulled into a supportive hug, completely enveloped.

"Sweetie, I'm so sorry. Fuck him. Right? Let him stew in his resentment forever if that's what he wants. Fuck him."

She nodded, knowing that's what she was meant to do. Fuck him, put him from mind, move on without another thought. "Right."

"The good news is there are plenty of spares out there. Siblings and grandparents. Put yourself in front of one of the teenages; they won't care if you serve the wagashi properly or not."

She nodded again, forced her mouth into a smile, and followed Yuriko to join the group.

Sumi didn't know why she was surprised. He hadn't returned her calls in days, and her text messages remained unread. She knew she could have simply gone to his shop, staked him out in the parking lot or in front of his house, but that would have been forcing a final draw, and her bravery had run out.

Her DMs, too, had been quiet.

Since she'd sent that last message to ChaoticConcertina, there had been no reply. *That* she had not handled with nearly as much grace as she was attempting to pretend for the ceremony. She had gone to bed that night tight with anxiety, too nauseous to sleep, too aware of what she was risking. *You might lose both of them.* Even then, knowing what she *knew* to be true, it was nearly impossible to separate them in her head.

When no reply came, she had sobbed. Cried over her silent laptop, wept under the hot blast of her shower, chest heaving at the thought of not having him there, notification appearing on her phone in the middle of the day. The thought of her days and nights being silent of that little chime, the notification that there was someone in the world thinking of her, someone who understood her to her core. A little chime, a message from him. And her whole world felt brighter.

She had felt the moment he'd flinched away from her in her bed. He'd asked if she was a teacher, only it hadn't come out of his mouth as a question. *An accusation.* His body had flinched, the same sharp reaction in her store over her knowing too much about his daughter's schedule. A pull-back, a ripple in the surface of the their two existences, and Sumi had known the time had come to meld them permanently.

And then he sent her that message.

Asking Pinky to meet, to solidify her existence, as if he were begging her for it to not be true. The realization that she may have lost them both was one she was not yet willing to face. Not until she got through her tea ceremony.

The group entered, bowing low to their guests, who bowed low in return. Each member of the group played a part in the ceremony. She was relieved that she had not been given the task of whisking the matcha, certain she would have slopped it on someone's shoes with her shaking hands, barely holding her composure together.

The chakin was just a little napkin, inconsequential and unimportant in the grand scheme of the world. But in this context, to this ceremony, it was a venerated tool, one worthy of study and mastery. She was responsible for wielding the napkin throughout the ceremony that afternoon, ensuring that it had achieved the appropriate level of wetness, that she wiped out the tea bowl fully, and that she didn't accidentally whip Yuriko in the face.

He wasn't there.

She didn't need to dwell on his absence during the ceremony itself, being fortunate enough to have a bored-looking tween seated in front of her, the younger sibling of the teen kitsune in their group. She didn't need to focus on his absence as she wiped out her tea bowl, and didn't have the embarrassment of an empty seat before her.

Afterward it was different.

Yuri gripped her wrist, putting on a bright face. "Come on, you're coming to dinner with us. We have a reservation. They can add in another —"

"No. I think I just want to go home."

Her friend pulled a face. "I don't want you sitting at home dwelling on this asshole. Come out with us, take your mind off —"

Sumi shook her head, already feeling the tears burning their way into existence. "Later, maybe. Later this week. I really just want to be alone right now."

She had parked at the shop. The benefits of having her own storefront in the downtown landscape meant that she wasn't forced to use the municipal lot, often crowded on weekends, as it was then. She had parked in her own little lot and walked up the hill, and now she was relieved for that as well. Sumi didn't want to face any happy families in the park, see couples strolling hand-in-hand, getting ice cream and sushi, being disgustingly in love. *Love is a fucking racket. So fucking Ohio.*

She had never considered her own rizz to be mid, but she supposed she was going to be forced to take the L in this case. Too bad the L meant a broken heart.

Letting herself into *Pink Blossom,* Sumi closed the door in relief, slumping against it. She might not even bother going home. *May as well just stay.* After all, she owed the demise of both her relationships to this place. May as well stay and work on tomorrow's orders, just sleep under one of the tables in her cinder block sweatshop. Making money was all she had to look forward to now. Never mind that she didn't have anyone to spend it on. *This is how billionaire sociopaths probably start. This time in ten years, you can have your own rocketship.*

She had just moved to the front of the store, when she saw it. Something near her front door, moving low against the floor, a great creeping beast. Grabbing a broom, she approached slowly . . . When a hand landed on her elbow from behind, making her scream.

Ranar scrunched his nose, wincing at the noise.

She dropped the broom. For what felt like a tiny eternity, all they did was stare at each other. Her heart crashed. Crashed against her lungs, crashed against her skull. She could scarcely believe he wasn't able to hear it.

"What do I need to do to get you to start locking your back doors? This is pathologically stupid, and I'm sorry to put it that way, but I feel like strong language is the only way to get it through your thick skull. This is how you get robbed or worse."

Her hand went to her throat, the laughter that burbled out of her sounding unhinged even to her ears. "I'll have to remember that. At least, I'll try."

"You'll *try*? You should *try* to remember to change your clocks ahead of daylight savings. This isn't something you try for. This is something you do."

"If only I had someone sensible in my life to remind me."

At that, he huffed, turning away. Ranar was quiet for a long moment, and when he spoke again, there was a bitterness in his tone that she'd never heard before. She'd inferred it, through text. She'd been able to feel the bitterness seeping out of each letter in his messages about his custody arrangement with his ex-wife, his bitterness over the giant that had steamrolled his industry. And now, bitterness for her.

"You know, I told my friend not long ago that I have discovered I am very suggestible. It was *suggested* to me some woman in my store was flirting with me, and I created this whole possibility around that. Just out of thin air. And if it had never been mentioned, I probably wouldn't be standing here, because I wouldn't have thought about you a second time after you walked out of my shop. It was *suggested* to me that I forgive the person who put me out of business, who, coincidentally, is that same woman from the first story. And low and behold, my stupid snake brain latched onto that."

He stopped, breathing hard. Sumi felt rooted to the spot, unable to even breathe.

"But I don't know if I can forgive the person who didn't invite *me* to her tea ceremony, because she was inviting some other jerk. I don't know if I can forgive my *friend* for not telling me the truth, however long ago she figured out whatever the truth is. I don't know if I can forgive being played with, like a puppet. Going through the motions, but not in on the joke. I can forgive a lot, Sumi. But I don't know if I can forgive that."

She couldn't move. Couldn't breathe. She would turn to stone here in this spot, in her shop, a cautionary tale of girl bossing too close to the sun, of being careless with a delicate heart, one she ought to have handled with gentler hands. *But he's here. He wouldn't be here if there was no chance at fixing things.*

"Why . . . why did you come here? Why here, of all places? Why meet me at my sweatshop?"

He laughed tonelessly. "I knew your car was here. I figured you'd come back." He paused, long and loaded. "I was going to go in. I wrestled with myself over it all morning. I wanted to throw your little invitation away, delete your number, block you everywhere. I really wanted to, because how *dare* you. Fuck you, Sumi." His eyes pinned her to the spot, glimmering black and full of hurt, and she hated herself for putting it there. "You're careless and selfish, and I really, *really* want to hate you. But I —" He broke off, swallowing hard, looking away again.

Sumi understood. It was hard to put aside the relationship they'd shared as two anonymous strangers, so much healthier than the tentative truce they'd created in person, full of false starts and disappointment.

"I made it all the way to the door. But I couldn't do it. I couldn't face you. How long have you known?" His voice was low and defeated, and *that* shook her to move more than anything she might have felt for herself. She hated hearing that tone from him. "Have you known from the beginning? Has this all been one big game?"

"*No*. Ranar, *please*." There were tears in her eyes when she crossed to him. She tried to remember his mother's words — his anger burned hot and bright and was always short-lived. *This*, though, was an entirely different kind of anger. Angled away from, looking at the wall, the floor, anywhere but here. This was a cold smolder, and she wasn't sure if they could survive it. *But he's here. He wouldn't have come if he was done.*. "I've only known for a bit."

"*How long?*"

Sumi winced as he snapped. She would freeze to death in this cold. Scorching anger was far preferable to this.

"Since just before that day in the rain." His eyes flicked to hers, full of hurt and recrimination. *That day in the rain that changed everything.*

330

"The afternoon I came to your shop. That night. I figured it out. I'd joined the owners' coalition server. I wanted to sabotage you, but then when I clicked on your name . . . I figured it out then."

He didn't pull away when she stepped into his space, laying hand on his arm. He was still avoiding her eye, but this was it, she realized, her chance to shoot her shot, and likely the only one chance she would get. If he left this afternoon still her adversary, that was all they would ever be, and this whole life changing journey would have been for nothing. *Maybe it's you. Maybe you're the reason things are like this. Maybe you're just unloveable.*

"I didn't mean to mislead you. I didn't know *how* to tell you. Either of you. If you only believe one thing, please believe that. I *never* wanted to hurt you." The tears overflowed, and she didn't bother to wipe them away. "How could I? You're the most important person in my life. You have been for months." He pulled away, but didn't shrug off her arm. Sumi tightened her grip, refusing to let go. "If you can forgive the person that put you out of business, how could you not forgive *me* for this teensy little thing? Didn't *I* mean more to you than that? Because *she's* guilty of fucking up your life. The only thing I'm guilty of is falling in love with you."

Ranar snorted, a disgusted shake of his head, but still didn't pull away. It was the best warming she was going to get.

"Is-is Ruma home with your mom?"

He looked away. She could *feel* the pain in his eyes without needing him to answer. He telegraphed his emotions so clearly, and Sumi couldn't understand how there hadn't been someone to come along all those years and appreciate what a precious gift that was. *Your gain.*

"She left yesterday. I don't know which of us was more upset. It makes me question if *any* of this is good for her . . ."

"I'm so sorry. I'm sorry that you're in pain and that you didn't have anyone to share it with. I told my friend online he needed to find someone who would take care of him. I want to *be* that person, Ranar. Here, in the flesh. And that's what I intend on doing. So if you can forgive that bitch who put you out of business, can't you forgive me? The one who wants to take care of you? Oh, how I wish you would."

He pulled away from her at last, a slow serpentine away, across the room to the coolers, away from her grasp. *That's that. You did this to yourself. You should have learned to bloom where you planted instead of running away. Instead, you ruined a bunch of lives for no good reason, including your own chance at happiness.*

"You told me once," he started suddenly, "that you thought maybe you were the reason for all the unhappiness in your life. That maybe things were like that because of you."

He'd picked a helluva time to be a mind reader, she thought, tears still slipping down her face, soaking into the neckline of her dress.

"And you are." At that, Ranar finally turned to face her. "You're a fucking menace, Sumi. You've been the arbiter of disaster in my life from the moment you came stumbling into it." He twisted before her, faster than his size should have allowed, never not shocking her, but now he faced her, his coils shifting beneath him to propel him forward. "But in that same conversation, I told you that I thought maybe everything going wrong in my life was because of me. Because I'm just unlovable."

"That's not true at all." Her voice was little more than a whisper, all the fight in her gone. "You're *so* easy to love."

She would never be able to stay here, knowing that he was so close and yet so closed off to her. She didn't think her heart could bear it. *You ruin things wherever you go. There's only one common denominator.*

"But if I'm wrong about that—" He was suddenly right there, swaying before her, hooking his finger with hers — "Then what else am I wrong about? Because I *want* to believe you . . ."

Her heart beat wildly, and she was once again possessed of that overinflated feeling, as if she might go floating away. She hooked an arm around his neck to tether herself to the ground and then a second, and still he did not pull away. Ranar was silent, and for a long, echoing moment, she wondered if she would be left standing here alone after all, watching him slither out of her life for good. When he finally met her eyes, they were glossy.

"I am going to develop *very* expensive tastes, I will have you know. So just prepare yourself."

Her own eyes blurred, fresh tears falling anew. *It had always been him.* "Only the best chili ingredients for my baby." The tip of his tail hooked around her ankle, a shackle she was glad to wear. "I'd like to ask you out," she began. "Because we need to do this properly. I don't know you and you don't know me. We're two strangers, who've met on chance."

"Chance. Yeah, I like that better already."

"A real date," she went on, ignoring his dig with a smile, "for two people who have never completed this rite of relationship passage together. You can tell me about your interests, and I'll tell you about mine. What books I love, what music you loathe. We'll commiserate over the scourge of well-meaning friends. And we'll both hide the fact that we're plant nerds until at least the third date, when it's safe to start letting our guards down."

"If you ask Grace, I act like I've never been on a date before, so I can't promise I'll know the rules."

Sumi beamed, stretching up on her toes, pressing the ghost of a kiss against his lips. "Well, I have the experience for both of us. We'll start with coffee. Then maybe dinner or drinks . . . For as long as we both shall live."

Also by C.M. NASCOSTA

ALSO BY C.M. NASCOSTA

Cambric Creek

(Suggested Reading Order)

Morning Glory Milking Farm

A Blue Ribbon Romance

The Mabon Feast (Wheel of the Year)

Sweet Berries

Run, Run Rabbit

Moon Blooded Breeding Clinic

Two For Tea

Hexennacht (Wheel of the Year – Coming Soon)

Girls Weekend

Girls Weekend

Parties

Invitations – (Coming Soon)

Talons & Temptations Historical Monster Romance

How To Marry A Marble Marquis

To Ravish A Rogue

About the author

C.M. Nascosta is a USA TODAY bestselling author of Monster Romance and a professional procrastinator from Cleveland, Ohio. She's always preferred beasts to boys, the macabre to the milquetoast, the unknown darkness in the shadows to the Chad next door. She lives in a crumbling old Victorian with a scaredy-cat dachshund, where she writes nontraditional romances featuring beastly boys with equal parts heart and heat, and is waiting for the Hallmark Channel to get with the program and start a paranormal lovers series.

For exclusive stories, signed paperbacks, bookish merch and more, visit (Updates weekly!):
https://linktr.ee/Monster_Bait

The best way to hear about all things Monster Bait before anyone else is to become a patron:

http://patreon.com/monster_bait

The second best way to stay up-to-date on release news and extras is to follow me on Instagram:

https://www.instagram.com/cmnascosta/

The best way to hear about things several days later when I get around to building an email is to join my newsletter:

http://cmnascosta.com/

Made in the USA
Coppell, TX
29 March 2025

47708290R00204